Praise for

the **Seems**

series

A Kidsreads.com Best Book
(*The Glitch in Sleep* and *The Split Second*)

★ "This is a rollicking tale, with great world-building and likable characters and a strong setup for further adventures. Unlike Garth Nix's conceptually similar The Keys to the Kingdom series, this story is upbeat and full of humor, seeming to draw a novel from David Wiesner's *Sector 7* template."
— *SLJ*, starred review for *The Glitch in Sleep*

"Offbeat exploration of a universe-tilting idea."
— *Booklist* on *The Glitch in Sleep*

"The high sense of adventure and an abundance of goofball humor should appeal especially to boys."
— *Publishers Weekly* on *The Glitch in Sleep*

"Hilarious wordplay, capitalized idiomatic expressions, puns, and figures of speech propel the plot along at a manic pace. . . . Advise readers to approach this book with a Grain of Salt and with Tongue firmly in Cheek for a wild ride."   — *SLJ* on *The Split Second*

"Likably friendly . . . humorous writing paired with mystical ingenious settings, top-notch action and thought-provoking thrills make The Seems a fantastic series, great especially for reluctant male readers."
— *Creators Syndicate* on *The Lost Train of Thought*

Books by John Hulme and Michael Wexler

The Seems: The Glitch in Sleep
The Seems: The Split Second
The Seems: The Lost Train of Thought

the SEEMS
the lost train of thought

John Hulme and Michael Wexler

illustrations by Gideon Kendall

BLOOMSBURY

NEW YORK BERLIN LONDON SYDNEY

First published in the United States of America in October 2009
by Bloomsbury Books for Young Readers
Paperback edition published in October 2010
www.bloomsburykids.com

For information about permission to reproduce selections from this book, write to
Permissions, Bloomsbury BFYR, 175 Fifth Avenue, New York, New York 10010

The Library of Congress has cataloged the hardcover edition as follows:
Hulme, John.
The lost train of thought / by John Hulme and Michael Wexler ;
illustrations by Gideon Kendall.—1st U.S. ed.
p.   cm.—(The Seems ; bk. 3)
Summary: Suspended for a year from his duties as a Fixer in the parallel universe
called the Seems, fourteen-year-old Becker is called back into service
when an entire Train of Thought is lost in the deserts of the Middle of Nowhere.
ISBN-13: 978-1-59990-131-2 • ISBN-10: 1-59990-131-5 (hardcover)
[1. Thought and thinking—Fiction. 2. Space and time—Fiction.
3. Technology—Fiction.] I. Wexler, Michael. II. Kendall, Gideon, ill. III. Title.
PZ7.H8844Lo 2010   [Fic]—dc22   2009002145

ISBN 978-1-59990-300-2 (paperback)

Typeset by Westchester Book Composition
Printed in the U.S.A. by Quad/Graphics, Fairfield, Pennsylvania
1 3 5 7 9 10 8 6 4 2

All papers used by Bloomsbury Publishing, Inc., are natural, recyclable products
made from wood grown in well-managed forests. The manufacturing processes
conform to the environmental regulations of the country of origin.

To David Kuhn, Titanium Deb,
and the kids with the safety-pinned shirts

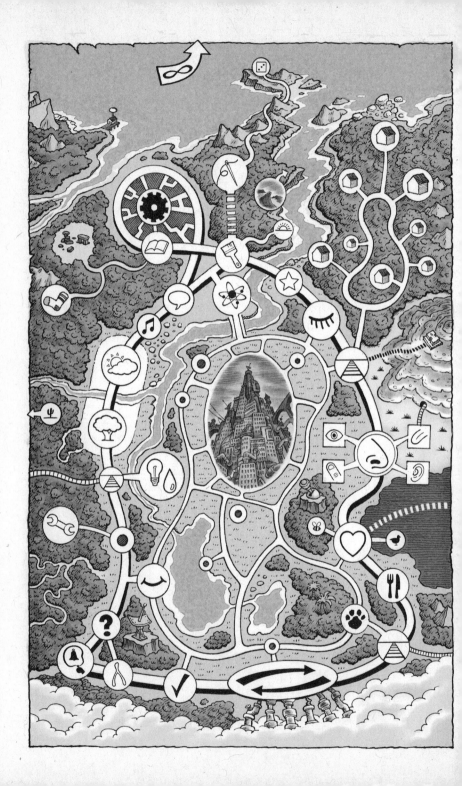

Contents

the Seems

the lost train of thought

POSTED!

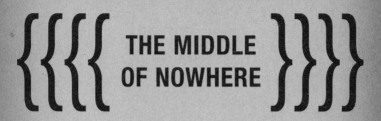

THE MIDDLE OF NOWHERE

NO TRESPASSING!

DO NOT ENTER!

GO AWAY!

UNAUTHORIZED HOPE PROSPECTING, IDEA SMUGGLING, BACK SCRATCHING, THOUGHT PROVOKING, AND SEARCHING FOR THE MOST AMAZING THING OF ALL STRICTLY PROHIBITED.

| | | | | | | | | | |

Violators WILL Be Prosecuted in the Court of Public Opinion

| | | | | | | | | | |

By order of the Powers That Be SPC § 30.01.6

Winds of Change

The Listening Post, The Seems

Beep! Beep! Beep!

Ralph Koohler lowered his sports page and let the half-eaten doughnut in his mouth fall to the desk. Was it his imagination, or had he just heard one of the long-range sensors go off?

"That wouldn't be good," he whispered aloud. "That wouldn't be good at all."

A few minutes of silence later, the forty-year-old father of three waited for his heart to stop racing. Ralph was not prepared to handle a crisis of any kind. He'd faced more than his share of those as an Air-Conditioner in the Department of Nature, what with the increase of smog and acid rain and the Powers That Be's insistence that it was all "part of the Plan." Thankfully, the transfer to the Listening Post had proved to be just what the Care Giver ordered.

In a small building that was remarkable only for the fact that it was covered with antennae and set atop a wooden pole nearly three thousand feet in the air, Ralph's sole responsibility was to monitor a series of safety beacons scattered throughout The Seems. These devices tracked the movements of natural phenomena like Purple Haze and Clouds of Suspicion—rare occurrences that, if allowed to go unchecked, could have significant effects on The World. However, in the month since he'd been reassigned here, not a single buzz, ping, or clang had—

Beep! Beep! Beep!

There it was again. Loud and clear and coming from a dusty transmitter that someone had stashed on top of the microwave oven. When Ralph rose from his desk and took a closer look, he noticed the only light on the metal box had flipped from red to green.

"Hey, Georgie, you're not gonna believe this." Ralph dialed down to his shift supervisor, who was stationed in the small shack at the base of the post. "Looks like I got somethin'."

"You're kidding." George sounded even more surprised than he was. The ex–Power Broker had retired from the Department of Energy a while back, and was just trying to keep busy by volunteering twice a week. *"Which sensor?"*

"Don't know. This thing's so old all it's got is a serial number on the side."

"Read it to me and I'll check the booklet."

"IB5944-WOC."

As Ralph waited for the supervisor to dig up the info, his left hand held his right to keep it from shaking. Twenty years ago, he had graduated from the School of Hard Knocks with dreams of making Air a thing of beauty again. In his mind, those dreams had failed to come true, and it had become harder and harder for Ralph to justify why The Seems didn't do a better job of keeping The World out of harm's way.

"You sure you got that number right, Ralph?" squawked George over the intercom.

"Yeah. Why?"

" 'Cause the booklet says that's the one hooked up to the beacon in the In-Between."

Now both of Ralph's hands were shaking.

"You're not sayin' what I think you're sayin', Georgie? 'Cause if you are, I'm quitting for good and moving out to the Sticks."

"You and me both."

Ralph took a deep breath, then turned on the old-fashioned dot matrix printer and plugged it into the back of the transmitter. Almost immediately, a stream of numbers began to churn across the paper, along with longitudes and latitudes and directional markers that Ralph didn't pretend to understand. In fact, the only piece of information on the rapidly unspooling document that meant anything at all were the three words written in modern Seemsian across the top . . .

"Winds of Change."

Ralph collapsed into his chair, and as he lifted the phone to his lips, he made a mental note to call his wife and tell her to start packing.

"Georgie . . . you better get the Big Building on the horn."

Red Square, Moscow, Russia

Becker Drane sat down on a bench in the northwest corner of Red Square and pulled his Transport Goggles™[1] off his head. Though it was late October, the unseasonably warm weather had caused the frost from the In-Between to melt off the lenses and soak his mop of hair. He wrung out a few drops of water, then turned his eyes to the fading light of afternoon.

Russia's largest public gathering place was neither red nor square, but as always, it was a cacophony of color and sound. A juggler on a unicycle struggled to balance both himself and the three balls that seemed to be spending way too much time on the ground. A barefoot songwriter was strumming "Back in the USSR" in the shadow of Saint Basil's Cathedral. And on the bench to Becker's right, a boyfriend and girlfriend were arguing about something so strenuously that he was glad he couldn't understand Russian. Ordinary people going through an ordinary day, none knowing what was about to blow this way.

"Fixer Drane to Briefer Frye, status report?" Becker tucked his Bleceiver™ into his pocket and pushed the wireless bud into his ear.[2]

---

1. All Tools copyright © the Toolshed, the Institute for Fixing & Repair (IFR), The Seems, XVUIVVII. For more information, please see: "Appendix C: Tools of the Trade."

2. After much debate, it was recently decided to combine the functionalities of the Blinker™ and Receiver™ into one all-purpose communications device. Hence, Bleceiver.

"Just arrived Department of Reality," the familiar voice of Briefer #356, aka Simly Alomonous Frye, came through crystal clear. *"Patch construction underway. I repeat, Patch is almost ready to go."*

"I want it done yesterday, Sim. According to the guys at the Listening Post, the Winds are coming through this Sector in"— Becker checked the update on the Bleceiver's view screen—"less than five minutes."

"Understood, sir. And sir?"

"What?"

"Can you believe it? Me and you? The Winds of Change?"

Becker hung up, smiling at this favorite right-hand man's trademark enthusiasm for the most dangerous assignments. But due to the complicated nature of this Mission, he didn't exactly share it.

Of all the natural wonders that originate in The Seems, few are more powerful than the mighty Winds of Change. These gusts of magnetic energy sweep at random intervals across the In-Between, causing wild shifts in the nature of The World. It was they that caused the invention of the wheel, the fall of the Roman Empire, and the social upheaval of the 1960s. But these events were the result of mere breezes that barely ruffled the Fabric of Reality. If the readings from the Listening Post were right, gale-force Winds were about to tear Sector 66 to shreds.

"Fixer Drane to Department of Nature."

"Nature here."

"Give me 20 percent more hold in the Grass Roots."

"Hold up twenty! Try it now."

Becker reached down and yanked at the small patch of

grass under his feet, which left the ground with little to no resistance at all.

"Still too loose. Kick it another 6." The sound of a hydraulic pump echoed over his Bleceiver and when he tugged at the grass again, it stayed firmly put. "Excellent. Now do the same for the trees and transfer me to Weather."

"Aye, aye, #37. Hold the line."

With twenty-two Missions already under his belt by the age of fourteen, saving The World had become just another day at the office for Fixer F. Becker Drane. But when he'd been called by Central Command and notified that Sector 66—an area populated by eleven million people—was in danger of a direct hit by the Winds of Change, he'd been forced to put on his Thinking Cap™. A quick spin of the beanie's propeller temporarily raised his IQ, and the Fixer landed on a plan: if the Winds themselves could not be stopped, then this entire sector would have to be battened down like a store in the path of an oncoming hurricane.

"Weather here." The familiar voice of Weatherman #1 chimed in over the line. *"Good to be working with you again, Fixer Drane."*

"Ditto." Becker closed his eyes and was about to tune his 7th Sense to Weather, but the sweat beading on his brow told him what needed to be done. "Nice of you to give the Muscovites a little Indian summer, but I think we're gonna have to drop 66 into the blue."

"Can't we just send a Cool Breeze to counteract the Winds?"

"Negative. The colder The World, the more resistant to Change."

"Good point. Weather over and out!"

Weatherman #1 was famously efficient, and only seconds after signing off Becker could feel the temperature plunging. Moscow was far from freezing, but the air was soon chilly enough to prompt the regulars in the square to put on their wool hats and sweaters and curse the dreaded Russian winter. Becker slipped on a hoodie celebrating Rutgers women's basketball and was about to dial the number for the Sound Studio when a voice almost made him jump out of his Speed Demons™.

"Your papers, please!"

The fourteen-year-old turned to see a tall man in a trench coat, black hat, and sunglasses sitting on the bench beside him.

"Pardon me?"

The mysterious figure smiled and repeated the request in a thick Russian accent. "I said, I would like to see your identification papers!"

Becker's heart leapt into his throat. For a second he thought he was about to be busted by a member of the dreaded KGB, who, upon finding out that the only "papers" in his possession were a Fixer's Badge and a card for the Highland Park Public Library, would no doubt arrest him and imprison him in the Gulag. But then he remembered two things: 1) there was no KGB anymore (at least not officially), and 2) even if there was, they wouldn't speak with Russian accents this bad.

"Very funny, Henry."

"Sorry, kid." The man's inflection vanished in an instant, a sheepish grin spreading over his mouth. "I just always loved those old Cold War movies, like *Firefox* or *The Spy Who Came In from the Cold.*"

"Watch them on your own time, dude. If we're not careful we're gonna have a front-row seat to *Apocalypse Now.*"

According to his Mission Report, the Winds were now only three minutes away, which gave Fixer #37 little margin for error.

"I got a few more calls to make and then you're on."

"Do your thing."

As the man who sometimes went by the name of Henry Steele crossed his legs and watched the juggler try and fail to add a fourth ball to the mix, Becker dialed the last few numbers on his list. He had the Sound Studio remix the Sound of Silence with a little more bass, the Olfactory sweeten the Smell of Success, and the Department of Energy crank up the pull of Gravity. All of which helped prepare this densely populated area of The World for what was about to happen.

"Why do you think they always hit the Russkies, kid?" asked Henry. "I mean, first they get stuck with Ivan the Terrible, then the Reds roll into town, and then that whole glasnost-perestroika thing. Why not Toledo or Walla Walla every now and then?"

"The Winds of Change follow a course all their own, Henry."

"As far as you know." The man in the trench coat pulled off his shades and threw Becker a wink. "Let's just hope they blow hard enough to help that guy's music career."

The earnest singer-songwriter had drawn quite an audience strumming Beatles and Cat Stevens covers, but now that he'd switched to his own material the crowd was starting to thin.

"We'll know in about a minute and thirty-seven seconds."

Becker pressed the gear icon on the Bleceiver's touch screen and made his final call.

"Fixer Drane to Department of Time."

"Time Management here."

"Ready for showtime?"

"Affirmative. But remember—we can only do this for thirty seconds, or we might not be able to get it started again."

"Roger that. One Day That Time Stood Still is more than enough for me."

"Just make sure you're wearing your Stopwatch™ and you're good to go."

"Got that, Henry?"

Henry held up his wrist, on which was strapped a red stop sign with Seemsian numerals up to twenty-five. "Never leave home without it."

"Good luck, #37," said Time Management. *"Hitting it in 3, 2, 1 . . ."*

The moment his countdown reached zero, everything in Red Square slowly ground to a halt. The pigeons that had been scampering about picking up scraps of popcorn and piroshki appeared to be turning to clay. The flags that flapped above Lenin's tomb gradually stopped rippling. Even the argument between the boyfriend and girlfriend started to sound more like a broken record. In fact, the only two things that continued to move in the entirety of Sector 66 were Becker and Henry Steele.

"What are the odds this plan of yours works?" Henry rose to his feet and gently placed his black fedora on the bench.

"People don't handle Change very well, but with Time on hold they should be able to weather the storm." Becker closed his eyes and inhaled deeply. He could already catch a whiff of revolution and hear a low howl from somewhere unseen. "The only question is whether the Fabric holds together."

"Well, maybe I can stack the deck in our favor."

Henry Steele may have looked like a private investigator or some bad B-movie spy, but in fact he was one of the few and the proud charged with disposing of the residue of Design. This substance is known to cause unexpectedly favorable Chains of Events in the Plan—be they as small as finding a parking space in a crowded mall or as large as a planet-killing asteroid narrowly missing the Earth. Hence, the Powers That Be formed a covert squadron whose sole mission was to dispense it with the greatest of care.

They called them the Agents of L.U.C.K.[3]

"Cross your fingers, kid."

As Becker did as he was told (not forgetting to cross his toes and knock on the wooden bench three times—and only three, in case the Jinx Gnomes were listening), the agent reached into a small leather pouch that was clipped to his belt. Out came a clenched fist, which he blew into once, then made a hand motion that looked suspiciously like someone throwing dice. But instead of two cubes covered with dots, the smallest amount of gold glitter escaped from his fingers and vanished into the air.

"Baby needs a new pair of shoes," was all he said.

"Thanks, bro." Becker pulled out two nylon straps and buckled them to the bench. "We'd better put on our Seat Belts™ too."

As Henry did as he was told, the air began to crackle and the invisible howl built into a deafening roar. Then Red Square itself

---

3. Little Unplanned Changes of Kismet. Note: For more, please see Appendix A: "Glossary of Terms."

started shaking so violently it reminded Becker of the train set he used to have in his grandparents' basement, and the way the miniature people and buildings would rattle when he and his little brother, Benjamin, wobbled the table and pretended "the end of the world was nigh." Thankfully, the extra gravity he'd ordered from Energy kept the real people and buildings of Sector 66 firmly rooted to their place in The World.

"It's working, Drane!"

"Don't book a table at Flip's just yet." A worminess in Becker's stomach was telling him that, though the pillars of Red Square were holding fast, something was not quite right. "My 7th Sense is ringing off the hook."

Becker's Bleceiver was also ringing off the hook and when he picked it up, the frazzled voice of Simly Frye was shouting on the other end of the line.

"I've got bad news for you, sir! We sewed the Patch into the Fabric but it's not holding! Repeat, it's not—"

"Tell me something I don't know!"

Much to the Fixer's horror, the ground began to bulge upward like a tin of Jiffy Pop. But instead of aluminum foil, the stone and brick of Red Square took on the appearance of cloth being stretched to the limit. In a matter of seconds, the bench to which Becker and the Agent were fastened rose several hundred feet in the air and if the Fabric pulled any tighter, they (and the rest of Sector 66) would soon be in a very unrealistic situation.

"Where's my L.U.C.K., Henry?"

"Have a little faith, kid."

Easier said than done, especially because in about fifteen

seconds Time would be restarting and a lot of Russians would be in for a rude awakening.

"I'm trying, dude. I'm try—"

But before Becker could express his struggle to believe that the impending catastrophe was all part of the Plan, the famous statue of Minin and Pozharsky unexpectedly tilted forward on its base and poked a tiny hole at the top of the distended square. Wind and Change rushed up through the opening, spouting like a geyser into the sky, while the very Fabric of Reality began to recede. By the time Becker and the bench had resumed their original position, not only had cloth returned to concrete and stone, but the bronze rendition of the butcher and prince who helped liberate Mother Russia in 1612 was proudly overlooking its homeland once more.

"Whoa," was all the Fixer could muster. But the last part of the Plan for this day had yet to be written.

Not one second later, there was a loud groaning noise, and just as Time in Sector 66 had slowed to a crawl, it now kicked back into gear. The pigeons resumed their gobbling, the lovers their quarreling, and the juggler his pedaling about the center of the square. Noticing Becker's jaw hanging loosely open at this miraculous stroke of good fortune, Henry tipped his fedora.

"Knew I was feeling lucky today."

"Nice work, dude. But we still gotta cross our i's and dot our t's."

Fixer Drane unbuckled his Seat Belt and sprinted across to the garden where Minin and Pozharsky had stood since 1936. In the grass beside the statue was the hole that had released the pressure from the Winds of Change, but instead of a window into the infinite highways and byways of the In-Between, all he saw was a small section of denim peeking through.

"That Patch held better than you thought," Becker informed his elated Briefer, and he could hear the cheers of the Seemstresses who manned the Department of Reality. "Just needs a little nip and tuck."

When Fixer Casey Lake had so famously sewn the Fabric back together, all she'd used for the job was a household needle and thread. But since this was more of a hole than a tear, Becker figured better safe than sorry. He used a Rounded Scopeman '4000™ to clamp the dirt around the denim, then wrapped a feathered Boa Constrictor™ around the apparatus and pulled Reality back together tight.

"Now call in the Cleanup Crew and tell them they've got a spill in aisle 66. All right, Sim?"

"Aye, aye, sir."

It wouldn't be easy to conceal the fact that an entire Sector of The World had mysteriously paused for over a minute—especially a Sector as prominent as this. Memories would have to be disguised as Dreams, pieces of Misinformation scattered, and any existing video footage edited for content, but the Cleanup Crew was renowned for their spotless record.

"There's one thing they can't hide, though." Becker looked up to the crystal blue sky. "The amount of Change that slipped through the Fabric."

"You can't stop The World from changing, kid." Henry smiled and gestured to the crowd. "Far as I'm concerned, that's a good thing."

Indeed, all was not as it once was in the heart of Red Square. The formerly talentless juggler was not only standing on the seat of his unicycle but had added a sixth and seventh ball to the mix. The lovers whose relationship was unraveling were locked in a warm embrace, and though not a single passerby was listening to the long-haired songwriter, a perfect arrangement of chords and heartfelt melody was emerging from his guitar.

It was hard to tell how far and wide these new possibilities would spread, but the two co-workers knew for certain that the Mission known as "The Winds of Change" was complete.

"Pleasure doing business with you, Drane."

"Likewise."

"And good luck in court tomorrow." Henry extended his gloved hand and Becker shook it with appreciation. "Everyone at the agency's pullin' for ya."

"Thanks, man. That means a lot."

With a final tip of the cap, Henry Steele, Agent of L.U.C.K., pulled up his coat collar and vanished into the crowd.

The late afternoon light was creeping toward evening and a group of Russian teenagers had begun to gather around the young guitarist, who was just beginning to test out some lyrics. The last thing Becker wanted to think about was what might happen tomorrow, so instead he busted out a Slim Jim and sat himself down to listen to the newly written tune.

"Noviy dyen' rassvetayet, noviy put' lezhit pryamo peredo mnoy."

Though the Fixer couldn't understand the lyrics without his Hearing Aide™, he knew the song wasn't the only thing that had been affected by the Winds of Change. Now that they

16

were here, he hoped maybe peace would reign on Earth. Maybe Pink Floyd would finally get back together and go on tour. Maybe Benjamin would even stay out of his room when the "do not disturb" sign was hanging on the outside of the door. (Fat chance.)

As per his orders, all the Seemsian departments had redialed Sector 66 to its original state, and he pleasantly sampled their wares. The grass felt soft and loose beneath him, the Smell of Success teased his nostrils, and the return of Indian summer allowed him and his fellow concertgoers to remove their sweat-shirts and gloves. Sooner or later, Becker would have to break out his Skeleton Key™ and get back to Jersey, where he would anxiously count down the hours until his fate was decided. But for now, all he wanted to do was close his eyes and listen to an ever-changing World.

Little did he know that winds of change were sweeping across The Seems as well.

The Court of Public Opinion

Court of Public Opinion,
Department of Legal Affairs, The Seems

Waldy Joels, Seemsian News Network's chief legal correspondent, straightened his perfectly coiffed hair and looked deeply into the camera.

"*We're inside the Court of Public Opinion, where a verdict is expected today in the trial of one of The Seems' most decorated Fixers. Should the defendant be found guilty on all counts, he faces the severest penalties under the law—immediate Pink Slip, incarceration in Seemsberia, and, worst of all, permanent unremembering of The Seems itself.*"

A murmur went through the packed courtroom as the door to the judges' chambers slowly creaked open.

"*Here come the judges now.*"

Waldy's cameraman trained his lens on the proceedings, where a grizzled old bailiff stepped to the front.

"All rise. The Court of Public Opinion is now in session." The crowd rose to its feet as the three members of the tribunal took their seats on the bench. "The Honorable Eve Hightower presiding."

Second in Command Eve Hightower, the highest-ranking official in The Seems, tucked in her robes and reviewed the motions submitted by the prosecution and defense. To her right was the Administrator of the Department of Legal Affairs, Alvin Torte, Esq., while on her left sat a sixth-grade teacher at the School of Thought by the name of Eleanor Altman, who, in accordance with Seemsian law, had been picked at random from the general population.

There was only one case on their docket today but it was a big one, and the hardwood benches were crammed with spectators. Most of them were holding battery-operated fans in front of their faces to combat the heat caused by a breakdown of the court's main air-conditioning unit. The one exception was the solitary figure sitting in the defendant's box, facing the crowd in a suit and tie his parents had bought him at the Menlo Park Mall.

"The court will now hear closing arguments in Case #00009876 BBJ-24, Fixer #37, Ferdinand Becker Drane III." Second in Command Hightower banged down the gavel, which loudly echoed off the high ceilings. "You may be seated."

Despite the fact that the same Ferdinand Becker Drane III was considered a rising star in Fixing circles, he had also become a figure of some controversy. Ever since his career began, he'd shown a tendency for bending (if not outright breaking) the

Rules that governed the conduct of all employees in The Seems. And though a certain leeway was given to Fixers—it was commonly known that their work often involved the gray areas of the Plan—#37's wiggle room had quickly run out when he had violated the "granddaddy of 'em all."

According to affidavits, "The defendant has systematically and repeatedly violated the Golden Rule by engaging in an unauthorized relationship with Jennifer Kaley of Sector 104, Grid 11—an association that began in a Dream world designed by the defendant himself after fully accessing Ms. Kaley's confidential Case File. Furthermore, when confronted with the allegation, Fixer Drane not only refused to remedy the situation but persisted in violating the aforementioned statute."

Although Becker was presumed innocent and allowed to remain on duty, the trial had fast become a media circus in the world that makes The World. Throngs of people had shown up on the steps of the Halls of Justice, while others routinely followed the proceedings via SNN, the *Daily Plan*, or CPO-TV.[4] But these viewers were more than just fans of reality TV, for they knew that in the Court of Public Opinion, their voice could make the difference.

In the Court of Public Opinion, every Seemsian had a say.

"In my opinion, the Golden Rule is golden for a reason!"

In the fourth row of the courtroom, a man in a three-piece suit twirled his walrus mustache.

"If it was bendable, breakable, or up for discussion, the

---

4. Court of Public Opinion Television.

original Powers That Be would have called it the Bendable, Breakable, Up for Discussion Rule!"

"Here! Here!" Several voices rang throughout the room, until Second in Command Hightower banged her gavel again.

"Please continue, Manager Dozenski."

Manager Dozenski had once been Administrator Dominic Dozenski of the Department of Sleep, but after a Glitch almost caused a devastating Ripple Effect, he'd been reassigned to the Flower Plant. Though the symbol on his lapel had changed from Sleep's closed eye to Nature's maple tree, his crusty demeanor had not. "I say send him to the Flavor Mines and be done with it!"

"I'm sorry, Dominic, but you're hardly an impartial witness." An attractive woman in a power suit rose to her feet on the other side of the room. "Fixer Drane's disagr—"

"All members of the public wishing to speak will raise their hands or be asked to leave the hall!" Clarence the bailiff had worked in the Hall of Justice since back in the Day, and he ruled the room with an iron fist.

"My apologies to the court."

"Please continue, Administrator Sandeye," said Eve Hightower.

"I'm simply pointing out that Fixer Drane's conflict with former Administrator Dozenski on the night of the Glitch is well documented."

"That has nothing to do with this!" shouted Dominic, his face turning bright red. "Rules are the foundation of any good organization—which is why I imagine you informed Fixer Drane that the Golden Rule would be invoked when he entered into the Case in question's Dream."

"Of course I informed him. But as you well know, Dreams can often be hard to let go of."

Carol Sandeye should know, for she was once VP of Dreams before being promoted to replace the outgoing Dozenski. From the obvious tension in the room, it was safe to say they wouldn't be sipping Love Potions together at The Slumber Party.

"Excuse me. I don't mean to interrupt but . . ." Judge Altman tentatively raised her hand from the bench. "Can I get a clarification of the Administrator's comment and specifically how it relates to the Golden Rule?"

"Perhaps one of my staff can better explain." Administrator Sandeye looked up to the mezzanine. "Dr. Seymour, will you please stand up."

In the back of the second-floor balcony, a pale lab-coated figure tentatively rose. No one sat within five feet of him, for few were the Seemsians who longed to be in the presence of one of the infamous Bed Bugs.

"Um. Well, you see . . ."

The technicians whose sole responsibility was to concoct the Nightmares of The World were not known for leaving their laboratory often (if at all) and the disheveled doctor's voice was quaking uncontrollably.

"Relax, Dr. Seymour." Eve Hightower lent some support from down below. "We're all co-workers here."

"Thank you, Your Honor." The Bed Bug lifted his green visor to reveal bloodshot and sensitive eyes. "When mixing a Dream, we use ingredients especially designed to create a heightened Reality—so the messages, experiences, and visions the recipients receive will stick with them until morning and beyond.

The Dream in question, which I believe was a modified #532, is especially difficult to shake because it also includes elements of a Nightmare."

"Does that answer your question, Judge Altman?" asked Administrator Sandeye.

"Oh yes, ma'am," said the little old lady, who still could not believe she was in the presence of so many Seemsian luminaries (let alone the Second in Command herself). "I believe that about covers it."

Administrator Sandeye nodded and turned to the rest of the tribunal. "I would only ask that the court consider leniency in this case."

"Your request is duly noted for the record, " Judge Alvin Torte coldly nodded to the stenographer, who was tasked with keeping track of every syllable in every trial. "But leniency is more of an issue for sentencing."

Whispers rippled through the press box, which was overflowing with Wordsmiths and reporters from the *Daily Plan*. Judge Torte was known to be a strict constructionist when it came to interpreting the Plan, which was why most experts believed he would come down hard on the side of a guilty verdict. But if the defendant was worried on the inside, he didn't show it. Fixer Drane sat expressionless on the stand, taking notes and waiting for Torte to continue.

"What I'd like to get are some opinions about the defendant's wanton disregard for the Rules, especially when it comes to the subject of his younger brother."

Torte, of course, was speaking of Fixer Drane's alleged violation of another sacred Seemsian law: the Keep Your Mouth

Shut Rule.[5] Upon his acceptance as a Candidate at the Institute for Fixing & Repair, Becker had been granted a semi-exemption of this clause, because he was only ten years old at the time and still living at home with his parents. This gave him the freedom to tell tall tales and bedtime stories about The Seems to Benjamin, who was often troubled by deep-seated fears and unanswerable questions.

But last summer, when Benjamin stumbled upon two identical versions of his brother—the real Becker and the inflatable Tool known as a Me-'2™—no mere semi-exception to the Keep Your Mouth Shut Rule would do.

"Zis is an outrage!" A flamboyant figure with smears of paint and Ingenuity all over his smock jumped to his feet in the eighteenth row. "I have had ze personal pleasure of instructing Benjamin Drane, and I tell you, ze boy is a natural!"

Figarro Mastrioni, the famed Maestro of Sunset Strip, was perhaps the greatest artiste to ever grace The World's sky at dawn or dusk. He also owed Fixer Drane a favor, which he was happy to repay by giving Benjamin art lessons.

"Someday zis Benjamin will make ze sky itself weep!"

"This isn't about Benjamin Drane's talent as an artist, sir," Torte replied from his place on the bench. "You of all people should know better than to disclose the secrets of The Seems to someone who hasn't been vetted by Human Resources!"

"Bureaucrats in their ivory tower! What about ze people of

---

5. "World-based employees of The Seems, in all cases regarding those without knowledge of The Seems, should (except when permission has been granted by the Powers That Be) keep their mouths shut."

Ze World? Have we forgotten zat zis should be our main concern?"

Figarro was as surprised as anyone when a round of applause exploded through the room.

"Order! Order in the court!" Second in Command Hightower angrily slammed down the gavel and brought the hall to silence. "I know a lot of people have strong feelings, but this trial is about more than one man's job. It's about who we are as The Seems and what kind of World we want to create."

"Hopefully not one filled with Rules and regulations." A disgruntled Nature Buff stood up without raising her hand. "Whatever happened to thinking for ourselves?"

"Sounds to me like you're surfing the wrong wave, sister." A Minuteman from the Department of Time got right in her face. "Maybe we should see what kind of necklace you're sporting."

Again, the Hall of Justice fell into disarray as the two workers charged at each other and had to be restrained by security. But this time, the pounding of gavels had no effect whatsoever.

"Order!" shouted all three judges to no avail. "Order in this court!"

While most in The Seems still had faith in the Big Building and its Plan, in the past year the underground movement known as The Tide had continued its alarming rise. Their efforts to remove the Powers That Be and take over The World had grown more brazen, and though few would publicly admit sympathies, the group's proposals were starting to gain traction with the public. Which is why fights like this had become all too common.

It was only when a tall man with steely blue eyes raised his hand from the very back of the room that the hall grew quiet once more. Slowly at first, then all at once, as each person in the crowd realized who was requesting permission to speak.

"The court recognizes Samuel Hightower." The Second in Command's voice remained decidedly professional, even though everyone in the room knew their relationship was anything but. "Do you have an opinion in this matter?"

The tall man leaned back against the wall behind him and smiled.

"It's my opinion that everyone should take a deep breath and remember that we're all on the same side."

When Samuel Hightower spoke, people in The Seems listened. His term as Second in Command had been the longest in recorded History and his approval ratings astronomically high. Though he had unexpectedly resigned his post seven years ago, he was still a consultant to the Powers That Be and with all the political upheaval, calls for his reinstatement had become louder and louder. Oh, and there was one more thing that made the gossip columnist for the *Daily Plan* lean forward in the press box.

Samuel was Eve Hightower's husband.

"These are tenuous times in The Seems, are they not?" He lifted a well-worn cowboy boot to the rail in front of him and polished the toe with his thumb. "Who among us thought there would come a day when metal detectors lined the doors to every department? When Special Forces roamed the Field of Play, checking every bag and knapsack? When brother and sister would turn on each other as they haven't since the terrible days of the Color Wars?"

Though he never looked at the Nature Buff or Minuteman, the reprimand was clear, and all who'd engaged in the scuffle dropped their eyes to the floor.

"It's no secret who is responsible for the situation we now face. And though we can all agree that The Tide's methods are distasteful—if not downright criminal—they've also forced us to ask some tough questions. Questions we've been avoiding since back in the Day. And trust me, no one avoided them more than I did, when I sat in the chair at the head of this room."

Heads shook throughout the hall, as if to exonerate the man who had led them for so many peaceful and productive years, but Samuel would hear none of it.

"In many ways, this trial is about our unwillingness to look in the mirror. A boy too young to vote or drive a car in his own world was confronted by the intractable Rules of another. Did Becker Drane break these Rules? Of course he did. Did he violate the 'granddaddy of 'em all'? Without a doubt. But in my opinion, that is not what we are here to decide."

"What then?" said Dominic Dozenski, anxious to be told what to do.

"What we're here to decide is what we, the people of The Seems, are going to do when the letter of the law and its spirit are at odds." Samuel dropped his foot back to the floor and gazed at the teenager who sat by himself in a small box at the front of the room. "And I for one cannot make that decision without hearing from the Fixer himself."

"Um . . ."

Realizing that everyone in the court was now intently staring at him, Becker stopped in mid-stroke and turned to a blank page in his Briefing Pad. The last thing he wanted anyone to see—especially at this point in the trial—was that the entire time he'd been on the stand, he had not been recording the opinions offered on or against his behalf. Nor had he been taking "notes to self" on case law for a potential appeal. Rather, he'd been pleasantly sketching the initials "J" and "K" in every conceivable combination and pattern.

"Fixer Drane." Eve Hightower laid her gavel back down on the bench and focused her piercing brown eyes upon the kid from Highland Park, New Jersey. "If you would like to make a statement on your own behalf, now would be the time."

By and large, Becker had kept his head down during the trial, both on his lawyer's advice and because this whole thing was really embarrassing. But when the Fixer brushed aside his lengthy bangs and scanned the courtroom, he was soothed by the sight of friendly faces smiling back.

Over there was Johnny Z, program director of radio station WDOZ, whom Becker had swapped mixes with ever since his first Mission to the Department of Sleep. And over there was Mellow, the barista at the Magic Hour coffee shop, who'd been sneaking Becker day-old scones long before he came to her rescue when the Time Bomb exploded. Flip Orenz had snuck away from the lunch rush at The Flip Side to lend his support, while leaning on his janitor's mop was Brooks, Becker's connection in The Know, who clenched a fist as if to say, "We're with you, bro."

"Well, I'm not going to lie to everybody," Becker said as he loosened his paisley tie. "I'm pretty much guilty as charged."

A low rumble went through the hall, but seemed to soften the mood.

"Talk to any Fixer who's ever gone on a Mission and he'll

tell you the same thing—if it comes down to saving The World or breaking the Rules, I'm gonna save The World every time. But obviously, the same logic doesn't apply to why I broke the Golden . . ."

Since Becker's fellow Fixers had been asked to recuse themselves, a handful of Briefers and Candidates had jumped at the front-row seats marked "reserved for IFR." All of them were shaking their heads at Becker, trying and failing to get him to change the direction of his testimony.

"I wish I could say I did it for some important reason or because I was trying to make a political statement, but the truth is, that had nothing to do with it."

Samuel Hightower leaned forward and asked the question that was on everybody's tongue. "Then why, son? Why did you do it?"

"I guess . . ." Becker flushed red and felt like he wanted to puke, but he had little choice other than to throw himself on the mercy of the court. "I guess because I really like this girl."

There was no response from the crowd, other than an instinctive turning toward Samuel, whose voice for so many years had been the most important in The Seems. For his part, the former Second in Command just sat back down on his chair and concluded:

"That's good enough for me."

Becker might've caught the present Second in Command rolling her eyes—just like his mom did when his dad pulled some sort of grandstanding move at a dinner party—but she quickly regained command of the floor.

"If there are no further opinions, then it's time to take

a Straw Poll in the case of Fixer #37, Ferdinand Becker Drane III."

In the Court of Public Opinion, each citizen was issued a packet of three different-colored straws. A red straw equated to "guilty" (and sentencing by the current tribunal), yellow to "guilty, with mitigating circumstances" (usually a slap on the wrist or community service), and green, "not guilty" (leave the courthouse steps a free man, woman, or child). One straw per person could then be deposited in any of the countless drop boxes used by SPS,[6] where they were rapidly gathered and tabulated in the Mail room.

All that remained to set the vote in motion was for each of the judges to ceremoniously bang their gavels and declare the hearing over. From the way Judge Altman and many others smiled at him, Becker was confident that his "honesty is the best policy" approach in the trial would land him a majority of yellow straws. The last thing he wanted was a sentencing hearing where Administrator Torte would no doubt be pushing for Seemsberia or a complete unremembering of everything he'd fought for and believed in these past four years. But just as he was about to button up his blazer and step off the stand, the doors to the courtroom swung open.

"If it pleases the court, Your Honors." A voice with the peculiar twang of southern Australia froze the gavels mere inches above the bench. "Central Command would like to offer an opinion in this matter."

"Of course." Eve Hightower and her two fellows leaned

---

6. Seemsian Postal Service: "When it maybe, hopefully, sort of, really needs to get there relatively on time^{SM}."

back in their leather-bound chairs. "The court recognizes Cassiopeia Lake."

Dressed in a smart pantsuit, her hair up in a bun for this formal occasion, was Fixer Casey Lake. Becker had never seen her in anything other than flip-flops and cutoff jeans or a sundress, and the wry look of amusement she usually wore on her face was gone. She looked deadly serious. But as she stoically handed Clarence the Bailiff a thin brown envelope stamped with a Wrench, Becker couldn't stop himself from celebrating the fact that his fellow Fixers were coming to his defense. Considering how much weight they were given among the Powers That Be, maybe a not guilty verdict was on the table after all.

"We, the undersigned Fixers"—Clarence pulled a single sheet of paper from the envelope and began to read aloud— "with one Fixer abstaining—submit the following opinion in the case of *The Seems v. Ferdinand Becker Drane III*."

Becker shot a smile at one of his closest Fixer friends, but when Casey did not return it, the suit that he'd worn to so many confirmations and bar mitzvahs began to feel abnormally tight and small. And that was before he heard the rest.

"Despite our respect for the defendant's skill and dedication to The World, each and every one of us swore an oath on the day we received our Fixer's Badge. A promise to protect the Plan for The World and live by the Rules that govern its enacting. And though every Fixer has been forced to bend or even circumvent those Rules with the fate of The World at stake, we believe that Fixer Drane's violations came not from any allegiance to our sacred oath or dedication to the Mission, but from a desire to meet his own selfish needs. Therefore, it is with profound disappointment that we recommend a verdict of guilty . . . without mitigating circumstances."

The bailiff looked up from the page and delivered the final blow.

"It's co-signed by Jelani Blaque."

Gasps shot through the Hall of Justice, as literally no one could believe that the IFR's legendary head instructor had thrown his weight behind the opinion. As for the defendant himself, Becker's heart started to pound so viciously that he thought he might pass out right then and there.

"The opinion of the Fixers is duly noted," declared Judge Alvin Torte, smug satisfaction dripping from every syllable. "Does anyone have anything to say in response?"

No one did, least of all Becker Drane. Thus, three gavels simultaneously banged down upon the bench, and Second in Command Eve Hightower rose to her feet. "Then let the Straw Poll begin."

Unremembering

Galaxie Diner, Caledon, Ontario

Jennifer Kaley put her wool hat in her pocket and shook a few stray leaves from her dirty blond hair. Caledon was cold this time of year and the fourteen-year-old was mad at herself for wearing her flimsy army jacket instead of the green parka with the furry hood.

"One for breakfast?" asked the waitress who greeted her by the cash register.

"Two. I'm meeting someone."

"Right this way."

The heavyset woman in the black and yellow apron grabbed two menus and led Jennifer toward the row of booths in the back. These were the best seats in the house, not only because of the soft red cushions, but because they came with their own individual jukeboxes.

"What can I get you to start?" asked the waitress.

"Water with lemon."

Being a single customer at a table with two menus always made her feel awkward, so Jennifer flipped through the jukebox that was filled with bands like Foreigner and ABBA and a bunch of others she'd never heard of. She finally chose "No Sugar Tonight" by the Guess Who (her dad's favorite band), which got a thumbs-up from the old biker dude who was working the Galaxie's grill.

The bell by the front door dinged loudly and Jennifer snapped her head around, hoping to see a teenage boy with shaggy hair and old-school corduroys walking in. But it was a party of Little Leaguers instead—the Caledon Fireballs—who poured into the surrounding booths, ready to celebrate another victory with a healthy breakfast of chocolate chip pancakes.

"Don't worry, honey." The waitress handed Jennifer a large glass of water, along with a knowing smile that said she too had waited for a mysterious man or two in her time. "If he doesn't show, it's his loss."

"Tell me about it." Jennifer smiled back. "This place has the best vanilla milkshakes in the world!"

"One vanilla, comin' right up."

The person Jennifer was waiting for had often spoken of the milkshakes at some beach-front burger joint as being the best he'd ever had, but since those were literally in another world, she felt quite confident in her opinion. Speaking of that person, he was now over fifteen minutes late and Jennifer couldn't help but be a little bit concerned. It had been two weeks since they'd last seen each other, and even though they'd spoken on the phone every night, it was hard to put aside the fear that the long-distance thing wasn't working anymore, or that maybe one of the girls at his new high school was much cooler or prettier.

Again the bell at the front jingled and when Jennifer saw Norm from Norm's Great Grocery entering with his family, she ducked under the table—mostly because she didn't feel like having to explain to her boss what she was doing here all by herself. But when she poked her head back up, someone else was standing by the door. He looked a little worse for wear—his shaggy hair a little shaggier, his corduroys cultivating a hole in one knee—but the smile that lit his face hadn't changed one bit.

"Hey," said Becker, plopping into the seat on the other side of the booth.

"Hey."

Ever since the night Jennifer and Becker shared a kiss in the woods on the outskirts of Caledon, they had been nearly inseparable. Well, that's not exactly true. The Fixer was determined not to break the Golden Rule again—especially after being reprimanded by his mentor Fixer Blaque—so their early relationship consisted mostly of e-mails, phone calls, and texts. But not seeing each other in person got old quick, and it was finally decided that one brief, innocent, face-to-face meeting could probably be arranged.

By the time the summer arrived, the Fixer was crossing the border on a regular basis—so much so that he and Jennifer even concocted a cover story that Becker was an American kid whose father's company had moved their main office to Toronto. This seemed to fly with her friends and family, and were it not for Becker's Me-2 pleading with him to stop using his Skeleton Key for personal travel, he probably would have started looking through the classifieds for a cheap apartment.

But that was before the results of the Straw Poll had come in.

"Is everything okay?" Jennifer slipped Becker's JV soccer jacket over her own as the two headed west on Henderson Street. "You seem a little weird."

"I do?" Becker shrugged, trying to avoid the conversation he knew was unavoidable. "Guess it's just been a crazy week."

"Everything good with Benjamin? Mom and Dad?"

"They're chillin'."

"Any cool Missions lately?"

"I did have one a couple days ago."

"You allowed to talk about it?"

"Not really." Even though Becker was willing to break the Rules time and time again just to be here, there were some things he wouldn't do: namely, reveal specific Mission details or take Jennifer to The Seems itself. "Let's just say the Winds of Change are sweeping across The World again."

"I knew something was up when my dad signed up for yoga!"

Becker laughed out loud, something he seemed to do a lot when she was around. "Seriously, Moscow almost got toasted."

"My hero! He saves The World and still has time to hang out with the little people."

Though Jennifer threw an arm around Becker's neck and gave him a hug, she'd known ever since he didn't finish his two eggs over medium at the Galaxie that things weren't quite right. She decided not to push it though. "Hey, did I tell you I had an idea for a new department?"

"Which one?"

"Education. They can teach us everything we need to know by playing audiotapes while we're sleeping. That way we never have to go to school but we end up twice as smart."

Becker cracked up—ideas like that came so easily to Jennifer. When they first started dating, he'd encouraged her to fill out a Seemsian Aptitude Test, since he thought she'd make a perfect Fixer. Her interests were much more geared to Case Worker, however, because they got to map out really intricate strategies to help people in their everyday lives (and also because the offices in the Big Building were supposed to be really plush).

But as Jennifer continued on about the Department of Ed's ability to allow each person to pick one thing they could be genius at, Becker could barely hear what she was saying. Instead of appreciating walking down the street with the coolest girl he'd ever met on an even cooler fall day, all he could think about was how horrible it would be if he couldn't remember any of it at all.

"Are you listening to me?" she asked, stopping outside the door to Paradise Bound Records, the best music store in Caledon.

"Totally. I heard every last word!"

"Liar." She kicked him halfheartedly in the shin. "What was I talking about?"

"Um . . . you were saying how great I am and how you wanted me to give you lessons on what it's like to be Becker Drane."

This time, the kick on the shin wasn't so light, and Becker responded with a nudge, which quickly escalated to a battle of nuggies, and then all gloves were off. But before a truce was declared and they strode into the pleasantly musty stacks of LPs, CDs, and eight-track tapes (three for a dollar) to find their friends, Jennifer turned to the boy who had made these past few months so great.

"Are you sure there's nothing wrong?"

Becker grabbed her hand and gave it a gentle squeeze.

"Nothing I can't fix."

Alton Forest, Caledon, Ontario

The group known as "Les Resistance" had been formed nearly two years earlier by a group of like-minded kids seeking refuge from the middle school grind. In a secluded corner of the Alton Forest conservation area, the founding members—Jennifer Kaley, twins Rob and Claudia Moreau, Rachel Mandel, and Vikram Pemundi—had built a clubhouse retreat where the business of resisting could be conducted undisturbed. Their number had recently grown to include the Moreaus' significant others—Neve and Miles—who, along with Becker, were forced to endure an initiation ritual far too clandestine for these pages.

This Sunday afternoon, the gang was kicking back on beanbag chairs and the velvet couch Jennifer "borrowed" from her parent's basement and doing what they usually did—talking about the meaning of life, the lack of the meaning in life, and everything in between.

"All I'm saying is that adding more seasons is a no-brainer." Vikram paced back and forth, like he was giving a lecture at a university. "You have Indian summer in October—and I'm not talking about Native American, I'm talking about the way it is in Ahmedabad, hot and humid—then there's splinter, which is between spring and winter. And if we're remaking the world, why not a seventh season?"

"Like what?" asked Jennifer.

"I don't know, like the season of the witch or this weird season where the sky is purple, the sun is blue, and Vikram Pemundi rules over the land with an iron fist!"

"We can see who's not gonna get invited to remake the world from scratch."

"Hey, I'm just trying to think outside the box."

"That's your problem, you think too much." Rachel Mandel cheerfully knocked on Vikram's head. "All the world really needs is girls to be in charge and chocolate chip cookies to grow on trees."

"Now you're talking!" Jennifer gave her friend a low five. "Toss in some doughnut bushes and lakes filled with Yoo-hoo and we're good to go!"

Ever since she'd supposedly found this weird pamphlet at the record store, Jennifer had enlisted her friends to help her answer the SAT's crucial Question #3.[7] Everybody had poured in their suggestions, and by the time she was finished filling out the questionnaire, it was the size of a book report. But even though Becker had hand-delivered her application to the Department of

---

7. "Pretend The World was being remade from Scratch. What kind of World would you create?"

Human Resources more than three weeks ago, the conversation was still going strong.

"I still say the most important thing is that bad things can't happen to good people anymore." Miles McQueen may have lettered in three sports at Caledon East, but Claudia's boyfriend was much more than the ordinary jock. "I'm sick of turning on the news and finding out another ten thousand innocent villagers got buried in a rockslide."

Claudia chucked a Cheez Doodle at Miles. "Hate to break it to you, sweetheart, but good and bad are in the eye of the beholder."

"I agree with Moreau," said Moreau (Rob). "One man's triumph is another man's tragedy."

"Whatever, dudes." Miles shrugged and ate the Doodle. "If a tree falls on me and breaks my legs, it sucks no matter which way you cut it."

Becker chuckled along with the rest of the gang, but as usual when the conversation turned toward Plan-related topics, he kept his mouth shut. Partially because he didn't want to spill any confidential material, but also because he was just happy to kick back for a change and let someone else do the wondering. Especially today.

"I say we make the world into a piñata." No one knew where this was going because Neve was a flophead[8] and flopheads think a little differently. "Then we take it to a kid's

---

8. Flopheads: a progressive tribe of teenagers known for wearing Doc Martens, listening to cool music, and shaving one side of their heads so the remaining hair will flop over.

birthday party, let a bunch of three-year-olds whack it with a stick, and see what kind of candy comes out."

At first, Les Resistance was stunned into silence, because this was only the third time Neve had ever spoken in their presence—but then they all burst into laughter. Even Becker forgot his troubles for a moment, especially when Jennifer leaned forward and elbowed him in the ribs.

"Let's go upstairs."

The coupling off of the group had been a relatively recent development, and each had selected their own private getaway. Rob and Neve would head off into the woods, while Claudia and Miles would "check on the waterfall" (as if it were going anywhere), leaving Vik and Rachel the downstairs portion of the clubhouse. And since Jennifer had been project coordinator of the second-floor observatory, it seemed only right for the group to cede this prime real estate to her and Becker.

"Don't you think it's ridiculous that Rach and Vik's parents are forcing them to have arranged marriages when they get older?" Becker was nervously pacing around the circular wooden platform, listening to the laughter that was bubbling up from the floor below. "I mean, wouldn't it be nice if they could just be with each other?"

"I don't know." Jennifer shrugged and popped another jujube. "Statistics show that arranged marriages are just as successful as so-called love marriages."

"That's not the point. I just think it's messed up when people try to tell other people how to live their lives."

Becker stopped to look into the telescope, which at this time of day wasn't good for much besides bird watching or spying on Rob and Neve.

"Come and sit down." Jennifer put her can of soda in the prefabricated cup holder that came with the theater seat they'd installed.

"In a minute."

"You're gonna drive yourself crazy if you keep bringing your work home with you."

"I know. But it's not just all these stupid rules and regulations that are so messed up, it's everything!" Becker pointed the telescope at the pale fingertip moon that was just revealing itself in the daylit sky. "The planet's falling apart, people are sick or dying or killing each other everywhere, and when I honestly ask myself, 'Is The World better than when I started this stupid job three years ago?' the answer is no! It's probably worse!"

Jennifer slowly closed up her box of candy and placed it back in the battery-operated fridge. She'd heard Becker talk this way before and knew he'd been struggling with doubts about his work ever since a Fixer friend of his had died on a Mission last year. But he'd never sounded as depressed as this.

"Becker." She patted the seat next to her, and made it clear she wasn't asking. "Sit down."

When the Fixer finally took his eye away from the viewfinder, it was difficult to tell if it was red from the eyepiece itself, or something else. Jennifer dusted off a stray acorn from the seat, and Becker finally let his body fall into the cracked and cushiony chair beside her.

"Do you wanna tell me what's really going on?"

"It's a long story," Becker finally choked out. "But I got in trouble in The Seems."

"What kind of trouble?"

"I broke some Rules . . . and one of them was kinda big."

"How big?"

"It's the Rule that says I'm, uh . . . not allowed to know you."

Jennifer's blood felt suddenly cold in her veins, even more so because Becker was having a hard time looking into her eyes.

"Why aren't you allowed to know me?"

"Because technically, when we met inside your Dream, I had access to the details of your Case File—your life—and there's nothing more sacred in The Seems than the privacy of the people in The World."

"But I want you to know the private details of my life. I want you to know everything about me. I mean, can't I just sign a permission slip or something?"

"I wish. The truth is, I've already been put on trial in The Seems."

"On trial?" Jennifer was flabbergasted. Becker had always spoken so glowingly of The Seems that she imagined it more like candyland or paradise, and never contemplated the fact that something bad could happen there.

"Yeah . . . in the Court of Public Opinion. I had a lawyer and everything."

"Had?"

"My trial ended yesterday."

Jennifer was afraid to ask, but there was nothing else she could do.

"And?"

"I was found guilty on all counts."

The official sentence had come down around four hours ago, when Becker was stewing in his bedroom at 12 Grant Avenue, still hoping for a guilty *with* mitigating circumstances verdict. And even though the message that flashed over his Bleceiver was text only, the words somehow echoed between his ears in the stentorian voice of Alvin Torte:

> *By order of the Court of Public Opinion, Ferdinand Becker Drane III has been suspended from active duty for a period of one year, effective midnight today Sector 33-514 time. In addition, Fixer Drane will be summarily unremembered of all knowledge pertaining to the existence of Jennifer Kaley of Sector 104-11.*

> *Ms. Kaley will in turn be unremembered of all knowledge pertaining to Fixer Drane. Secondarily, Benjamin Q. Drane will be unremembered of all knowledge of The Seems, and any/all association with the Department of Public Works suspended posthaste.*

> *Lastly, Mr. Drane will have his Seems Credit Card revoked until further notice.*

Becker's first reaction had been to smash his Bleceiver into a million pieces, which, though satisfying in the moment, brought little long-term comfort. He could stomach losing his unlimited account to all the best stores in The Seems, could face returning to the days when he told his little brother it was all just a story he'd invented, could even tolerate being unemployed for a year. But Jennifer? How was he going to tell the first girlfriend he'd ever had that everything they knew about each other, everything they had done, and (because of the previous two) everything they'd felt was going to disappear from their memories in less than seven hours?

For several long seconds neither said a thing, and together they listened to the sounds of Alton Forest. A *Picus canadensis* pecking the wood of an unseen tree. Squirrels chattering about their plans. Finally, Jennifer forced a smile.

"They're looking for a stock boy at Norm's Great Grocery."

"At what?"

"The deli where I work."

"You don't understand, Jenny. This is really serious."

Jennifer was afraid to ask. She remembered Becker talking about some awful place called "Seemsberia," but would they really send a fourteen year old to prison? Or worse?

"How serious?"

"Well . . . the truth is . . ."

The mighty young Fixer who had stared down a Glitch, who had chased a Split Second through Frozen Moments of Time, who had even earned the respect of Melvin Sharp (the toughest/scariest kid in Highland Park) by beaning him in a game of bombardment, could not even bring himself to speak.

Then, out of nowhere, somebody spoke for him.

"Hey, Becker!"

It was a young man's voice, echoing from somewhere down on the forest floor. Jennifer and Becker looked at each other, wondering if they were imagining the very same thing, because it didn't sound like any member of Les Resistance.

"Becker, it's me! Are you up there?"

As Becker leaned over the side of the platform to take a gander below, his only thought was, "It can't be!" But it was.

"Simly?"

"In the flesh, sir!"

Impossibly standing at the base of the tree and snapping off a sharp-wristed salute was Briefer #356, also known as Simly Alomonous Frye. His trademark Coke-bottle glasses covered his eyes, while a bright white Toronto Maple Leafs jersey stretched from neck to knees—a clear effort at "fitting in" with the Canadians.

"What the heck are you doing here?"

"They sent me to find you and bring you back to the, um, ahem . . ."

Even from twenty feet above Becker could see Simly's face turning bright red when he noticed Jennifer peeking down at him too.

"Don't sweat it. She knows the whole deal."

Jennifer waved and smiled. "Hey, Simly. Becker's told me all about you."

"He has?" Simly brightened up like a Christmas tree. "Well, he's told me all about you too, and personally, I think this whole unremembering thing is a total—"

"Simly!"

The Briefer coughed a few times, realizing he was about to pull another Frye-paux,[9] then bit his tongue hard. "Sorry."

---

9. Frye-paux (n): 1. A violation of accepted although unwritten Rules. (From the Seemsian, meaning "Another foot-in-mouth moment, courtesy of Simly Alomonous Frye.")

"Who sent you to find me?"

"Central Command, sir! They've been trying to reach you for, like, hours, but for some reason, your Bleceiver's not responding."

"Um . . . yeah . . . it's a little bit on the fritz." Becker tried not to think about the wastebasket in his bedroom where what was left of his communications device blended with paper clips, junk mail, and gum. "Why, what's wrong?"

"I don't have high enough clearance to know for sure, sir. But word on the Street is that T&E lost an entire Train of Thought!"

"They lost what? But my 7th Sense[10] didn't pick up a thing."

"Neither did mine." Though Simly Frye was Seemsian by birth, he was one of the rare few of his kind who'd managed to unlock a Fixer's greatest Tool. "That's what scares me."

Becker backed away from the railing, feeling the same fear as his favorite Briefer. But as his mind played out the possible consequences of the event, the Fixer found it hard to escape what *he* was about to lose in just a few hours.

"Isn't there someone else they can call, Simly? I'm kind of busy right now, if you know what I mean."

"It's okay." The last thing Jennifer wanted to do was get in the way of the fate of The World. "Why don't we just hang out when you get back?"

"Because we can't! I mean . . . of course we can, it's just—"

Jennifer watched Becker angrily stomp to the other side of the platform, then peered down at the Briefer, who helplessly

---

10. An innate sense or feeling that something in The Seems has gone wrong and will soon affect The World. Fixers often use this skill to track the location and/or nature of a Malfunction.

shrugged back at her. To be honest, part of her was glad that Becker wanted to stay, because she had this weird feeling that if he walked away right now, she would never see him again. But the look on Simly's face said this Mission was a lot bigger than either of them.

"Maybe if you fix this thing, you won't be in so much trouble anymore," she whispered.

Becker wanted to shout back that Jennifer didn't understand and that this was probably the last chance they would have to hang out together, but at the same time, maybe she had a point. Maybe the Powers That Be had reconsidered and were offering him a second chance.

"Are you sure?" he asked.

After the slightest hesitation, Jennifer nodded, and Becker quickly gathered his belongings. Meanwhile, down on the forest floor, a Toronto Maple Leafs fan was anxiously awaiting his orders.

"Get your Skeleton Key ready, Sim."

"Yes, sir!"

As Simly happily scrambled to find a secluded spot to create a portal into the In-Between, Jennifer slumped back into her chair. She was happy that she'd done the right thing, but that awful premonition was still there, stuck inside her chest, and it made her feel like crying. Sadness had descended over the Fixer's heart as well. Chances were good that the next time they met, they wouldn't even recognize each other, and he still didn't have the courage to tell her. So Becker pulled Jennifer close and kissed her instead, hoping it would say everything he wanted to say right now but couldn't.

"I'll call you when I get home."

The Second Team

With the discovery of the fields of Thought and correspon-
ding Wells of Emotion, The Seems was confronted with a
new set of ethical challenges. While providing Good Night's
Sleep, tying Rainbows, and combining the H_2 and the O
were virtual no-brainers, introducing these powerful new
elements threatened to violate the spirit of personal freedom that the original Powers That Be were determined to
guarantee. In the end, it was decided that The World should
think and feel for itself, and the architectural firm of Mind,
Body & Soll, LLC was finally allowed to break ground on
one of their most innovative departments to date.

—From *A Penny for Your Thoughts (and Emotions):*
The True Story of How T&E Almost Didn't Come
to Be by Sitriol B. Flook (Copyright ©
Seemsbury Press, MGBHV, The Seems)

Office of the Administrator,
Department of Thought & Emotion, The Seems

Eve Hightower stepped to the front of the executive suite, having exchanged her judge's robes for the business casual attire of her office. But there was nothing informal about the way she cleared her throat and began to address the four others who'd been asked to join this classified briefing.

"I know you probably expected the administrator of T&E to run this meeting, but as you'll soon see, Dr. Thinkenfeld's absence is not a coincidence."

The Second in Command grimly turned to the first page of the Mission Report and continued.

"Yesterday morning at exactly 7:35 a.m., a train loaded with all The World's Thought for the next six weeks departed on schedule from the End of the Line. Unfortunately, it failed to reach the next station stop in Seemsberia—let alone deliver its precious cargo back to this department."

The gasp that slipped from Becker Drane's mouth wasn't the only one in the room.

"When all attempts to reach conductor or crew proved futile, the decision was made to assemble a team of Fixers whose combined skills made them uniquely qualified to locate and retrieve the missing train."

Eve Hightower pressed the intercom button at the head of the table.

"Kevin?"

As the AV Mechanic dimmed the lights, Eve swiveled her chair around to face a flat-screen display.

"Central Command received the following transmission early this afternoon."

The images that flashed onscreen shook like a home movie— barely focusing on a flip-flopped foot, a mound of sand, and the bright blue sky above before tumbling crazily toward something new. But whoever was operating the camera soon got her bearings, and a wide and barren landscape finally came into view.

"I hope you guys are getting this."

Becker immediately recognized the Australian accent of Casey Lake, and deduced that the footage had been shot via the wireless Seeing-Eye attachment available on all the Toolshed's latest optics.

"We lost radio contact with Central Command approximately one hour ago, but we'll continue broadcasting just in case." A gust of wind caused Casey's microphone to pop and skip, but the audio quickly recovered. *"Update is as follows."*

The camera began to march slowly up the rise of a sand dune.

"Away team arrived End of the Line to find station staff absent and no visible sign of the missing train. Initial sweep yielded no evidence of theft or intrusion, but following a hunch, Fixer Simms uncovered a set of tracks leading directly into the Middle of Nowhere—"

Becker was stunned to be looking at actual footage of that forbidden wasteland on the very edge of The Seems—especially when Casey crested the hill and peered down upon the other side.

"This is what we found when we followed those tracks."

Stashed in the valley formed by a ring of towering dunes was a rusty red caboose, half-buried in the sand. The train it had once been attached to was nowhere in sight, nor were the rails it must've ridden to get there. In fact, the only other things visible onscreen were the sweeping sands and two figures scrambling around the car, both wearing Extremely Cool Outfits™ to protect themselves from the heat.

"How in the name of the Plan did it get there?" asked the white-haired old woman who was sitting directly to Becker's right. "I don't see any train tracks."

"Please hold your questions until we reach the end of the clip, Sylvia," answered a voice with a thick African accent.

"Sorry, Jelani."

Becker bit his own tongue and refocused his attention onscreen, where a massive figure was poking his head from beneath the abandoned caboose.

"Locking clamp snapped like twig." As usual, the Sprechen-einfaches™ struggled to translate the Fixer known as Greg the Journeyman's obscure Yakutsk dialect. *"What could do such thing?"*

"Smell that Scratch?" Casey sniffed the air, and the Journeyman did the same. *"It's London to a brick that a Brainstorm came through there."*

Fixer Lake tilted her eyes (and the camera) up to the roof, where the third member of the away team was sitting in the lotus position, eyes closed, arms extended.

"Po, you picking up anything?"

The inscrutable Li Po, #1 on the Duty Roster, silently shook his head no.

"Me neither." Casey spat with frustration, then spoke directly to whoever might be listening to her broadcast. *"If you're getting this back home, we're pretty much flying blind out here when it comes to the 7th Sense. Can only assume that stories about Middle of Nowhere are true, and will compensate accordingly—"*

"Cassiopeia!"

The voice of an Englishwoman called out, and Casey turned the camera toward where the caboose would be heading if it were still attached to a train. A slender figure was emerging from a path that cut between the dunes.

"No more tracks, as far as my Trinoculars™ can see," said Fixer #11, Lisa Simms. *"But I do see puffs of smoke in the direction of the mountains."*

"Then that where we must go," said Greg, and despite the shadow that came over Fixer Simms's face, she agreed.

It was easy to see why the Powers That Be had assigned this particular group of Fixers. Casey was a shoe-in for team leader, and if there was any chance of 7th Sensing where the missing train might be, Li Po would be the one to feel it. Greg the Journeyman's physical strength was the stuff of legend, while Lisa Simms was the only active Fixer to have entered the Middle of Nowhere and lived to tell the tale. With such a mighty collection of talent, Becker couldn't fathom what went wrong.

He was about to find out.

"All right, mates." Onscreen, Casey Lake was pulling a hand-painted Turf Board™ out of her Toolkit. *"Let's get after these whackers . . ."*

But their departure was interrupted by the sight of Fixer #1 rising to his feet atop the caboose and extending a finger off toward the horizon.

"What's wrong, Po?"

Casey and the others turned in the direction he was pointing to see a strange light emanating from somewhere on the other side of the dunes. Whatever the source, it was almost as bright as the sun shining over their heads.

"It is . . . werry beautiful," whispered Greg the Journeyman, and when he turned to the increasingly shaky camera, there were tears rolling down his bearded cheeks. As if to confirm his opinion, Casey turned her gaze back toward the light, which was so bright now that it hurt to look at even in the screening room.

"Cover your eyes, people!" The broadcast was starting to flicker and skip. "Cover your eyes!"

Greg directly ignored her order, stumbling even closer to the source of the eerie illumination, while Lisa Simms had switched over to Night Shades™ and was desperately flipping to the darkest setting.

"Cassiopeia, I think we should—"

But the woman who was the first violinist for the London Philharmonic in her "real job" could not muster the strength to finish the sentence. Fixer Simms collapsed to the ground with her hands over her eyes and rolled into a little ball. And the light got brighter still.

"What is it, Po?" Fixer Lake shouted, and for the first time since they'd met three years ago, Becker heard fear in her voice. "What's happening?"

On the roof of the caboose, Li Po was also wiping streaks from his eyes, but from the smile on his face, he appeared to be laughing, not crying. Then the unquestioned master of the 7th Sense turned toward the camera and did something he hadn't done in almost thirty years.

He spoke.

"The Most Amazing Thing of All."

The last thing Becker saw was Casey Lake digging a hole in the sand beneath her feet—as if she might claw her way to some refuge from the unbearable brightness. And then, in a flash . . .

. . . the video went white.

When the lights came up, Becker leaned back in his chair, shocked by what had taken place onscreen. Not only had Li Po broken his vow of silence, but the most experienced Fixers on the Roster had been reduced to stumbling shells of themselves by some unknown force. And judging from the faces of the others at the table, they were just as disconcerted by the transmission as he.

In addition to Eve Hightower and Sylvia (aka the Octogenarian), Becker was joined by a dashing Persian man. Shahzad Hassan was a professor of literature at Tabriz University, and was best known for having spent his entire life searching The World for an ancient artifact. But though Becker hadn't encountered #19 in over a year and knew almost nothing about him, it was the presence of another colleague in the room that put him decidedly more on edge.

"I suggest we begin with questions," said Jelani Blaque, rising to his feet with the help of his famed Igbo stick.

"That mysterious light . . ." Hassan gathered his jet black hair and pulled it back into a tight ponytail. "Could it be Hope?"

"That's what I thought at first." Blaque rewound the

broadcast to the moment before it was shut down. "But look at the color and texture of the light. Hope is softer, more yellow . . ." Onscreen, the light that overwhelmed the first team of Fixers was harsh and white, and having seen and felt a Glimmer of Hope firsthand, Becker could not argue with his mentor's assessment. "I fear we may be looking at a weapon the likes of which we've never seen before."

"Po had a theory about what it was," suggested the Octogenarian, raising a curious eyebrow.

"Fixer Po was also under great duress. But I concur, it cannot be ruled out."

This piqued Becker's interest. "The Most Amazing Thing of All" was the answer to an ancient riddle—"If The Seems is building The World, then who's building The Seems?"—and some thought that answer could be found in the Middle of Nowhere. Many more, however, believed it to be a myth.

"What about Dr. Thinkenfeld?" asked Hassan. "Do we have any idea where she could be?"

"Negative," said Second in Command Hightower. "At last report, she was assisting in the Thought harvest—but we haven't been able to raise Contemplation either."

Fixer Blaque grabbed the clicker and rewound the tape all the way back to the discovery of the caboose.

"As for the culprits, this may be premature, but I see no evidence that The Tide was responsible for the theft."

Everyone leaned forward for a closer look, for they all bore scars from their battles with the followers of Triton—especially in the last few months, when it seemed like every day brought a new Tide assault upon the machinery of The Seems. But nowhere on the body of the caboose was painted their dreaded symbol of a black wave cresting and about to crash upon the shore.

"Then who?" pressed the Octogenarian. "The Time Bandits are behind bars, and this is way beyond the capacity of a few Idea smugglers."

"That's what we're here to find out."

As Becker's mind began to speculate who besides The Tide would steal six weeks worth of Thought, and what they wanted to do with it, his own thoughts were overwhelmed by a host of strong emotions. Things like anger and hurt and disappointment, all of which drove him to slam his fist down upon the conference table and shout in a voice much louder than he'd intended.

"Hold on a second!"

When everyone snapped their head around in his direction, Fixer Drane had little choice but to ask the one question for which there seemed to be no viable answer.

"I get that this is a serious crisis and all, but what am I doing here?"

All eyes in the conference room turned back to Fixer Blaque.

"The Powers That Be asked me to come out of retirement and put together a second team to go after the lost Train of Thought." The lead instructor at the Institute for Fixing & Repair turned to arguably the greatest student he'd ever taught, and smiled. "I'd like you to be on it."

"You'd like me to be on it? After you and every Fixer on the Roster sold me out in court?"

As Blaque nodded, Becker fought to hold himself back from saying all the things he wanted to say (but knew he shouldn't) since the verdict came down. Unfortunately, he lost.

"I'll tell you what you can do with your second team . . ."

Central Shipping,
Department of Thought & Emotion, The Seems

As the elevator descended from the Administrator's office to the shipping room floor, Becker's hands were still shaking from what he'd just done. Just like his dad and his brother and particularly Uncle Ferdy, when Drane men got going, boy, they really got going.

"I'm sorry about my behavior up there, Madame Second. That was very unprofessional of me."

"It's understandable." Eve Hightower put a hand on the shoulder of her youngest Fixer. "You've been on quite an emotional roller coaster lately—and I don't mean the one at Awesomeville."[11]

"I appreciate that, ma'am. It's just . . . yesterday I'm public enemy number one and now, because you need me, I'm supposed to drop everything and put my life on the line again?"

The muzak that piped over the elevator's speakers was a Seemsian cover of "Don't Worry, Be Happy," but the song he kept hearing in his head was Johnny Paycheck's classic anthem, "Take This Job and Shove It."

---

11. The most popular amusement park in The Seems, featuring an Awesome Place to Eat, Awesome Things to Do, and the Most Awesome Ride Ever.

"First," the Second in Command confessed, "let me say it gave me no great pleasure to side with Judge Torte in imposing such a harsh sentence."

Just hearing the name of the Administrator of Legal Affairs brought Becker's blood back to a sauté, but this time he restrained himself.

"However, if you're honest with yourself—and from what I've heard, Fixer Drane, that's one of your finest attributes—then I think you'll agree that your conviction and punishment were richly deserved."

"With all due respect, ma'am, I beg to differ."

As the elevator dinged to a stop, Eve patiently waited for the doors to slide open.

"Let me show you something."

When Becker and the Second in Command stepped into Central Shipping, they were immediately handed hardhats and goggles. All around them, raw Thought was being pressed into pokerlike chips and stacked for easy shipment, while Ideas were strung with a filament of Mind and wrapped in blown-glass bulbs. Even bottles of Emotion—brought up from the wells in wicker Basket Cases—were rolled onto palettes destined for The World.[12]

But things were far from business as usual in the Department of T&E.

"Since the new delivery hasn't come, we're being forced to tap into our reserves of Idle Thought." She motioned to the

---

12. 99.9% of all Thought and Emotion is shipped in its raw form for people to do with what they will. The remaining .1%, however, is reserved for Case Workers to offer their clients Helpful Hints, Emotional Rescues, Songs You Can't Get Out of Your Head, etc.

floor, where the Brain Trust was scraping resin off the sides of empty hoppers. "But we only have enough to last for three days."

Becker's mouth suddenly got a little bit drier.

"We're not talking about a potential Ripple Effect here, are we?"

"Let's hope not. But it's possible the Unthinkable could happen."

Becker didn't even want to think about that. Without the higher faculty of Thought, there would be nothing to keep the baser Emotions from raging out of control. The collective Jealousy, Anger, and Frustration of millions of human beings would boil over and it wouldn't be long before the people of The World literally tore themselves to shreds.

"Why can't we just keep everybody happy for a while?" asked Becker. "Pump a little extra Love into the air?"

The Second in Command smiled as if she wished it were all that easy, then plucked a random Thought from a hopper. In its unrefined state, it looked like a sticky clump of tree sap, and she held it up next to a jar of Sadness.

"We here in The Seems have the power to do anything we want with these. With one Thought or Emotion, we can push people left or right, up or down, toward a good day or bad. But the people of The World weren't meant to be controlled by joysticks."

She replaced the items and continued down the walkway.

"It's the Rules that keep us from playing with that joystick, Fixer Drane, and it's the Rules that keep us from tampering with the Plan."

"I understand all that, Madame," Becker interrupted. "It's

just . . . it's hard to see the line sometimes. When we're allowed to help and when we're not."

"It is." Eve smiled, as if she'd wrestled with that same issue many times herself. "At the end of the day, I guess it comes down to one thing: do we believe in the goodness of that Plan, with all its mysteries and imperfections? Or do we not?"

A young Mind Blower approached, clipboard in hand.

"Sorry to bother you, ma'am, but since Administrator Thinkenfeld's MIA, could you sign off on a Head Trip for Sector 109?"

"Certainly."

While the Second in Command initialed the order, Becker fired up the replacement Bleceiver that the Toolshed had sent down for him and flipped through the Cases that would be affected should the Unthinkable happen. His hope was that in one of them, he could find a Mission Inside the Mission that would give him the inspiration to get back in the game. But he still couldn't stop thinking about his own troubles.

"Oh, and in case you were wondering"—Eve returned the clipboard and led the young Fixer back toward the elevators—"regardless of whether or not you accept this Mission, your sentence is set in Stone.[14] The suspension will take effect as soon as you return, as will the unremembering."

Becker knew the Second in Command wasn't a Mind Reader, but it sure felt like she was leafing through his.

"I hope you'll look past your own concerns and join the

---

14. The hallowed piece of marble onto which all Court of Public Opinion decisions are irrevocably engraved.

second team. But if not, don't let it bother you—it's only the Unthinkable, right?"

The elevator doors again slid open and the Second in Command stepped inside.

"It's not the end of The World."

Trans Central Station, Beyond, The Seems

Forty-five minutes later, a man in a blue hat and red tie scanned the platform one last time, then pulled a pocket watch from inside his blazer. "15:59." Oh well. Time to get the old girl going . . .

"All aboard the Trans-Seemsberian Express!"

A throng of excited travelers hopped off the wooden benches and up the steps of the train. Most, the Conductor figured, were headed out to the Black Market—which at this time on Sunday was just rolling out its best bargains—but he was quite sure the man with the old Air-Conditioner's belt and his family were headed out to the Sticks.

"This is the local train, making the following station stops: the Outskirts, Obscurity, the Sticks, Seemsberia, and the End of the Line!"

By the time he announced the last stop, the only people left in the station were three owners of a Badge with a double-sided Wrench, none of whom seemed anxious to board the train just yet.

"All aboard!"

"Any chance we can get you to hold it for five more minutes?" asked the Octogenarian, still sitting on her handbag-style Toolkit.

"Sorry, ma'am." The Conductor was unmoved by Sylvia's famously sunny disposition. "The Trans-Seemsberian hasn't been a single minute late since MJGVXXIII, and I'm not going to be the one to break the streak."

"What's the point?" Shahzad Hassan lifted his twin attachés. "Clearly, the child is not coming."

The Octogenarian nodded sadly, and even the mysterious Hassan was disappointed at the fact that Becker Drane was nowhere to be found in this moment of need. But Fixer Blaque seemed more surprised than anything else.

"It appears you are right, Hassan."

Blaque threw his weatherbeaten Toolmaster '45™ over his shoulder, then leaned on his walking stick and headed for the crowded train.

"Don't we need to call in someone for backup?" asked Sylvia, following him up the steps.

"I planned for this eventuality, although I hoped it would never come." Blaque slowly led his colleagues through the train car, searching for an empty three-seater. "Fixer #2 has been living in Obscurity for quite some time now, and he's agreed to meet us should the need arise."

The Octogenarian looked at Hassan, who was as intrigued to hear that the reclusive Mr. X might be joining a multi-Fixer Mission as she was. But there would be plenty of time to discuss this and other developments on the long trip out to the End of the Line. The first order of business was finding a seat.

"Perhaps there is room in the dining compartment?"

As the three Fixers stepped between cars, the Trans-Seemsberian dragged itself into motion. The chandeliers jingled as they had for nearly a century, and the red velvet walls and sepia-toned photographs told stories of a long-vanished era. Unfortunately, every high-backed dining booth was full—all except for one, that is, where a single head leaned against the window.

"Excuse me." Fixer Blaque approached the lone traveler, who was lost inside a dog-eared text. "Would you mind if we joined you?"

The teenage boy put down his copy of Agatha Christie's *The Orient Express*, took another sip of his iced Certain Tea, then turned to face the three weary Fixers. They were a strange lot to be sure, but for a Mission to the Middle of Nowhere, Becker Drane figured they would do.

"What took you guys so long?"

Trans-Seemsberian Express

The Black Market, The Outskirts, The Seems

On Saturdays and Sundays between 9:00 a.m. and 6:00 p.m., a normally muddy field in the thinly populated area on the edge of The Seems is transformed into a thriving metropolis of tents, tables, and vendors displaying wares of every shape and size. Most of the trinkets and keepsakes found here are of the perfectly legal (though often junky) variety, but for those who dig a little deeper, the Black Market offers items of a different sort.

"Seven Bucks?"[15] The crusty, gold-toothed merchant angrily pushed away Fixer Blaque's coin-filled hand. "I couldn't buy my grandmother a dazzleberry pie for seven Bucks!"

Fixers Blaque and Drane stood before a foldout table stocked with jars, glass bottles, metal pots, and tins, each containing a

---

15. A unit of Seemsian currency named after Bucky Buckerson, first Administrator of the Department of Miscellaneous, and inventor of dirt.

powder, oil, or extract from some far-off corner of The Seems. Becker even recognized an unused ounce of Sleep, which only underscored the truth of the handwritten banner that hung above the merchant's head:

"Man of Substance(s)."

"I didn't know your grandmother liked dazzleberry," Blaque needled the merchant, then took another look inside the tarnished locket in his hand. "I'll give you eight."

"We're talking the essential building block of Reality here, my friend. Be reasonable. The lowest I can go is a Bill."[16]

Fixer Blaque closed the case, then handed it back to the merchant.

"Maybe I'll just go see Powderfinger. He knows how to treat a customer."

Blaque threw a subtle wink at Becker, as if to say, "Sometimes you have to be willing to walk away," and started to do just that.

"Hey! Where you going, buddy? I'm just trying to make a living here." The Man of Substance(s) threw up his hands. "Since it's for a good cause, I'll do it for nine—but that's my final offer."

"And a very generous offer it is. I shall accept."

Fixer Blaque handed the coins to the vendor and the locket to Becker, who packed it into his Toolkit, along with the battery-powered Calling Card they'd purchased in case their Bleceivers malfunctioned in the Middle of Nowhere. The small

---

16. A unit of Seemsian currency named after William "Bill" Mahoney, first Administrator of the Department of Nature and composer of the four seasons. (*Note: 1 Bill = 10 Bucks.*)

metal square allowed users to project holographic images of themselves across great distances, usually to another Card holder.

"Your uncle's a real skinflint!" the Man of Substance(s) crankily called out to Becker as he and Blaque walked away. "Tell him money only grows on trees in A Better Place!"

The Black Market totally reminded Becker of Englishtown—this outdoor shopping extravaganza in Jersey where he and his grandfather used to go—except much bigger and more exotic. There were endless rows of tables and booths, where shady characters hawked used Fixer Tools, pirated copies of the Plan, hubcaps, and square-cut french fries in brown paper bags. There was even an old Tinker selling T-shirts that read: "Stem The Tide: Bring Back Samuel!" And judging from his half-empty cart, business was booming.

"How many more stops do we have, sir? The Trans-Seemsberian should be done switching over from coal to electric in about ten minutes."

"Plenty of time, son. Only one more item on the list."

Jelani Blaque hobbled forward on his walking stick as a group of licensed Bargain Hunters toting nets and coupons passed by.

"I know you won't believe this, Becker, but I signed that petition for your own good."

Becker wasn't going to bring it up, but now that the proverbial elephant in the room was out in the open, he wasn't going to avoid it.

"So everyone keeps telling me."

"Take my word for it, when you start Fixing for yourself instead of The World, it's a slippery slope. That's how Hadley

Eure lost her way, and Zachary Lake, and of course you know the story of Sir Reginald."[17]

"I think I'm starting to catch your drift, sir. But imagine if you had to unremember Sarah or your kids. Even if you knew it was justified, would it make it any easier?"

"No, it wouldn't."

The two Fixers strolled silently for a while, cutting down a dark and trash-strewn alleyway. There were no tables here, only shadowy figures in dark alcoves, whispering of Fantasies and Frozen Moments stolen from the people of The World. Becker made eye contact with a woman in heavy makeup and costume jewelry who claimed to be a member of the Future Oriented, and she waved him toward her parlor. With a gentle tug from Blaque, he kept walking.

As soon as they stepped back into the light, the duo found themselves in the Tamishantery, a district on the edge of the market where men in brightly colored robes did battle to offer the latest in Seemsian hat wear. Bee Bonnets, Chrome Domes, Big Wigs—even an old World-Beater baseball cap—were all hanging from hooks and ready to be placed upon prospective heads. But when Fixer Blaque approached an old man too wrinkled and hunched over to even hold up a sign, Becker could tell he was looking for something that wasn't on display.

"What is your pleasure, oh mighty Fixers of the World?"

The old man's skin was the color of brown that can only be painted by a lifetime under the unforgiving sun, and his eyes were the milky white of blindness. Yet the unmistakable gleam

---

17. A Fixer in fifth-century Europe who tried to save England by restringing a Chain of Events but ended up causing the Dark Ages instead.

of a born salesman was still behind them, a gleam that bright-ened considerably when Fixer Blaque began to speak to him in a language Becker had never heard before. It was harsh and gut-tural, one that the old-timer clearly understood, for it was only a matter of seconds before he flashed a toothless grin and called out in the tongue common to all Seemsians.

"Grandsons!"

Two teenagers sending text messages on their SeemsBerrys snapped to their feet, and with a whisper from their grandfather, disappeared behind an ornate tapestry. When they reemerged, the boys were juggling four brass helmets that looked like they belonged on an old-fashioned deep-sea diving suit. One by one, Becker plopped them into his Toolkit—which, although it had plenty of extra Space, didn't have unlimited weight. It was start-ing to get awfully heavy.

"What kind of helmets are these, sir?"

Fixer Blaque checked his Time Piece™, which indicated their train would be departing for Obscurity in less than three minutes.

"Let's hope you never find out."

"Next station stop: the Sticks! All aboard for the Sticks, Seems-beria, and the End of the Line!"

As the wellness colony of Obscurity slowly receded into the distance, Becker and Fixer Blaque retired to their sleeper cabins to sort through the gear they'd scored in the market. Mean-while, Hassan and the Octogenarian were finishing up light lunches and watching the landscape shift from rolling green hills to marshlands and thicket. The crowd in the dining car had noticeably thinned since they'd left the Outskirts—most of the remaining passengers congregated on the stools around the lunch counter—leaving the two Fixers a booth to themselves.

"Why do you think Blaque selected you for this Mission?" Hassan asked his counterpart, mouth half full. "I understand why he took the boy genius—but with all due respect, you're not exactly in your prime."

The Octogenarian had already finished her grilled cheese and was happily knitting an afghan from balls of multicolored yarn. "Actually, I was wondering the same thing about you."

"How so?"

"Honey, the only way we're going to survive the Middle of Nowhere is if every member of the team knows they can count on one another." Fixer #3 switched colors from larkspur to huckleberry. "Considering no one on the Roster trusts you as far as they can spit into the wind, I find you to be an even more unlikely selection."

"Touché."

Hassan didn't need to be stabbed by a knitting needle to know this was a dig at his life's work. The Fixer had been born to a proud and storied people whose beliefs and customs were contained within an ancient book. But over two thousand years ago, the thirteenth and most critical chapter had mysteriously vanished, leaving the text tragically incomplete. In the centuries that followed, a tribe that once stretched across the face of The World dwindled to a few thousand . . . and could soon become but a footnote in the annals of History.

"It's been years since I turned down a Mission to pursue the chapter, Sylvia."

"All I'm saying is, some of us wonder what comes first: your worldly Mission or your Mission to save The World?"

The only answer was the steady and hypnotic *click-clack* of wheels against rails.

"And as far as *my* age is concerned, let me just say this." The Octogenarian held up the afghan, frowned, then got back to work. "Every year on the third Wednesday of October, I take a trip to Canaima National Park in Venezuela, climb to the top of Angel Falls, and tell myself the same thing: 'Sylvia, if you can't bring yourself to base-jump off The World's highest free-falling waterfall, parachute down the eight-hundred-meter drop to the bottom, and still dig the rush, then you'll know it's time to hang up your handbag.'"

Since the third Wednesday in October had already passed, Hassan assumed she still dug the rush.

"What of Blaque?" The Persian steered the conversation away from himself. "I had no idea he'd returned to active duty."

"He hasn't." Sylvia concentrated her energies on a particularly difficult section of drop stitching around the blanket's back edge. "I guess because of Hope Springs Eternal, the Powers That Be felt he was the appropriate choice."

In fact, Sylvia was worried about the entire second team. How were a convicted child, a crippled instructor, a cutthroat treasure seeker, and a resident of the Gordon's Bay Retirement Community going to accomplish what a team of The Seems' most formidable Fixers could not? As was her nature, she pushed those negative thoughts aside, preferring to concentrate on the way Hassan's fingers idly found their way to the amulet of a winged sun around his neck.

"Are you any closer to finding it, Shahzad?"

"Almost there, Sylvia." Hassan smiled sadly and tucked the necklace back beneath his shirt. "Always almost there."

The Trans-Seemsberian Express didn't have much in common with New Jersey Transit, but just as when he occasionally hopped the Trenton Local from New Brunswick to New York's Penn Station, Becker leaned his head against the glass of his sleeper cabin and watched the world go by. Instead of Metuchen, Elizabeth, and Rahway, the Fixer was treated to the Sticks—a forest of tall yellow reeds that stretched as far as the eye could see. Somewhere out there was a utopian settlement founded by dropouts determined to escape the rat race of The World project, and when the train pulled to a stop, a handful of travelers—with all their Seemsly belongings strapped to their backs—got off.

The Sticks put him into a gloomy state, mostly because it reminded him of the time he and Jennifer Kaley went to a corn maze outside Toronto. They got intentionally lost and found a dead-end corner where the stalks reached high enough that they could hide and listen to the kids laughing and the parents running out of breath. When it was over and he got back to Highland Park, he could smell Jennifer's bubble gum lip gloss on the collar of his flannel shirt, and he couldn't bring himself to wash it for weeks.

Knock. Knock. Knock.

"Come in!"

Becker expected to see the ticket taker, who often checked the sleeping cars for stowaways or hoboes, but it was Hassan's ponytailed head he saw instead. "Briefing in Blaque's compartment. Five minutes."

"On my way."

Fixer Drane splashed some cold water on his face, then hoofed it over to Blaque's cabin, where the rest of the second team had already coalesced.

"The Powers That Be have asked me to reiterate that this is *not* a rescue Mission." Fixer Blaque was reading from a message on his Bleceiver. "As much as we want to find our friends, our first priority is making sure the Unthinkable doesn't happen."

Everyone nodded their assent, though the way he tossed his Bleceiver onto a pile of clothes said he had no intention of leaving anyone behind.

"I also wanted you to know that I put in a request to have extra Twinkle and Refreshment added to our Good Night's Sleep packages tonight. Considering the likelihood that tomorrow we will have to enter the Middle of Nowhere, I thought it prudent."

"As long as I get my Snooze." The Octogenarian smiled widely. "It's the key to a long and healthy life."

"Last but not least." Blaque turned his gaze toward the window, where the first hints of snow were scattered on the rocky ground outside. "Be advised that this train is going to be making an unscheduled layover at Seemsberia station."

"For what purpose?" asked Becker, in no hurry to spend more time in that awful place than he had to.

"I have arranged a brief meeting with one of the inmates. It shouldn't take more than twenty minutes and the conductor has kindly agreed to hold the train for that duration."

"If you don't mind me asking, sir." Hassan crossed a curious leg. "Which inmate?"

"Thibadeau Freck."

For the second time today, the team gasped in perfect harmony. But Becker's was just a little bit bigger than the rest.

"You're meeting with Thib?" he whispered. "What for?"

Fixer Blaque placed a hand on the cold glass and looked as if he were a million miles away.

"That's between me and him, Mr. Drane."

Seemsberia, The Seems

Before the TSE even pulled into the Seemsberia station, Becker donned the cool-looking Hot Head he'd picked up as a parting gift from the Tamishantery. Hassan buttoned up his sheepskin coat, and Octo (as her friends and fellow base-jumpers called her) wrapped herself in the thick wool afghan she'd been knitting the whole way. Temperatures in Seemsberia routinely dipped fifty degrees below zero.

"Station stop: Seemsberia! Next stop, End of the Line."

The Fixers followed Jelani Blaque onto the granite platform, where icicles hung off a solitary ticket machine and sparse wooden benches offered little comfort from the cold. All they could see for miles upon miles was frigid, unforgiving snow, interrupted only by the occasional glacier of ice, and the one unforgettable contrast. Far in the distance, a sprawling, high-walled prison made entirely of stone.

As Becker watched a medley of convicted felons negotiating their shackles and stepping onto the platform single file, he could only imagine the chills that were going down their spines. He himself had narrowly averted a stint in Seemsberia during his own trial, and he put himself in the soon-to-be prisoners' shoes—emerging from a sealed car after a long ride and glimpsing for the first time the storied penitentiary where their rehabilitation and reintegration into mainstream society would take place.

"I'll be back in thirty minutes." Fixer Blaque joined two Corrections Officers who stoically waited to transport him to the main gates. "Be sure to hold the train."

"I agreed to twenty minutes, friend," the Conductor quickly corrected him. "One second longer, and you should think about where you'll be sleeping tonight."

Fixer Blaque didn't argue with the Conductor, just handed him a business card, upon which was printed a single name and number. "If you have any problem with my request, I suggest you contact Madame Hightower on her direct line."

The Conductor had no idea who Jelani Blaque was or why he was here—keeping his beloved TSE on schedule was his sole reason to be—but the Second in Command was an entirely different matter.

"On second thought, I'm sure the boys in the coal car could use a little Pickmeup."

As Jelani Blaque commandeered a jeep and disappeared into the tundra, his fellow Fixers huddled together and watched a host of uniformed personnel board the caboose. Standard operating procedure for the Department of Corrections was to scour the train for contraband every time it arrived, and today was no exception.

"Why do you think he wants to see Freck?"

Hassan pointed to the distant gates of the prison, which were slowly opening to admit the vehicle bearing Fixer Blaque.

"Who knows?" The Octogenarian pulled the afghan tighter. "Maybe Jelani thinks The Tide stole the train after all."

For Becker's part, he was just trying to stay warm and keep cool. Thibadeau Freck had been the most talented Candidate in Becker's class at the IFR (not to mention Becker's best friend) until he'd faked his own death and resurfaced as a prominent member of The Tide. Now he was serving a thirty-year sentence in Seemsberia for his role in the devastation of Time Square[18]— and Becker swore he'd never speak to the young Frenchman again.

"I hope he rots in there."

Even though Hassan and the Octogenarian were shivering, they could feel Becker's white-hot rage.

"Don't worry," the Persian again glanced toward the windowless complex. "He's as much a pariah in there as he is out here."

"Sergeant Linney, over here!"

The Fixers turned to see a gaggle of guards and dogs come running down the platform, all gathering around something a Corrections Officer had thrown from one of the storage cars.

"I think we've got something, sir." The Officer showed his square-jawed staff sergeant a long printout filled with item descriptions and serial numbers. "This wasn't on the requisition list."

It was a large suitcase—more like a chest, actually—one of those steamer trunks that Becker imagined merchant marines would carry on their voyages across the seven seas. Upon hearing the commotion, the Conductor, the crew, even the lady who ran the newsstand crowded around the bulky antique.

"Everybody stand back," Sergeant Linney said as he warmed up his baton. "I'm gonna crack this thing open."

18. See *The Seems: The Split Second.*

As the inspector got ready to bust the lock, Becker had the strangest feeling that he'd seen this chest before; not on imaginary ocean voyages or underneath the cot of one of his bunkmates at Camp Walden, but in a dorm room at the IFR. The sloppy carving of a double-sided Wrench on one of the sides confirmed his suspicions, as did several others that said simply "I ♥ CL/#23."

Crack!

The lock split open and everyone who'd been told to stand back pushed forward to see what was lurking inside. But of all the people on the platform, the only one who could positively ID the illicit cargo was Becker Drane himself.

"Simly?"

"In the, uh . . . flesh, sir."

Briefer Simly Frye dropped his head into his hands, which were rudely cuffed to the back of a seat on the prisoners' bus.

"But I was only trying to help!"

"I know that, dude, but you went about it the wrong way!" Becker paced up and down the center aisle. "Fixer Blaque had to cut his meeting short to speak with the warden on your behalf, and take my word for it, he is *not* psyched."

Outside in the frozen air, Jelani Blaque was still locked in heated negotiations with Inkar Cyration, the feared Administrator of the Department of Corrections. From the stony look on the Warden's face, it did not appear to be going well.

"Why would you do such a thing?"

"You said it yourself, Becker! I'm the only one you can trust!"

"When did I say that?"

"Back in Thought & Emotion, when you read everybody the riot act. You said that every Fixer on the Roster had betrayed you, and if they wanted you back they'd better let you bring along Milton Frye's favorite grandson so there's at least one person on the Mission who's got your back instead of trying to stab you in it!"

Becker cringed at the memory of his temper tantrum.

"I really said all that?"

"Word for word. I probably shouldn't tell you this, but I, um . . . had a Fly on the Wall™."

Becker shook his head with dismay, because eavesdropping with that old and decommissioned Tool was a serious infraction.

"Dude, you can't just break every Rule in the Briefer's handbook 'cause you feel like it."

"Why not? You did."

As Fixer Drane marveled at the ripple effect of his bad life decisions, the door to the bus swung open and in walked a not very happy looking man wearing blue-tinted shades that had frosted over white.

"It took a great deal of bargaining, Briefer Frye." Fixer Blaque sat in the empty driver's chair and turned to Simly. "But I managed to keep you out of the Clink."

Becker and Simly whispered "yes" at the same time, until—

"Unfortunately, seeing as the Trans-Seemsberian will not be making its return trip until tomorrow, it looks as if you will be spending some time in the Pokey."

Simly turned a whiter shade of pale. The Pokey was not the Hokey Pokey of birthday parties and roller-skating rinks, but rather the short-term holding cell where hardened criminals awaited processing and small-time hoods learned lessons they wouldn't soon forget.

"But sir, wouldn't it be better if I came along on the Mission? There's four Fixers and not a single Briefer!"

"Out of the question."

"But—"

Fixer Blaque silenced Simly with an angry bang of his stick.

"You're right, sir. A few nights in the Pokey is just what I deserve."

"It'll be okay, Sim." Becker patted his favorite Briefer on the shoulder. "Just do what they tell you and keep your mouth shut."

"Yes, sir. I won't say a word." Simly tried to sound convincing, but everyone knew he'd attempted a vow of silence before, and with dubious results. "And good luck, sirs."

The two Fixers gave short and sympathetic nods, then headed off the bus, having already overstayed the Conductor's ten-minute extension. Simly watched them hop aboard the train, and with a belch of black smoke, the Trans-Seemsberian was off on its overnight journey from the snows of Seemsberia to the scorching desert at the End of the Line.

"All right you scoundrels! Everybody take a seat!"

Simly turned to the front of the bus, where Inkar Cyration had claimed the driver's seat, and two dozen of the most vicious crooks in The Seems were dragging their shackles up the steps. Unlike Simly, their eyes were focused on the floor or the ceiling or the green vinyl seats that they took one by one—anywhere but on the dreaded prison that loomed ahead. The Warden flashed them all a Cheshire grin, then pulled the metal handle that closed the doors tight.

"Welcome to your new home."

Contemplation

End of the Line, Department of Transportation, The Seems

The morning sun beat down upon the old terminal station known as the End of the Line. It was not as merciless as it would be several hours from now, when only gila monsters and sandpipers would risk venturing outside, but it was already hot enough to send the Dust Bunnies scurrying under the passenger platform. From the cool shade beneath the wooden slats, they watched pebbles and tumbleweeds sweep across the Thought Tracks and listened to the desert moan.

Directly above, the station sign was squeaking in the breeze, while the door to the signal box gently banged against its hinge. On a typical day, two signalmen would be behind that door, trying to ensure that no two trains arrived on the same track at the same time, while the famously cranky Wheel Tapper would duck his head in and lament the fact that Quality Control still hadn't fixed the vending machine.

But this was no typical day.

"I think I found something!" Becker yelled from inside the Yardmaster's office, which had also been left wide open. Upon the cluttered desk a reading lamp was still on, a mug of Pick-meup half drunk. "Looks like his Time Piece stopped at exactly 7:37!"

The voice of Fixer Hassan replied from within the signal box.

"Same with the clock in here! Mark my words, whatever happened in this place, it happened at that moment."

Becker returned to the desk and sifted through the papers that were laid about in several stacks. Judging by how meticulously they were arranged, he assumed the first team of Fixers had already gone through these documents—but if they'd found anything of value, they'd clearly taken it with them.

"No dice."

The door to the office swung open, and in walked the Octogenarian, waving a paper fan across her face. "The time cards say six people were on duty, but I can't find a single soul."

"Any sign of Dr. Thinkenfeld?"

Sylvia removed her sunhat and wiped some sweat from her white hair, then shook her head no. "I think we have to assume the worst."

The two headed out onto the platform, where Hassan was now squatting behind the busted vending machine. Judging by the way he was banging around inside, he appeared to be trying to fix it. "Where's Fixer Blaque?"

"He's looking for the tracks that Casey mentioned in her

transmission." Sylvia pointed to the westernmost portion of the station, where giant rubber stoppers had been placed to keep the Trains of Thought from rolling into the desert. "Seems to think they might be over there."

"Blaque's wasting his time," mused Hassan. "The Listening Post picked up storms raging all across the Middle of Nowhere last night. Any footprints or trails the first team might've followed would be long gone by now."

As the Fixers silently considered what that might mean for their Mission, Hassan made a slight adjustment to the coin slot on the vending machine, then closed the back panel and plugged it back in. It flickered for a moment before firing up with a soothing electrical hum.

"Anybody want a Zagnut?"

The Octogenarian purchased a Powers That Be Bar instead, then found her way to the laquered map that was posted on the platform.

"Still nothing from Contemplation?" she asked, pointing to the southernmost portion.

Becker shook his head no. "The phones are all dead, and when I try to Bleceive them, all I get is this weird clicking."

"What's the difference?" inquired Hassan. "Whoever stole the train took it into the desert."

"Maybe somebody saw something when they were loading it up," countered the Octo. "Even if they didn't, there might be some excess Thought lying around that could buy us a little more time."

"Good call," Becker concurred. "Let's go down there and take a look."

"You and Hassan go. I'll keep an eye on Jelani."

As Sylvia put on a pair of big green sunglasses devised not for the brightness of the Seemsian sun but for her troublesome cataracts, she polished off the final bite of her nougat-wrapped, caramel-coated treat.

"Be careful, boys. We don't know what we're dealing with here."

Back behind the rubber stoppers, Fixer Blaque watched two members of his team disappear in a cloud of dust, then refocused his attention to the parched ground at his feet. He had hoped to locate some evidence of where Fixer Simms had made her discovery, but the violent weather of the previous evening hadn't done him any favors. A thick layer of sand covered every last corner of the station, and even his Vindwoturelukinvor™ had failed to uncover a sign. What was really fouling up the search, however, was the buzzing in his own mind.

Though his meeting with Thibadeau Freck had been brief, it had also been quite illuminating. If what his former student said was true, then Fixer Blaque's own time window had closed considerably, and a plan years in the making was rapidly approaching its day of reckoning.

"Any luck?" The Octogenarian had snuck up behind him, looking for all the world like a giant green-eyed bug.

"Nothing yet. Why don't you do a sweep along the edge of Track #3."

"What am I looking for?"

"Any marking that would indicate where the first team went in. Lisa knew the dangers out there from personal experience. She never would have embarked on such a journey without leaving some kind of sign."

Sylvia nodded in agreement, but something in Blaque's voice troubled her.

"Are you all right, Jelani?"

"I'm fine. This place just brings up a lot of memories, is all."

That seemed to alleviate Sylvia's concerns, and she sauntered off to explore the northernmost Thought Track. But for Jelani Blaque, walking along the border of the Middle of Nowhere, it was hard not to be thrown back to that time twelve years ago—when he, Lisa Simms, and the late Tom Jackal were charged with bringing back Hope for a despairing world. He had lost so much on that Mission, and even though it had ended in success, he was never truly the same.

Behind the rubber stopper for Track #3, something reflected in the sunlight. It was a small knob of wood sticking out of the sand, which he wouldn't have spotted were it not for the long piece of string attached to it. Upon closer inspection, the filament that danced in the breeze was actually a fine strand of horsehair, and the knob the tip of a violin bow that someone had stuck into the ground. Considering it was crafted from the finest Brazilian Pernambuco wood, he had a pretty good idea of who that someone was.

"Well done, Lisa. Well done."

Contemplation, Department of Thought & Emotion, The Seems

The only way to the mining colony of Contemplation, save a day's walk through the desert, was a set of rails that ran due south from the End of the Line. Being that there were no trains running, Becker and Hassan had pulled on their Speed Demons instead. They hadn't planned to turn the trek into a race, but their competitive natures soon took over.

"Lookin' a little rusty, old man!" shouted Becker over his shoulder as he momentarily pulled ahead.

"Slow and steady wins the day." Hassan stayed just off to the right to avoid sand being kicked up by his young peer. "Or aren't you familiar with *The Tortoise and the Hare?*"

The "old man" took a shortcut through a gulch and soon it was Becker who was eating a faceful of dirt. The young American reminded Hassan of his son, Cyrus, who tried to best his father at every turn. Hassan hadn't seen the boy in six weeks— not since he'd followed a false tip that the missing chapter was buried near Thebes—and he promised to make up for lost time as soon as this Mission was done.

"Yeah, I'm familiar with that story!" Becker clicked the back of his heels together and shifted into fourteenth gear. "But in this version, the rabbit kicks the turtle's butt!"

Fifteen minutes later, the two Fixers were skidding to a stop.

"Let's call it a draw," said Hassan, and the two bumped fists (though in his heart, Becker thought he'd beat him by a step). Up above, a buzzard stared down at them from a cracked and peeling sign:

WELCOME TO CONTEMPLATION: WHERE THE THINKING PROCESS BEGINS!

Unfortunately, the colony itself looked far more like the end of something than the beginning. Torn canvas tents dotted the horseshoe-shaped canyon, pickaxes and sifting pans were strewn across the ground, and a thin trickle of water plinked off the tin roof of the refinery. And much like the dusty station at the End of the Line, no one seemed to be on duty here at all.

"Hello! Anybody here?"

The only thing that boomeranged back was the echo of Hassan's own voice.

"This place is creeping me out," said Becker, and he could tell his partner was feeling the same way. "It's like a ghost town."

"I don't even think the ghosts are here anymore."

"Let's hope not."

Since the welcoming committee was conspicuously absent, the duo made a quick decision to split up and search the canyon on foot. Hassan took the Refinery and the Foreman's office, while Becker made sure that no damage had been done to the Thought mining process itself.

"Hellooo!" Becker called out to the maze of abandoned rail-cars and wafting tent flaps. "I know splitting up was probably a stupid thing to do, but I figured calling attention to that might get me off the hook!"

Again, he was greeted only by the sound of an echo.

"Not that anyone out there *has* a hook . . ."

The unnatural silence was starting to get under his skin, so he began humming aloud as he followed a grass-covered set of train tracks that cut through the center of camp. They took him to a boarded-up mineshaft, which Becker immediately recognized as an old In-Betweener tunnel. The Seems hadn't shipped Thought (or anything) to The World that way in years, but the Fixer closed his eyes and imagined what it must've been like when automated freight trains, piled high with Goods & Services, cruised back and forth.

Shucka, shucka.

A gentle banging drew his attention to the open end of the canyon, where the only gate through a barbed-wire fence had been left open and unlocked. On the other side were rows and rows of enormous cactuses, with thorns the size of arrowheads serving as warning to anyone who wished to extract the precious Thought inside. Judging from the fact that some still had taps sticking from their branches, they were finishing up a harvest when whatever happened here went down.

Becker did a quick loop around the field and was pleased to see that the basic pillars of the operation were still intact. Though it took weeks to load an entire Train of Thought, in the three days they had left before the Unthinkable happened, there might still be enough time to fill a boxcar or two. They would need to call in at least two teams of Provokers—the meticulous tradesmen who tapped the cacti with little hammers to locate deposits of Thought, then patiently teased out the amber substance within—and a third squad of Collectors to get it over to the Refi—

Shucka, shucka, shucka.

Becker wheeled around, certain he'd just heard that banging again from somewhere over his shoulder. But when he turned to investigate, all he saw was a drop cloth attached to an empty scaffold, an open lunchbox overrun by Buzz Kills, and a transistor radio with a dead battery melting in the afternoon sun.

Shucka, shucka, shucka.

It was coming from inside one of the discarded Think Tanks, and Becker wasn't taking any chances—he pulled out his trusty Sticks & Stones™. But when he approached the rusty metal cylinder and cautiously popped open the hatch, it was not a Collector or a poltergeist or even an ax-wielding maniac that he saw inside. It was a bespectacled woman in a tie-dyed skirt and beaded necklace, completely lost in Thought.

"Dr. Thinkenfeld?"

In the cool shade of Contemplation's mess hall, the Administrator of Thought & Emotion looked up at Hassan with grief and terror in her eyes. "They're all gone."

"Who's gone, Doctor?"

"Everybody! I'm the only one who—"

Dr. Laura Thinkenfeld burst into tears and crumpled into Hassan's arms, as if crushed by the guilt of her own survival. Becker threw Hassan a look like "maybe we should give her a few more minutes," but the Persian shook his head no.

"Pull yourself together, Laura. We need to know what happened here."

The weary Administrator wrung out a few last sobs, then did her best to recover. This was no easy task, since her hair looked like she'd stuck her finger into a wall socket, and her face was burned by something other than the sun. She was also badly dehydrated from being locked inside the Think Tank, but a few swigs from Becker's canteen seemed to restore her strength.

"It's a thankless job, y'know? Toiling away in the hot sun, day after day, hundreds of miles away from air-conditioned offices and the Field of Play. That's why I always come out here to help with the harvest . . . because these people work too hard not to get some kind of recognition. I mean, all they really ask is for someone to shake their hands and say, 'You matter.'"

"Laura, please . . . ," urged Hassan.

"I'm sorry."

She limped over to the window of the mess hall to have a look outside.

"The train had just left for the End of the Line—every boxcar stuffed to the brim—and even though it was early in the morning, some of the boys had already broken out kegs of Cheer. But then I heard someone say—I think it was Mendenhall, the Foreman—'What do you make of that, ma'am?'"

"Make of what?" said Becker, unable to bite his tongue.

"A strange light . . . on the horizon." Dr. Thinkenfeld turned toward a westward-facing window, as if she could still see something unexpected approaching. "At first, I thought it was some kind of explosion way out in the Middle of Nowhere, but I didn't hear any sound. I would've heard if it was a bomb or something, right?"

She squinted and raised a hand to her face, shielding herself from whatever it was she'd seen two mornings ago.

"All I remember is people running everywhere, screaming, looking for some place to hide before whatever it was that was coming hit us. And I swear, I tried to stay outside until all my people were safe. But Mendenhall, he wouldn't listen to me, he just grabbed me and threw me in the tank and told me to wait there until he could—" Dr. Thinkenfeld abruptly swiveled toward Becker. "I swear, I didn't desert my people."

"I believe you, Doctor. We just need to know where everybody went."

"Where they went?" Dr. Thinkenfeld began to laugh, as if Becker had just reminded her of a very funny joke. "Where do you think they went?"

The joke ended poorly.

"They're dead! They're all dead!"

Before she could say any more, the Administrator of Thought & Emotion collapsed from exhaustion. Hassan scooped her off her feet, then gently laid her on one of the wooden picnic tables. "We need to get her to a Care Giver ASAP."

"I'll call it in," said Becker, already dialing the emergency hotline to the Department of Health. But even as he punched 8-1-1 into his Bleceiver, the fact that the entire staff of Contemplation had potentially been vaporized was starting to make him feel a little queasy about this Mission. And there was an even more grim reality to face: if these people had met with the fate that Thinkenfeld said they did, then it was likely the first team of Fixers had perished the same way.

"Look at her Time Piece, Drane." Hassan lifted the doctor's limp wrist. "Just like the End of the Line."

Becker looked down at the hands of her watch, which came together to form the numbers 7:37. "What kind of weapon is powerful enough to strike two locations twenty miles apart at the exact same time?"

"Nothing I'd like to see firsthand."

#37 was about to start digging through his Manual when his Bleceiver beeped, indicating another call was coming in.

"Becker, it's me . . ."

"Hey, Octo. Listen, I gotta call you back, 'cause the Department of Health is on the other line and—"

"It's Fixer Blaque, dear," interrupted Sylvia, her voice filled with both excitement and fear. *"He found the tracks."*

End of the Line, Department of Transportation, The Seems

Fixer Blaque was leaning on his walking stick, peering directly into the Middle of Nowhere. Only now it wasn't just wind and sand and mesquite grass that made up the desert before him. Now there was something else that reached into the vastness of the west.

"Train tracks?" Becker knelt before his former instructor, completely befuddled. "But there was nothing here before!"

"Wasn't there?"

Inexplicably, beyond the rubber bump stop that marked the end of Track #2, another set of iron rails stretched out toward the vanishing point. These were much newer than the ancient I-beams that carried trains back and forth from Thought & Emotion, and Fixer Blaque had used his Brush Duster™ to uncover fifty feet or so from beneath the sand.

"How far do they go?" asked Fixer Hassan, walking out to where the rails disappeared.

"Hard to say," Blaque speculated. "But I suspect at least as far as that caboose the first team found."

Hassan gave one of the beams a slight kick, as if to prove its reality, then turned back to face the team leader. "It makes no sense."

"As you'll recall, Casey said that Fixer Simms had uncovered some tracks that led to the Middle of Nowhere. At first, I thought she was referring to footprints left by the thieves . . . but then I realized, she was talking about train tracks."

"But the map says the End of the Line is the end of the line." Even the Octogenarian, who had been by Blaque's side ever since he'd let out a whoop of delight some forty minutes ago, still couldn't figure out what the tracks were doing there.

"It *was*. Until someone made them go farther."

Fixer Blaque pulled out the same locket he'd purchased from the Man of Substance(s), then flipped it open to reveal a blue powder inside. There wasn't much of it, perhaps a thimbleful, but what there was had a slightly phosphorescent glow.

"Scratch," said the Octogenarian, shaking her head at Blaque's ingenuity. "Of course."

At the very mention of the basic building block of The World, Becker and the others began to grasp how the thieves, whomever they were, had managed to make a brand-new set of rails. When heated even a few degrees, Scratch could literally bring thoughts into existence. All one needed to do was place the powder between thumb and forefinger, generate a modicum of friction—and there were simply no limits to what the volatile substance could be used to create.[19]

"Plan help us if The Tide's got their hands on Scratch."

Hassan gave voice to his teammates' greatest fear.

"Let's not jump to conclusions." Fixer Blaque closed up his case, and with the help of his walking stick, finally rose to his feet. "All we can do is have faith in the Plan, and see where these tracks lead us."

Like a flash, the second team was in motion. While Blaque handed out Extremely Cool Outfits, the Octogenarian wrapped Administrator Thinkenfeld in a Security Blanket™ to ensure she was safely tucked away until the emergency Care Givers arrived. Meanwhile, Fixers Drane and Hassan found a rusty old handcar that someone had parked behind the switchman's hut and lugged it over to the tracks.

"Now remember, our 7th Senses will be virtually useless out there." Fixer Blaque dropped his Toolkit onto the front of the car and motioned to the Middle of Nowhere. "It'll be like a compass that can't find its way north."

A gust of wind arose, whipping sand and dirt in their faces and underscoring the warning that was posted on a single "No Trespassing" sign.

"Jelani." The Octogenarian folded her umbrella, which had been shielding her from the sun. "Look at the sky."

They all looked to the heavens, where a once crystalline blue was slowly darkening. Huge black storm clouds had gathered above the mountains to the west—as if somehow called by

---

19. For more on this delicate process, see Appendix B: "Making Things from Scratch."

their defiance of the warnings—and were now rolling toward them with alarming speed.

"Maybe we should wait till it blows over, sir," said Becker, leaning upon the seesaw lever that powered the car.

"No can do, Mr. Drane." Their leader removed his blue-tinted glasses and wiped the sweat from his eyes. "Unprocessed Scratch only has a half-life of three days. Which means these tracks could disappear at any moment."

Fixer Blaque replaced his shades, then reached into Becker's Toolmaster 3000 and began to remove the strange brass helmets he'd purchased at the Black Market.

"It also means we better put these on."

Powers That Be

12 Grant Avenue, Highland Park, New Jersey

As soon as Benjamin Drane got home from school, he dropped his bike on the front lawn and trucked up the wooden steps of 12 Grant Avenue. His trusty easel was waiting for him in the foyer, and after ditching his bookbag and sneaks, he lugged it straight upstairs to the door with the Bob Ross poster out front.

"Not so fast, half-pint!" babysitter Samantha Mitchell shouted from her favorite spot by the cordless phone in the kitchen. "No painting till after you do your homework!"

"Sorry! Ze artist formerly known as Benzamin cannot hears you. But he shall be in his room should anyone needz him."

Ever since he was little Benjamin had drawn everything in sight, and the walls of his room had been covered with napkin portraits, crayoned menus, and pencil sketches of downtown Highland Park. But when his older brother had hooked him up with private Sunset painting lessons from Figarro Mastrioni,

Benjamin raised his game to an entirely other level. "The Maestro" had trained him in all aspects of the profession—from horizon to clouds to the Emotion instilled within—and the wallpaper had quickly disappeared in favor of glorious panoramas, painted directly on the plaster itself.

Knock. Knock. Knock.

Benjamin tied on his smock and picked up his pallet from atop a pile of dirty underwear. "Come inz!"

The door swung open, and in walked what looked remarkably like his brother, Becker. So remarkably that it could only have been that lifelike invention of the masters at the Toolshed known as a Me-2.

"Hey, Me!" Benjamin bumped elbows with the replica like they were old pals. "What's shakin'?"

"Chillin' like a villain," Me-2 said as it plopped down on Benjamin's race car bed.

"Hey, guess what?"

"That's what?"

"Better." Benjamin dipped his brush into a spot of Alizarin Crimson and laid down a base. "Figarro says all I need is one or two more signature pieces and I'll be ready for my show."

"When's your show?"

"Next week. Administrator Nye from Public Works is gonna be there and if everything goes well, I could totally get a job as a Junior Scenic."

"Sweet."

"Tell me about it. If you play your cards right, I might be able to score you an original Benjamin Drane at half price."

Me-2 smiled proudly. With Becker gone as much as he had

been, the lifelike Tool had become almost a brother to Ben, and seeing his excitement and his blossoming artistic ability gave its mechanical heart real joy. Which only made what was about to happen that much harder to swallow.

"What's wrong, Me?" Benjamin dabbed a small blob of Phthalo Blue into a patch of sky on his canvas. "Why the long face?"

There were a few things that weighed heavy on the Me-2's mind that day. First and foremost was the fact that the precocious Sunset painter would probably never have his long-awaited show. Because of the Court of Public Opinion's ruling, Benjamin would never remember that there *was* a Seems, except as a figment of his brother's imagination. But if that brother had no L.U.C.K. in finding the Lost Train of Thought, unremembering would be the least of their problems.

"Actually, I'm a little concerned about this whole Unthinkable thing."

"I thought you said Becker's team had it under control?"

"They do, it's just—" Me-2 held up in midsentence, not wanting to let on that just minutes ago it had abruptly lost contact with its real self. "The last update from Thought & Emotion wasn't so hot."

The other Becker grabbed the remote control off the night table and fired up the TV that had been installed on Benjamin's ninth birthday.

"C'mon, Me, I'm trying to get some work done here!"

"I just wanna see what's going on in The World."

As Benjamin tried to tune out the video and get back to his sunset, the Me-2 flicked between the nine-hundred and seventy-one available channels. And if what it saw on CNN and BBC was true, things on the ground were even worse than feared.

Someone had started a wildfire in the hills of Santa Barbara, and the flames now stretched across a hundred-mile radius. The fans of two soccer teams had clashed outside a stadium, and the resulting riot had left scores of people injured and three innocent bystanders fighting for their lives. Worst of all, the rebels were on the move in the Congo again.

"I told you, B. CLOTs are popping up left and right!"

"What's a CLOT?"

"Complete Lack of Thought!" Me-2 threw up its synthetic arms. "From there, it's only a hop, skip, and a jump to the—"

"Those aren't CLOTs, doofus—that kind of stuff happens every day. Why do you think I never watch the news?"

"Then explain Zurich!" Me-2 pointed to the picture-in-picture, where the capital of Switzerland had erupted in a torrent of political protests. "The Swiss are neutral about everything!"

"You're crazy, Me. In fact, you're doing exactly what my science teacher Dr. Isakoff says *not* to do: come up with a theory first and *then* find evidence to support it!"

The Me-2's liquid crystal eyes took another glance at the events transpiring around the globe.

"Yeah, maybe you're right, B. Maybe it's all just part of the Plan . . ."

"That's the spirit!" Benjamin yanked the clicker away from his alternate brother and turned off the boob tube. "Now beat it and let me get back to work."

Seemsberia, The Seems

After the bus carrying Simly had passed through the gates of Seemsberia proper, he had been escorted down the steps and led directly to processing. Like every other Seemsian whose fate it was to reflect on their deeds behind these stone walls, he was searched, showered, relieved of his personal property, and issued a standard jumpsuit and prisoner ID number. Then, per Fixer Blaque's agreement with the Warden, the Briefer was locked in the relative safety of a twelve-by-twelve holding cell until the next morning. That agreement had suddenly changed.

"But why can't I stay in the Pokey?"

Simly Frye's feet were in shackles, which didn't exactly help him keep up with the Corrections Officer who was leading him down the long, dank hallway.

"New batch a'inmates comin' in," said the guard, ignoring the catcalls coming from the cells that lined both walls. "Gotta make room."

"But I'm only here for one day!"

"Sorry, kid. Warden's orders." The Officer stopped before a tall steel door, then brusquely undid the shackles. "Suggest you wear these."

He handed Simly a thick wool jacket and cap, pulled a fat brass key off the rings on his belt, and inserted it into the heavy latch on the door.

"Is it safe out there?" asked Simly. His teeth were already chattering, but not from the cold.

"Long as you don't get on nobody's bad side."

With that, the guard opened the door and pushed the prisoner outside.

"Don't do the crime if you can't do the time," Simly whispered to himself. But when his eyes adjusted to the harsh light and he took the first look at his home for the next twenty-five hours, he was pretty sure he couldn't.

Fenced in on all sides by barbed wire and overseen by four separate guardposts was a football-sized yard of frozen tundra. Inmates dressed in heavy layers were scattered across the ice and mud, pumping iron, playing chess, and engaging in the ancient sport of Distraction. Most were broken into clearly delineated cliques, and Simly recognized people in The Know, as well as the infamous Rocky Road Gang and even a crew of Seems Firsters.[20] But as he tucked his hands in his pockets and found a quiet corner, there was one posse that scared the Briefer more than all the others combined.

There were at least a hundred of them, all congregated on the stone stairs that overlooked the east side of the yard. At first glance, there was little they had in common with each other, for Pencil Pushers sat alongside Reality Checkers who chewed the fat with Drifters and Degenerators. But upon closer inspection, even the casual observer could spot somewhere on each prisoner's body a tattoo or patch or piece of jewelry depicting what would have been a mark of shame in mainstream Seemsian society, yet here was considered a badge of honor:

A sinister black wave.

---

20. A radical group of environmentalists who believe that the natural resources of The Seems should not be "wasted" on The World.

"You must be a newbie!"

Simly turned to see an old man with a Seemsberian monkey on his shoulder limping toward him and extending a gnarled hand.

"I'm Bill. Bill the Lifer, they call me."

"Simly Frye." He hadn't forgotten Becker's admonition not to talk to anybody, but the man's wrinkled smile made it hard not to say hello. "I'm only in for one more day."

"Time is relative, young fella. Some people live an entire lifetime in a day! Ain't that right, Fumbles?"

The old convict petted the monkey on his shoulder, which disturbingly turned out to be a mangy stuffed animal. Even worse, a few eyes in the yard were beginning to turn their way.

"Well, it was nice meeting you, Bill."

Simly started to look for another spot, but Bill followed.

"What you in for, if you don't mind me askin'?"

"Trespassing," said Simly, not wanting to get into the embarrassing details.

"Got caught with my hand in the Cookie Jar,[21] myself."

"Sorry to hear that, bro. Listen, I don't mean to be rude, but I just wanna pay my debt to society in peace and quiet."

"C'mon, Fumbles! We can tell when we're not wanted!"

As Bill the Lifer and his closest friend stormed off in a huff, Simly did his best to tuck into the shadows and make himself invisible again. Unfortunately, the damage had already been done.

---

21. The locked safe where the Food & Drink Administration keeps their sweetest treats.

"Well, well, well. Look what Seemsberian Snow Cat dragged in."

Much to Simly's horror, the entire Tide clan was drifting in his direction. The way they moved was like a sailboat tacking, plotting just enough of a circuitous route as to avoid the suspicion of the guards, who sat with their binoculars in the towers above. But in a very short amount of time, they had formed a semicircle around where he was standing.

"If it ain't Kid Fixer's string-bean sidekick!" An ex–Flavor Miner whose beard was tied with a rubber band got right in Simly's frostbitten face. "Looks like Seemsmas came early this year, eh, boys?"

"I'm not lookin' for any trouble," muttered the frightened newbie, backing up the two inches that separated him from the wall behind him.

"Well, it's looking for you."

As The Tide started to roll in, Simly instinctively reached for the Fists of Fury™ that were clipped onto his belt. But then he remembered the collection of Tools that were normally strapped all over his body were now sitting in two cardboard boxes in Seemberia's property room. So he put up his dukes—just like his grandpa Milton had taught him—and prepared to take his lumps.

"Les partir suel!"

En masse, the gang turned toward the voice of a gaunt figure that was approaching from the other side of the yard. His hair and beard were disheveled, and he was rail thin—though what there was of him was rock hard. Whoever he was, The Tide didn't turn on him, which meant he merited respect.

"This don't concern you, Frenchy," the miner whispered under his breath.

"But it does concern them."

The scraggly inmate unexpectedly hucked a rock up at the nearest tower, enough of a signal to catch the guard's attention.

"There a problem down there?" The Corrections Officer took off his mirrored shades and shouted over a bullhorn. Nobody said a word, because nobody wanted to be tossed into solitary confinement or given extra sessions on the Couch. "I didn't think so. Now break it up!"

He didn't have to ask twice, and one by one The Tide began to reverse course and trickle back into the yard. But not before one of them gave Simly a vicious shove, knocking him into the wall and off his feet.

"I don't care if you are Triton's boy." The Flavor Miner stepped right up to the one called Frenchy and spat directly in his face. "I'm personally gonna send you to A Better Place."

"But I'm already there, *mon ami*."

As the chess masters returned to their clocks, the bearded prisoner grabbed the newbie by the elbow and lifted him off the ice.

"Simly Alomonous Frye. What's a nice guy like you doing in a place like this?"

Simly hadn't recognized his savior at first glance, but the accent born of summers in Paris and winters in Chamonix left no doubt in his mind about who this stranger was. The two had trained together on the hallowed grounds of the IFR and faced the same gauntlet of challenges thrown at all his Candidates by instructor Jelani Blaque. But the Briefer shuddered at what terrible events could have transformed that debonair French teenager into the battle-scarred convict who stood before him now . . .

"Thibadeau?"

Executive Conference Room, The Big Building, The Seems

Eve Hightower sat one chair to the right of the head of the conference table, numbly clutching the twelve ballots in her hand.

"Eight to four?" She had already counted the anonymous votes reflected on the small white squares of paper twice, but she couldn't stop herself from doing it again. "Eight to four?"

Since the other eleven members of the Powers That Be had already excused themselves, the Second in Command was left alone to figure out what had gone wrong. Only a single issue had come up on the docket today, that being whether or not to intervene in the matter of the Blue Poison Dart Frog. The amphibian indigenous to Sector 419 was on the verge of extinction, but the Rules governing Animal Affairs clearly stated: "*tampering with the success or failure of any species is strictly prohibited.*" Eve was beyond stunned, however, to find that hers was one of only four votes that advocated letting Nature take its course in this matter.

"How is this possible?"

She angrily tossed the ballots across the table, not because the actual issue had won approval, but because of what the results said about the Powers That Be themselves.

"What were you expecting, dear?" Out of the shadows in the corner of the conference room stepped an older woman with long silver hair. She was dressed more casually than the Second in Command—in a simple white blouse and jeans, with sandals on her feet—and she seemed far more amused by the vote. "A landslide?"

"Just the usual seven to five." Eve's annoyance only increased at the sight of the older woman's smile. "But to flip-flop that far the other way?"

"Surely this isn't the first vote that caught you by surprise." The new arrival sat down upon the edge of the table and pointed to a famous painting on the wall. "You should've seen my face when the original Powers shot down my proposal for extra Time off for good behavior."

"Mother, please! If I wanted to hear stories about the good ole days, I would call Sitriol Flook!"

Sophie Temporale quietly let Eve's fury wash over her. No matter how hard she tried to be helpful, the woman known as "the Time Being" still couldn't avoid getting under her daughter's skin. "I'm sorry, sweetheart. I thought you wanted me to be here."

"I did. I do." Eve took a deep breath, feeling typically guilty about flipping out on her mom. "But what I really need from you right now is advice."

Ever since her mother had made an unexpected return to The Seems after fifty-plus years of exile, Eve had sought Sophie's council. These were dangerous times, what with the rise of The Tide, and the Second didn't know who she could trust anymore. "You saw the vote, heard the arguments. Who do you think sold me out?"

"If you ask me, the question is not who, dear, it's why. Why would they approve a motion that is so obviously and noticeably against the Rules?"

"And I'm sure you have an answer for that too."

Sophie nodded. "The Powers That Be have always been and always will be mere reflections of what's happening in The Seems at large. And any fool can see that the people are beginning to lose faith in the Plan."

"That sounds more like Samuel talking." Eve was surprised by the coldness of her own voice. "Or Triton."

"Ignore the truth in your enemy's words at your own peril, sweetheart. And speaking of Samuel, you might want to consider heeding his advice instead of dismissing it, else those who sold you out take it as a sign that you fear his popularity."

"First of all, it was I who asked him to be a consultant to the Powers That Be. And secondly, the day I'm afraid of Sam Hightower is the day pigs fly."

"Then why isn't he living at home anymore?"

This time Sophie knew she'd crossed the line that safely separates mothers and daughters, especially when it comes to personal matters.

"Y'know what, Mom?" Eve calmly rose to her feet and headed for the exit. "I liked you better when you lived in New York."

She slammed the door shut behind her, then angrily made her way back to the corner office from which she oversaw the operations of two entirely different but intricately connected worlds.

"Hold all my calls, Monique."

Eve's personal assistant nodded without looking up, then

handed her a fistful of messages. Once inside the frosted glass door, the Second in Command tossed those messages onto the ever-increasing pile in her inbox and collapsed into the chair behind her desk.

"Stay calm, Evie. Stay calm."

As she opened up a tin of Tiger Balm and rubbed it on her temples, Eve knew it was easier said than done. She had lost control of the Powers, that much was for certain, and her mom was right about one thing: all that mattered was finding out why. Were the eight members who had voted against her wishes merely sending a message that it was at last time to revisit the Plan? Or was it more insidious than that? Were they flat-out planning to oust her and bring back her husband? Either way, she wasn't going down without a fight.

"Ma'am, I have Human Resources on line one."

Eve pressed the intercom button, irritated.

"I thought I said to hold my calls."

"I know, ma'am, but Director Dejanus says it's an emergency."

"Of course it's an emergency," she thought. An entire Train of Thought is lost, a CLOT just popped up in Zurich, and her mother was driving her up the wall. She reluctantly picked up the phone.

"Second in Command."

"Sorry to bother you, Madame Second, but it just couldn't wait."

"Not a problem, Nick. How can I help?"

"Madame, are you aware of the existence of Proposition HR 1647-14?"

"The new internship at the Big Building?"

"Exactly. The first time a person in The World will be given

the opportunity to observe the Plan in action. After a lengthy review process, I'm delighted to inform you that a consensus has emerged as to the best Candidate for the position."

"Great. So what's the problem?"

"Ahem. Well . . . you see, the thing is . . ."

"Out with it, Nicholas. I have a lot on my plate right now."

"Of course. It's just, there appears to be a conflict of interest with a recent decision handed down by the Court of Public Opinion."

"What's the Case number?"

"Number 423006-74634, A as in apple, V as in Victor, 323."

The Second in Command rolled her chair over to the set of Windows on her desk and toggled directly to the Case File database. But as she was typing in the encrypted sequence, Eve realized she already knew the associated name. It was one she had heard for the first time in a briefing about the Glitch in Sleep, and it had nearly become a household name during one of the most celebrated trials in the history of The Seems. It had to be a mistake.

"You don't mean Jennifer Kaley?"

Brainstorm

Far-Out Saloon, Who Knows Where,
The Middle of Nowhere

Crackoom!

Thunder rolled and lightning flashed outside the dusty windows of the Far-Out Saloon. The sawdust on the creaky floorboards jumped and danced, the bottles lining the mirrored bar rattled, and the gaslit chandeliers that hung from the barrel-gilded ceiling flickered on and off. Just as they had all night.

"Today's my lucky day, Emmett." A man with a crinkled '49er hat, muddy boots, and suspenders polished off his drink and slammed the empty glass on the bar. "I can feel it!"

Emmett the bartender cracked a smile and poured the old prospector another shot of Sunshine. "Hope so, Hopeless."

The grizzled old-timer knocked back another one, then tried to pinch the waitress as she passed.

"Get yer paws offa me, you ol' buzzard!"

The rosy-cheeked young woman slapped the prospector with the hand that wasn't carrying a tray, then headed upstairs to deliver some much-needed sustenance to the patron in Room #1.

"Wish I'd lost *my* marbles out there, Charity. Then maybe you'd make a bowl'a soup for me!"

"In your dreams, old man."

When Hopeless wasn't scouring the Middle of Nowhere for the Eternal Springs of Hope, he could usually be found right here in his favorite watering hole in his favorite frontier town. Who Knows Where was the last of a handful of such outposts that sprang up during the Head Rush, when Seemsians had flocked to these parts with dreams of fast fortune. But tonight the aged prospector wasn't the only one seeking solace in the Far-Out Saloon. Tonight, thirtysome-odd people had gathered here to collectively ride out a wicked Brainstorm.

Crackoom! Crackoom!

"Think this place is gonna hold up, Emmett?" A Back Scratcher who was sitting with four other men at a card table called out when the windows and ground stopped shaking. "Haven't seen one this bad since Ophelia."[22]

The bartender twirled his handlebar mustache, then shrugged. "Ophelia was bad, but she warn't no Lulu."

"Right about that. Lulu was one mean lady!"

One of the other players in the poker game tilted up his Stetson. "Son, is you playin' cards, or is you swappin' spit?"

---

22. Brainstorms in The Seems, like hurricanes in The World, are given alternating male and female names.

When the blowing winds and shifting sands of the Brainstorm had kicked up, so had a friendly game of Who Knows Where high-low. The Back Scratcher was joined by the town doctor, a Snake Oil salesman, and two Idea Smugglers who had cut short their run when the skies above had darkened. By now, deep stacks of Miracle Cures, Strokes of Genius, and Chips off the Old Block had formed a massive pot.

"Call," said the Scratcher. "I trust Time in a bottle will suffice."

As Doc dealt the hand's final card, a boy no more than seven in his best bib and tucker ran up to the bar.

"What's the worst Brainstorm you've ever seen, Mr. Emmett?"

"Levi McCoy, you hobble your lip!"

The boy's mother chased after him and brought him back to the corner table. In addition to the outlaws and mudsills, Who Knows Where's few respectable citizens were anxiously waiting out the storm as well.

"Nothin' but a thing, Eudora." Emmett wiped his hands on his apron, then leaned his elbows on a faded spot on the bar. "Tell the truth, boy, worst storm I ever seen was Malachi . . ."

The boy's eyes went wide as he jumped up onto his pa's lap. Even the three figures robed in black who had slipped into town with the first gusts of wind and done little but quietly whisper among themselves turned to hear the tale.

"Thing about Mal' was, when he come through, there warn't no warnin' t'all. No clouds, no rain, no nothin'. Just dropped right down on our heads. We tried to run, crammed the whole damn town into this here cellar, but ol' Mal just reached down and ripped the roof right off."

The boy called Levi looked up at the ceiling, quaking in his little boots.

"And I don't gotta tell you what happens in a Brainstorm when all that Scratch is heated up and whippin' 'round your head." A dark shadow passed over the barkeep's face at the memory. "The worst things you can imagine literally come to life."

The loudest crack yet seemed to snap Emmett out of it.

"Come to think of it, this here storm kinda reminds me of Malachi. Don't it, Percy?"

The bartender swiveled to his right, where an old piano player stroked the keys of a grand piano, as he'd done every night since back in the Day.

"Sho 'nuff, Emmett. Sho 'nuff."

As Percy's bony fingers effortlessly switched to a haunting version of "Riders on the Storm," Hopeless had to chuckle, for he'd heard Emmett spin this tall tale before. Besides, he had other things on his mind, like—

Bang! Bang! Bang! Bang!

Thirty-two heads slowly turned toward the boarded-up front door of the saloon.

"What was that?" asked the Snake Oil salesman.

"I didn't hear nothin'," whispered the Back Scratcher.

"Me neither," one of the Idea Smugglers agreed, but he joined his partner in pulling out a Pea Shooter just in case.

"Everybody take it easy," said Emmett. "Just the blowin' of the wind."

But when the banging came a second time, louder and unmistakable, there could be little doubt as to the cause: someone was on the other side of the door. Or some*thing*.

"We have to let them in, Emmett," said Charity from the top of the stairs, her voice trembling with fear.

"The heck we do!" The Snake Oil salesman grabbed his winnings and ducked beneath the card table. "We don't know if it's a man out there or a man's worst fear!"

"But what if they need our help?"

Charity looked down at Emmett, who only dropped his eyes and polished up his bar. "Far as I'm concerned, anyone stupid enough to be out in a Brainstorm deserves what's comin' to 'em."

From the nods that rippled through the room, most of the patrons who had sought sanctuary in the Far-Out agreed. In fact, only Hopeless the prospector begged to differ, getting off his stool and ambling over toward the door. Something in his old bones told him that the break he'd been looking for all these years had finally arrived, and if he could just keep everyone's britches from getting in a snit, this would indeed be his lucky—

Bang! Bang! Bang! Bang!

It was louder this time, and more urgent. Outside, the winds had whipped into a frenzy.

"Charity's right, Emmett." Hopeless reached for one of the boards that had been nailed across the door. "We gots a responsibility."

But Hopeless's fingers stopped short when he heard a loud click behind him. He didn't have to look to know that Emmett had exchanged his barman's towel for a sawed-off I'llshoot-youdeadwhereyoustandyoulowdownnogoodsonuva Gun, which he was now pointing directly at the prospector.

"I'm the sheriff in this town, Hopeless—not to mention

the mayor, the Bill collector, and the justice of the peace—and my only responsibility's to the people who elected me. Especially when there's women and children involved." Emmett gave the 'Sonuva Gun a second pump. "Door stays locked."

"Here, here!" said the salesman, taking a sip of Liquid Courage just in case. But even though the decision had been made on the inside, whoever or whatever was on the outside had different ideas.

Crash!

When the smoke finally cleared, the barricade was gone, and the two swinging doors of the saloon blew back and forth on their hinges. Wind and rain and blue-tinted sand gusted through the entrance, followed closely by four figures that looked as if they'd stepped right out of a deep-sea diving expedition. They wore strange bodysuits and brass helmets, and though they were tethered together by what for all The World looked like toilet paper, the last one in line was being dragged facedown along the floorboards.

"Everybody get back!"

As Emmett hopped over the bar and trained his weapon on the new arrivals, he didn't have to ask his customers twice. Everyone piled to the back of the saloon or cowered beneath their tables, utterly convinced that a fisherman in the Sea of Confusion had been lost in the gales and seen his or her worst Nightmares come to fruition.

"Shoot 'em, Emmett!" someone shouted. "Shoot 'em!"

The sheriff/bartender was aimin' to do just that, when the leader (and shortest) of the sand-encrusted pilgrims reached up and began to unsnap the buckles on his metal hat. Steam hissed out and no one in the saloon breathed or moved a muscle until the helmet fell to the floor, revealing a sweat-soaked teenager with a shaggy mop of hair.

"Is there a doctor in the house?"

Becker Drane had been to some pretty fantastic places in his time, but when he wiped away the sweaty bangs from his eyes, what he saw might've taken the cake. He and the second team had somehow stumbled onto an Old West show run amok, with cowboys and townsfolk and a mustachioed sheriff ready to settle things the old-fashioned way. There was even a little "Sinbad" thrown into the décor, ornate tapestries hanging on the walls beside stuffed animals and wagon wheels, and three robed Bedouin-looking dudes pointing curved swords in his direction.

Luckily, this place also came equipped with its very own Doc.

"How long was he out there with a broken Head Case?" The pale man in the bifocals lifted the cracked helmet off Hassan's head and listened to his heart with a beat-up stethoscope.

"Impossible to say," answered Fixer Blaque, picking out sand from the ornate carvings on his Igbo stick. "After the storm hit, we got separated, and we weren't able to locate him for, what, an hour or so?"

Blaque looked to Becker for confirmation, and #37 nodded. "When we found him, he was already out cold."

Doc scraped some bluish sand off Hassan's helmet with a scalpel and rubbed it between his finger and thumb. Head

Cases had been protecting travelers from Brainstorms ever since the first Bandwagon trains had come this way, but once they lost integrity, you were out there on your own.

"Lotta Scratch got in there, fellas. Not a good thing."

Doc held up his stained fingers at Emmett, who was boarding up the doors of the Far-Out for the second time today.

"Not a good thing at all."

Ironically, the second team's foray into the Middle of Nowhere had started auspiciously—those ominous clouds holding off as Becker and Hassan hand-pumped the old seesaw trolley and its passengers as far as the hidden tracks would go. In the deep valley of dunes featured on Casey Lake's transmission, the team had found the same caboose, along with two additional items: Greg the Journeyman's Toolkit and the cloth pouch that once carried Li Po's precious speaking tiles. But when the tracks had suddenly disintegrated and blown away in the wind, so had their luck, for the tempest regathered and fell upon them with twice the wrath.

"How'd you fellas even find this place?" asked Charity, who'd been kind enough to assist Doc with his Smelling Salt and cotton swabs. "Surely ain't on any maps."

"It's on this one."

Becker held up the crinkled piece of parchment that Fixer Blaque had given him when they'd become hopelessly lost in the swirling sands. The hand-drawn diagram had been useless at first, the team unable to locate a landmark, but when they'd stumbled across a fork-shaped cactus that looked suspiciously like the one Blaque had sketched, Becker led his fellows on a last-ditch effort toward the town labeled "Who Knows Where."

"Mind if I get a gander at that?" Hopeless snatched the sheet before Charity could even get a look, and when he studied its contours, his eyes glowed like they'd just seen gold. "Where'd you say you got this here map again?"

"He didn't." Fixer Blaque held out a hand, making it quite clear to the old prospector what he expected to be put in it. "It's just a few pictures I drew last time I was here."

"Well, why didn't you say so?" Hopeless flashed a rotten-toothed grin and handed the map over without a fight. "To whom do I owe the pleasure?"

"You can call me Fixer Blaque."

Up until now, there had been too much commotion for Becker to feel out the vibes in the saloon, but at the mention of the word "Fixer," the tension became palpable. The patrons who had gathered around the injured Hassan quietly slinked back to their tables—keeping their eyes on the floor and their mouths shut—and it was pretty obvious why. Anyone who called the Middle of Nowhere home had something to hide . . . or someone to hide from.

"Tell your customers not to worry, Emmett." Fixer Blaque sidled up to a stool by the bar. "We're here to find a lost Train of Thought, not to make trouble for honest, hardworking people."

"Mighty nice of you to say, Jelani." Emmett reached across and shook the retired Fixer's calloused hand. "And mighty nice to see you again."

"Been too long."

Blaque's familiarity with this of all places caught Becker by surprise, and it was becoming increasingly apparent why the Powers That Be had insisted upon him as team leader.

"You and your men must be dyin' of thirst." The bartender wiped his hands on his apron and cordially handed out menus. "No offense, ma'am."

"None taken." The Octogenarian smiled, happy to finally be free of that dreadful helmet. "And make my Shot in the Dark a triple."

As Becker perused the drink list and wondered if they checked IDs in this joint, he took another covert glance at the three robed men. When Blaque mentioned the lost Train of Thought, everyone in the bar did a double take—but the Bedouins hadn't reacted at all. Becker leaned in for a closer look and noticed that one of them appeared to be injured—the bottom portion of his robe was soaked with blood—and his friends were forced to prop him up lest he fall out of his chair.

"I think he's coming around!"

Doc put the Salt shaker back into a black bag that still bore the faded symbol of the Department of Health, and all attention turned to the man on the floor, who was starting to emerge from his trance.

"What happened?" Hassan tried to sit upright, but quickly abandoned that idea when the sudden rush of blood forced him to grab his temples in pain. "Where am I?"

"You're in Who Knows Where, son."

Doc eased the Fixer's head onto a velvet pillow, and Becker dragged his Toolkit over to his fallen teammate.

"You look like you could use a Breath of Fresh Air™."

Hassan sat up on his elbow and helped himself to the Binaca-like blast.

"Don't mind if I do."

"Listen, son . . ." Doc leaned in close, gravely concerned.

"You didn't happen to see nothin' . . . strange out there, did you?"

"Like what?"

"Oh, I don't know . . . somethin' you wish you hadn't?"

Unlike earlier, when every man, woman, and child in the saloon was pretending to be invisible, now they were transfixed. Hassan looked toward the front door, which was still being pounded by the wind and rain.

"I remember nothing except getting lost in the storm, my visor breaking, and a suffocating blueness . . ."

Everyone eyed the Fixer skeptically, but it was Emmett who said what was on their minds. "You're sure now, mister? 'Cause some real bad things come to life in a Brainstorm."

The Persian's steely brown eyes revealed little of what was behind them.

"I said I saw nothing."

"Hassan is a liar!"

A deep and throaty voice called out from above, and all looked up to see a huge, half-naked man standing at the top of the stairs. His flesh was sunburned and his hair sizzled, and judging from the bandages that covered his eyes and hands, someone had been giving him a great deal of medical attention.

"Sweetheart, I told you to stay in bed!" Charity scrambled up the stairs and hastily tried to lead him to his room. "You're still burnin' up with fever!"

The waitress pulled at a heavily muscled arm, but even in his weakened condition Greg the Journeyman was not an easy man to move.

"Hassan has always been a liar!" The giant Fixer looked

directly at Hassan, as if he could see right through the blindfold. "Most of all to himself."

Becker couldn't stop himself from checking to see how closely the Yakustkan's comment had struck its mark. But Shahzad Hassan only squeezed the rain from his long black hair and started up the stairs.

"It's good to see you, Greg. We feared the worst."

The first of the missing team of Fixers to be found by his brethren reached out a mighty paw and blindly shook Hassan by the shoulder.

"Fear not, brother. For I have seen the—"

And then Greg the Journeyman crashed to the floor.

"Help me get him back to his room!" cried Charity, and two more Fixers bounded up the stairs. But when Becker joined Blaque and Hassan in lugging the more than three-hundred-pound man down the hallway, he was surprised to see that the burn on Greg's torso was not caused by the sun at all.

"Is that what I think it is?" Becker pointed toward the seared flesh, where an oversized teardrop and lightbulb had been seared into Fixer #6's chest like he was a branded steer.

"It is. But there will be time to discuss it in the morning."

Fixer Blaque seemed to know exactly what was on his protégé's mind. Of course there were other possibilities, but chances were that way out here in the Middle of Nowhere, there was only one place that this proud icon could be found at a temperature sufficient to cause such a wound. It was on a steampowered juggernaut whose black smokestack was emblazoned with just such an icon, and whose precious cargo provided the raw materials for The World to ponder, ruminate, and muse . . .

A Train of Thought.

By the next morning, the winds had died, the sun shone brightly, and seeing that no crawling eye or swarm of giant roaches had shambled out of the storm—as they had during Brainstorms Mathilda and Persephone—it was business as usual in Who Knows Where. The Snake Oil salesman shilled his latest tonics, Back Scratchers sifted the sand for specks of blue, and the Idea Smugglers stuffed their saddlebags for another illicit run to the Black Market.

"What a difference a day makes," observed the Octogenarian, joining her fellow Fixers on the bench outside the General Store. "And what a charming little town."

Though Sylvia always looked on the bright side, she also knew that this was not the moment to indulge her favorite hobby of scoping out exotic travel destinations. The Brainstorm had cost the Mission precious Time, and while Hassan was getting a final once-over at Doc's Apothecary, the rest of the team anxiously waited for Greg the Journeyman to awaken from his slumber.

"Here he comes now."

Becker pointed to the swinging doors of the saloon, where the Yakutskan strongman was stretching his huge arms. He seemed to be in a good deal of pain, however, and Charity the waitress emerged to give him a shoulder to lean on as he made his way onto Main Street.

"Those two are awfully cozy, don't you think?" The Octogenarian peered across the street from behind her copy of this morning's *We Know Where Gazette*. "I wonder how she feels about him resuming his duties?"

"I think we're about to find out," said Fixer Blaque, spreading a smear of Seems Cheese on an Anything bagel. After a few heated words were exchanged, Charity headed back through the swinging doors, and Greg lumbered across the street to meet his comrades.

"*Dobraye ootra*, my brothers and sister!"

The Fixer's eyes were still covered with a blindfold, and it took both Becker and Blaque to guide his massive frame over to the bench.

"Good morning to you, Greg." Fixer Blaque patted him on the back. "I take it you're feeling better."

"Much better. Doctor say fever break."

"And your eyes?"

When Greg removed his blindfold, even Blaque found it hard to stifle a wince of horror, for the once hazel irises had been scorched white.

"What was it, Greg?" asked the Octogenarian, gently reaching up to touch her comrade's wounded face. "What did this to you?"

"Something more beautiful than you could ever imagine."

As the Journeyman recounted everything that had happened since the coming of the strange light, a childlike wonder graced his weather-beaten face. Becker had assumed the first team (as well as the staffs of Contemplation and the End of the Line) had been eradicated by some sort of secret weapon, but Fixer #6 told a different tale.

"Everything Gregor fear, as soon as light wash over him, gone. So into light he walk—straight toward mountain—until he find it . . . half buried in sand."

"Find what?" asked Blaque, though he hoped he knew the answer.

"Lost Train."

A silent satisfaction settled over the General Store's front porch.

"What about Casey and Lisa and Po?" asked Becker, worried for his friends.

"Do not know, Becker Ferdinanovich. Others go separate way, as we must all in life."

"#6, this is Fixer Octo talking."

"Is great pleasure not to see you again, Sylvia."

Both Fixers laughed, and the respect Greg had for his elder was evident.

"I was curious if before you lost your vision, you were able to ascertain the identity of the thieves."

"Yes, when find train, robbers digging out from nasty Brainstorm." Greg ripped open his shirt to reveal his badly burned chest. "Perhaps Gregor should buy ticket instead of hold on to smokestack, but pain of burn nothing compared to glory of light."

The Journeyman's smile bespoke the truth of that statement.

"Can you describe them?"

"Men, robed in black from foot to head. Was they who threw me off train—but not before I throw three of them first. Is only by grace of Plan does Gregor survive and end up Who Knows Where."

Becker's heart jumped. The teenager had suspected the black-robed figures in the Far-Out Saloon from moment one, and kept a watchful eye on them all night. The party of three never said a word, and never got up from their table until Emmett had unsealed the doors at six a.m. Even then, they had only requested some bandages for their wounded comrade, whose injuries surely could've been caused by a fall off a moving train.

"If y'all are wondering about them Nowherians, they done skedaddled out the back door 'bout an hour ago."

From the alley behind the General Store, a voice with a definite Middle of Nowhere twang rang out, followed closely by an old codger with a '49er hat and a long piece of straw between his yellowed teeth.

"And b'lieve you me, once they get back into the desert, might as well be huntin' Dust Bunnies without a broom."

Nowherians? Where had Becker heard that name before? He looked at the Octogenarian but she seemed just as perplexed as he was. Fixer Blaque didn't seem to have the same problem, though.

"Let me guess." Blaque threw Hopeless a wry grin. "You're the only fella in town who can help us find them?"

"Dang tootin'!" The grizzled prospector winked. "Alls I ask in return is a few minutes with that map you got there."

Blaque unfolded the twelve-year-old piece of parchment and dangled it in the air.

"It's yours."

"Whoo hoo!"

"*After* you take us where we need to go."

"Done!" Hopeless jumped into the air and clicked his worn-out boot heels together. "Lemme just roust my partner, Zebulon, and we'll head for the mountains!"

While Hopeless skipped off toward the stables, the second team busted out Turf Boards and Cross-Country Skis™ for the journey that lay ahead.

"Put these on, Greg." Fixer Blaque pulled a plastic case from his Toolkit and offered it to his old friend. "I think you'll find blindness as a handicap is overrated."

"Is not necessary, Jelani. Gregor will not be coming with you."

The team stopped in their tracks, and wistfulness filled the crags of the Journeyman's face.

"Gregor has had long and fruitful voyage in this life. From town in middle of nowhere to Middle Nowhere itself, and always he move on. But today he finally know where journey end."

"But what about the train?" Becker knew what Greg's strength could do for this Mission, and hated to see it wasted.

"Plan will provide, boychik." The Journeyman placed a leathery paw on the shoulder of his youngest comrade. "Never has Gregor known that more than he does now."

As Greg bid his fellows good-bye, none among them could deny he had earned the right to choose this ending. For three decades he had served The Seems' cause, and his mighty shoulders had literally carried the weight of The World on several occasions. But even Atlas had to shrug.

In the doors of the Far-Out Saloon, Charity nervously gnawed at her fingernails, searching Greg's body language for whether or not he was planning to stay. But when she let out a holler and jumped into his arms, Becker knew she'd gotten the answer she'd been hoping for instead of the heartbreak that had passed through town so many times before. Heartbreak that Becker himself began to feel—for he'd given someone else a different answer—and he pushed it from his thoughts as fast as he possibly could.

"While I'm young, boys." The Octogenarian affixed her umbrella to one of her ski poles and opened it high and wide. "Time to saddle up."

The second team fanned out onto Main Street, heading for the Apothecary to round up Hassan. But halfway there Fixer Blaque stopped, as if some important task had somehow slipped his mind. He turned to face the Far-Out Saloon, and when he shouted out to the blind man who sat on the steps, Emotion that can only be felt by those who have shared a higher calling was dripping from his voice:

"Live to Fix, Greg the Journeyman!"

The red-haired giant clenched a fist and raised it proudly over his head.

"Fix to live, Jelani Blaque!"

Au Contraire

"Wake up, Simly!"

"Just five more minutes, Mom!"

Simly Frye tucked a pillow over his head and tried to hustle back to dreamland.

"Simly, *wake up!*"

Someone gave the mattress beneath him a swift kick.

"Who? What? When?" The lanky Seemsian sat up like a shot, banging his head against the ceiling. "Where am I?"

"In my cell." A soothing French accent calmed his nerves from the bunk below. "They're about to do the count, so make sure you're dressed and ready to go."

"Thanks, Mom. I mean, Thib."

Simly wiped the twinkle from his eyes and thought for a moment he might be dreaming, and that he really was back at the Frye family compound in the Seemsian suburb of

Everywhere. But when he saw the bars on the window and realized his Jinx Gnomes comforter and allergy pills were nowhere to be found, the reality of his situation came back with force.

After the new arrival narrowly escaped a brawl in the yard, his old friend Thibadeau had paid off a Corrections Officer to let Simly serve out the remainder of his sentence in the safety of the Frenchman's cell. "Safety" was a loose term, however, for the Protective Custody wing not only housed some of the most dangerous criminals The Seems had ever known, but it had been sequestered from all other wings for a single purpose:

To protect those inside from the rest of the prison population.

"All right, convicts! Up and at 'em!"

As Simly stumbled from the cell and lined up beside Thibadeau, he tried his best to keep his eyes locked straight ahead. Last night he had only caught brief glimpses of the other inmates, but in the morning light he was able to get an all too illuminated view.

"Hey, kid . . . over here."

Someone was whispering to his right, and the Briefer couldn't resist turning to see a scraggly prisoner with shaking hands and bloodshot eyes.

"Got any Knockout Punch? I swear I'm gonna lose it if I don't get some shuteye!"

When a guard came over to see what the ruckus was about, the jittery con pretended to be a model citizen, but it didn't take Simly long to realize he'd just come face-to-face with the infamous Insomniac. The former employee of the Department of Sleep had been caught rerouting Wake-Up Calls and spiking the Snooze, and when asked on the witness stand to defend his countless acts of sabotage, had infamously offered: "If I can't sleep, nobody can!"

"Are you present, Lenny?" demanded the Corrections Officer. "Because if you're not, I can get you in touch with the Inner Child again."

"I'm present, I'm present, I'm present!"

That threat alone was enough to slap the Insomniac into shape, and the guard moved down his list.

"Remote Gremlin!"

"Here!"

"Sock Goblin."

"Yo."

"Freck!"

"Oui!"

As the count continued with military precision, Simly heard name after name that sent chills down his spine. Son of Seems. Rack the Jipper. Even Drew Keloggian, the dreaded Cereal Killer who had been the scourge of the FDA. But what shocked the incarcerated Briefer most was the sight of a fair-skinned and wispy-haired man four cells up the line.

"Is that . . . ?"

"C'est lui," whispered Thibadeau. "Time is no longer on his side."

"Neverlåethe!"

"Present."

Even in his orange jumpsuit and without his trademark pocketwatch, Permin Neverlåethe was easy to recognize. Simly had watched every second of the deposed Administrator's trial on SNN, including his full confession of the role he played in creating the bomb that laid waste to Time. Nonetheless, a court of his peers had sentenced him to three consecutive life terms— a punishment that had left him a visibly beaten man.

"Frye!"

"Huh?"

Simly snapped out of his daydream to find the Corrections Officer right in his grille, spittle forming at the corner of his mouth. "I said, Frye!"

"Here!"

"That's right, you're here! And you're gonna stay that way for twelve more hours *if*—and that's a capital IF—I don't add a few more days to your sentence. Understood?" The fear behind the Coke-bottle glasses told the guard the answer was yes, and he brought the count to a close. "Everybody back inside!"

Simly was still shaking as he followed Thibadeau back into the cell, and when the bars automatically slid shut behind them, the Briefer took his first real gander at how far one of the best Candidates in the history of the IFR had fallen. Beside the bunkbeds, the cinderblock square was also home to a steel toilet, a naked lightbulb, and some old graffiti that had been mostly scrubbed away. In fact, the only hint that anyone in particular lived there were two oversized photographs taped to the wall—one of a beautiful girl somewhere in Paris, and another of a picture-perfect World.

"I don't know how you do it, Thib."

Simly climbed back up to the top bunk and buried his head in the pillow.

"Do what?"

"Survive this place."

Thibadeau lay down on the bottom bunk and placed his hands behind his head. "One day at a time."

Neither spoke for a while, the only sounds the ticking of a clock and the Frenchman's foot tapping against the bed frame. It was unheard of for a World resident to serve time behind these walls, and at Thibadeau's trial his lawyers had opted for a guilty plea, fully expecting a sentence of "unremembering." But Judge Alvin Torte wanted to make sure the defendant "never forgot the screams of his victims," and made prisoner #566-PC3 only the second Flip-Sider in history to call Seemsberia home.[23]

"Why, Thib? Why'd you do it?"

"Join The Tide?"

"Uh-huh."

"You would not get it, Simly. You are not from The World—"

"You'd be surprised what I get."

The sharpness of his voice caught even Simly off guard. Maybe he wasn't born in The World, but he loved it just the same, and deeply resented The Tide's willingness to put it in danger for political gain.

"It is a powerless feeling to grow up in a place you don't understand, *mon ami*. To take it on faith that there is something good behind all the terrible things that happen there. Triton promised a chance to make those terrible things go away."

"Tell that to the people who died in Time Square!"

---

23. The first was Stu Ivar, aka "the Accidental Tourist," but that's a Story for Another Day.

"Do you not think that weighs upon my conscience every day?" Simly winced at the sound of Thibadeau pounding a fist against the cinderblock wall. "I was told that the bomb was a decoy, and that no one on either side would be hurt!"

"Then you're even stupider than I am."

"Très vrai." The voice below grew heavy and tired. "On this we can agree."

The silence between them returned, broken only by a harmonica warbling behind the bars of some distant inmate's cell.

"What of Becker? How is he handling his conviction?"

"You know about that?"

"News travels fast—even in this Plan-forsaken place. I'm just glad he wasn't given a one-way ticket on the Trans-Seemsberian Express."

"Yeah, but he's pretty depressed about the whole unremembering thing. As soon as they find that Train of Thought, the Memory Bank's gonna freeze all his—"

Simly abruptly sat up in bed, seeing the same guard who had put them through the count appear outside Thibadeau's bars. For a moment, the Briefer thought he was about to get that threatened extra time, but then he realized the Corrections Officer had something else in mind.

"Let's go, Freck. Captain Marcus wants to see you."

Maximum Security Wing, Seemsberia, The Seems

Though there hasn't been a war in The Seems since Green and Blue fought Purple and Red, peace and security are still maintained by Special Forces—an elite battalion functioning under the leadership of a single Captain. Only a handful have held this post since back in the Day, and Robert Marcus was the most formidable of all, a shining light who kept Seemsians ever safe from harm. That is, until he was sentenced to life in Seemsberia for releasing moths into the Fabric of Reality—the heinous act that announced the arrival of The Tide.

Now Marcus and several hundred of his fellow friends of Triton were sequestered in an old gymnasium that served as the Maximum Security Wing, spreading out in concentric circles of workout benches and beds.

"Thank you for joining me on such short notice, Mr. Freck."

"It is my pleasure, *mon Capitaine*."

Thibadeau watched in amazement as the nearly fifty-year-old man tore through a final set of upside-down stomach crunches. The Captain's head was shaved bald, his muscles were taut and lean, and the enormous tattoo of a cresting wave, which spiraled around his body like a black cape, seemed to rise and crash upon the shore every time he yanked himself up.

"So, what did Jelani Blaque have to say?"

"Pardon nez-moi?"

"During your not-so-secret meeting?"

Thibadeau did his best to keep his face calm, but he knew the Captain saw through it.

"It was hardly a meeting, *Capitaine*. More like an interrogation."

"Did it have anything to do"—Captain Marcus released the bar and landed on his feet in one spectacularly coordinated motion, then accepted a towel from one of his two muscle-bound bodyguards—"with a missing Train of Thought?"

"Indeed. He wondered if The Tide was responsible for stealing it."

"And what did you tell him?"

"That I had no idea." Thibadeau followed the trio over to the captain's cot. "As you know, I do not exactly have Triton's ear anymore."

The fact that the disgraced soldier already knew about a classified Mission only fed Thib's suspicion that Marcus was, in fact, Triton himself. During the time the Frenchman had been in good standing with The Tide, he had spoken with its enigmatic leader via Calling Card numerous times, though on those occasions, the transmission was always garbled to protect Triton's identity. The way the Captain carried himself, though, and the authority with which he spoke were eerily similar.

"And still Jelani interrupted his first active Mission in over ten years to see you."

The Frenchman looked away. This moment he had to tread carefully.

"I believe he was fishing for information about the deluge."

Marcus finished toweling off the sweat, then sat down and lifted a barbell off the floor. "How so?"

"He fears the train is an opening salvo—a diversion that will leave the Big Building vulnerable to a larger attack."

"If only he knew how close he was." The Captain methodically curled the weight up and down. "But not close enough."

Thibadeau's breath grew shallow and thin. "So it is still on?"

"It was never off."

From the very first night of his recruitment, when Thibadeau had been offered the chance to "answer all the unanswerable questions," there had been whispers of The Tide's final stroke.

The covert insurgency had gradually infiltrated every department, every corner of The Seems, and once Triton gave the word, it would seize control of the means of production to build "a new and better World." But only one man knew when that day would come.

"Jelani knows it is coming. They all do, and they are frightened." Marcus's eyes gleamed like two black jewels. "They should be."

"What amazes me, *Capitaine*, is that you fail to see your own hypocrisy." A rage long swallowed came vomiting out of Thibadeau. "The Tide has degenerated into a mélange of power-hungry vandals who seek nothing but to destroy, destroy, destroy! Not for the sake of anything worthwhile, but for the satisfaction of their own petty desires!"

If the Captain was moved by the accusation, he didn't show it. He simply switched the barbell to his other hand, and continued pumping iron. "You'll have to take that up with Triton himself."

"Will you stop this charade?" Thibadeau shouted at the top of his lungs. *"Everyone knows that you and Triton are one and the same!"*

Heads throughout the chamber whipped in Thibadeau's direction, though it was hard to tell whether it was due to the nature of the outburst or the accusation it contained.

"Me, Triton?" The Captain laughed, and his loyal body-guards followed suit. "I am but a soldier in his army, anxiously awaiting my orders." He dropped the barbell to the floor and checked the Time Piece on his wrist. "Which I believe are about to arrive."

As steely arms grabbed Thibadeau and drove him facedown

to the floor, Marcus put two fingers to his lips and emitted a high-pitched whistle. Seconds later, a wiry kid with glasses and a hoop earring was jerry-rigging a homemade Calling Card on the parquet floor.

"Good to see you again, Sketch." Thibadeau recognized the prisoner as a former Drifter who'd been his co-defendant at trial. "Have you spoken to Lena lately?"

"I got nothin' to say to you, Freck, and neither does she."

"Yes, I too was disappointed that she didn't attend our tr—"

But Thibadeau was cut short by a former Flavor Miner's knee in his back.

"Why are we wasting time with this traitor, Cap? Let's waste him instead."

"Because Triton appreciates those who question authority. For if we stifle every voice of dissent, will we not become as corrupt as the Powers That Be?"

Captain Marcus gave the go-ahead, and the Drifter plugged a power cord into the square metal plate on the ground. There was a brief surge of electricity, followed by a high whine as the Calling Card struggled to pick up a remote signal. But with a twist of the antenna, the broken-up image of the man they all knew as their leader shimmered into view.

"The rising Tide raises all ships!" said Triton in an eerily garbled voice.

Two hundred voices shouted back their response, so loud that the very floors of the gymnasium shook—and so united that it only sounded like one.

"All ships raise the rising Tide!"

"Mon Dieu," whispered Thibadeau, struggling more against his own fear than with those that held him down. For even though the image and voice were masked with digital fuzz as always, something about the way Triton clenched a fist and raised it into the air sent cold shivers down the Frenchman's spine.

"The word is given," was all he said.

"Attention! Attention all prisoners! This is Captain Robert Marcus speaking . . ."

Simly tightly gripped the bars of the cell block door to the Protective Custody Wing, listening to the voice that boomed across the Seemsberia-wide loudspeaker.

"As of precisely twelve minutes ago, The Tide has assumed command of this facility!"

Smoke from scattered fires made his eyes burn, but Simly could still make out panicked squadrons of guards running everywhere. Yellow lights in glass cases spun like carousels, belting out ear-splitting alarms, while pieces of Department of Corrections paperwork floated aimlessly in the air.

"Corrections Officers looking to join our cause, report to Cell Block Q for further instructions. Those who'd rather cling to an old and tired system should vacate the premises or be dealt with accordingly."

A man's scream in the distance punctuated the Captain's threat.

"Marcus over and out."

Simly backed away from the tall iron bars, trying to stifle the fear that was growing in his stomach. Not fifteen minutes ago, the Briefer was sitting on his perfectly made bed waiting for a guard to hand him his Walking Papers, when pandemonium had broken loose. Every cell door in Seemsberia swung open, instantaneously freeing Simly and a host of villains from their cages. The main entrance to Protective Custody remained locked, however.

"Simly, come inside." A wispy-haired old man beckoned from inside his open cell. "It's not safe for you out there."

"Don't worry, Permin. These guys are too crazy to worry about little old me!"

Simly glanced over his shoulder where the Insomniac was banging his head against the wall in an effort to get some rest and the Cereal Killer and Son of Seems were squaring off over the rights to the coveted title of "most infamous criminal in The Seems."

"I'm not talking about this cell block, son. The Tide will not be kind to a company man."

Permin again motioned to his cuckoo clock–filled cell and this time, Simly accepted.

"Maybe you're right."

During Thibadeau's absence, the Briefer and the former Administrator of Time had struck up a conversation through the bars of their cells. Permin Neverlåethe was pleasantly surprised when Simly claimed to have read every single page of his famously long treatise, *A Not-So-Brief History of Time*. For his part, Simly had found Permin not the monster he'd been portrayed as, but rather a man of deep conviction, haunted by his own crimes.

"I don't understand this, Permin. What are they rioting for?"

"The Tide will do anything to accomplish their goals. I only hope they had the foresight *not* to open the doors to the Heckhole."

"What's the Heckhole?"

"The ward for the criminally insane." Neverlåethe struggled to moisten his lips. "That's where they keep all the Glitches."

So terrible was the idea that a swarm of those malignant creatures who'd almost destroyed The World a thousand times over could be loosed into the Seems again that Simly almost fainted right there on the spot. But then loud footsteps could be heard approaching the cell block. "Someone's coming!"

"Hurry, boy!" Permin ran to a tall grandfather clock that he'd built from popsicle sticks and egg crates. "I can hide you inside Grandpa!"

Simly knew he should do as his new friend said, but if he had one Achilles' heel (well, he probably had more than one) it was his insatiable curiosity. So instead of climbing into the belly of Permin's latest invention, he poked his head outside the cell to see who was using a heavy ring of keys to unlock the doors to Protective Custody.

It was the Corrections Officer again, joined by the disgraced Flavor Miner, whose rubber-banded beard had been singed by the fires. And dangling between them, his thin frame battered with fresh welts and bruises, was a barely conscious Thibadeau Freck.

"Back to the Holiday Inn, Frenchie." The Miner threw Thib roughly to the ground. "As soon as we take care of the Warden, I'll be back to put you out of your misery."

"Triton's orders were clear," cautioned the Officer. "Nobody puts the kibosh on the frog."

"I wouldn't dream of it, but everyone knows accidents happen in a riot."

The two Tide members flashed each other evil smirks.

"Same goes for you, string bean!" Out of the corner of his eye, the Miner spotted a lanky neck poking out of Permin Neverlåethe's cell. "Enjoy your last few minutes on the face of The Seems!"

As soon as the duo locked the door and disappeared into the fray, Simly and Permin scrambled to Thibadeau's aid. Though his left eye was closed and his beard smattered with blood, he was starting to come around.

"I guess your meeting with Captain Marcus didn't go so well?" Permin grabbed an arm and helped him up to a sitting position.

"Let's just say we agreed to disagree."

"But what's he after? He has to know the Powers That Be will never submit to his demands!"

"The riot is only the first step, *mes amis.*" Thibadeau spat a mouthful of blood to the floor. "A distraction for the deluge to come."

Simly's already strained heart sank another inch lower.

"Once the Powers That Be turn their attention to Seemsberia, Triton will activate his deep-cover agents, shut down The World one department at a time, and seize control of the Big Building itself!"

"You almost sound like you admire him," whispered Simly.

"I respect Triton's goal. But not his methods of achieving it."

"Fool me once, shame on you; fool me twice, shame on me." Permin Neverlåethe dropped the toilet paper he was using to dab Thibadeau's wounds and clenched an angry fist. "I'm not going to stand by and let another Time Square happen on my watch!"

During their shared imprisonment, the two had never spoken of the roles they'd played in the tragedy of the Split Second. But all the guilt and sorrow they shared finally passed between them in this silent moment.

"If we wish to save The World we adore, not to mention ourselves, then there is only one option." Thibadeau shook himself free of the cobwebs and rose to his feet. "We must escape from Seemsberia."

"Escape from Seemsberia?" Simly laughed, though there was nothing funny about it. "Nobody's *ever* escaped from Seemsberia, and the reason no one's ever escaped from Seemsberia is because there *is* no way out of Seemsberia!"

Bandaged but not beaten, Thibadeau leaned on Simly's shoulder, and the Briefer saw a long-forgotten sparkle returning to his eyes.

"*Au contraire,* Simly. *Au contraire.*"

The Middle of Nowhere

The Middle of Nowhere

Since the Unthinkable would happen in less than twenty-four hours, the second team didn't have the luxury of following an old coot and his partner on a painstaking journey from Who Knows Where to the mountains. When that partner turned out to be a bowlegged and cantankerous mule, the Fixers had no choice but to make certain "travel arrangements" to get where they needed to go in a timely fashion.

"How them sneaks, Zeb?"

Zebulon waited for Hopeless to hop out of his saddle, then gave an unimpressed shrug. Too tight.

"Mebbe so, but you ain't never moved that fast in your life, less'n it was to snatch a bite a'Thought when someone warn't lookin'."

The prospector was referring to the twin pair of size 12 Speed Demons that Fixers Blaque and Drane had slipped over the beast of burden's badly cracking hooves. Several hundred miles of creosote and Nothing had been covered in less than an hour, but now that the travelers had entered the tall crags that lorded over the Middle of Nowhere, it was a slow and steady climb up the one pathway to the top.

"How much farther?" asked the Octogenarian, tilting her hat against the glare.

"Still got a ways to go, ma'am." Hopeless removed his own hat and wiped the sweat from his wrinkled brow. "These Nowherians is dug in deep."

Half a dozen yards behind them, a chiseled figure limped up a grassy foothill. "Assuming you actually know where they are."

"Just keep that there map nice and dry, and ol' Hopeless'll take you straight to 'em."

Jelani Blaque motioned up the mountain, as if to say "after you," but the retired Fixer was clearly struggling. The leg he'd injured during his last excursion to the Middle was acting up, and the crumbly silt at their feet rendered his walking stick nearly useless. Still, he powered forward without complaint, followed closely by Fixer Hassan, who had barely spoken since the Brainstorm. Wherever his mind was, it wasn't on this pebble-strewn path as it suddenly reached its end.

"Path picks up again on the other end of this dale!" shouted Hopeless, hopping back in Zebulon's saddle. "Don't dilly-dally now, ya hear?"

Toward the back of the line, Becker thought he detected a hint of nervousness in the voice of their guide. The prospector had led them to a valley surrounded by cliffs on all sides, and from the way he gave Zebulon a not-so-gentle knee to the ribs,

Hopeless was obviously uncomfortable at being so exposed. But it wasn't until he emerged through a small glade of eucalyptus that the teenager started to get an inkling of why.

Scattered across the dale were dozens of stone slabs, each about ten feet high and covered with runes and glyphs. Lying naked on top of each, their bones picked clean by vultures and bleached by the Seemsian sun, were the skeletons of the dead.

"They're called Towers of Silence." Fixer Blaque appeared over Becker's shoulder, his voice hushed and solemn. "It's a Nowherian burial ground."

Blaque approached the nearest slab and pointed to the pile of personal items someone had placed around the desiccated corpse. There were dried-up flower petals, pieces of jewelry, even an old piece of parchment with the stick-figure drawing of a family on it, clearly made by a child's hand.

"You have to remember, Becker, Time doesn't exist out here. So it's a rare and sad occasion when someone actually dies."

Becker checked his Time Piece, and just as Fixer Blaque had suggested, the First, Second, and Third hands had all stopped dead. Other than a slight tingle in his scalp, it didn't feel any different to be in a timeless place, but there was no telling what prolonged exposure would do to his body or mind.

"I ain't jokin' around, back there!" Hopeless's exasperated voice echoed back at them from a few hundred yards ahead. "This ain't no place to be sightseeing!"

"He's right," said Fixer Blaque, scouring the cliffs on all sides. "If the Nowherians catch us here, we'll be getting towers of our own."

As the two picked up their pace to catch the rest of the

team, Becker recalled a strange night he'd had once at the IFR library. While doing some research for a paper on what The Seems was like before the World Project, he'd come across an off-handed mention of a mysterious clan that called the Middle of Nowhere home. But the two books in the card catalog whose subject line contained "Nowherian" were checked out, and the one paragraph he finally found in Sitriol B. Flook's *A Little About the Middle* had been blacked out "By order of the Powers That Be."

"What's the deal with these people, sir?"

"All I can tell you is what I was cleared to discuss by the Second in Command." Blaque dropped his voice so Hopeless wouldn't hear. "That at the End of the Day, there was an extended period of conflict between those who were inspired to craft a brand-new World and those who felt it was an abuse of power. This war was long and bloody, and only ended when a truce was declared and a line drawn in the sand between them."

They silently passed another tower before Fixer Blaque continued.

"Jackal, Simms, and I were the first emissaries of The Seems to cross that line in a millennia, and it nearly cost us our lives. Truth is, when they had us cornered at the Eternal Springs, Tom and I were ready to give up the Hope. It was only Lisa who kept us . . ."

The instructor's voice suddenly caught in his throat.

"I'm sure she's okay, sir." Becker still held out hope for Fixer Simms, not to mention Lake and Po. "I'm sure they're all okay."

The ground beneath them began to gently slope upward, as the team was finally approaching the other side of the valley.

"As to why the Nowherians stole the train and broke the truce now?" Fixer Blaque cleared his throat. "I haven't the foggiest i—"

But before he could finish his thought, he snapped his head up toward the hillside to their right.

"Did you hear something?"

Becker listened but didn't hear a sound until he slapped on his Hearing Aide to discover the audio signature of small stones rolling down the slope.

"I done tol' you so!" A few yards ahead, Hopeless had heard the noise too, and stopped the rest of the team in their tracks. "Now them freaks is gonna skin us alive!"

"Relax, Hopeless." Fixer Blaque was calm, but he kept his voice to a whisper. "They rarely monitor this side of the mountain. Let's just get to higher ground."

Higher ground was only about a football field away and the squadron of Fixers wasted no time in slaloming their way through the remaining Towers. When they finally reached the continuation of Hopeless's path, the prospector threw his hat to the ground and kicked up some dust.

"No one ever listens to ole Hopeless, do they, Zeb?"

Zebulon shook his head sadly. *No they don't, pardner.*

"Well, they better start if they want to make it off this blasted rock alive!"

The team laughed at the old crank's histrionics, happy to be out of the open field and back in the mountain's embrace. In fact, only one in their number seemed unmoved by the experience, quietly heading up toward the summit and into the coming night.

"What's up with him?" whispered Becker, to no one in particular.

Fixer Blaque pointed back at the grinning skulls that lay motionless on the funeral slabs. "These are not the only ghosts that Hassan has seen in the Middle of Nowhere."

Shahzad Hassan crested the Peak of Experience and steadied himself for the long and arduous descent. At this altitude the temperature had dropped precipitously, and it was all he could do to keep from being swept to his doom by the blasts of frigid wind. Fortunately, his Extremely Cool Outfit not only shielded him from excess heat, but per its description in the Catalog, "the breakthrough garment is extremely cool in every sense of the word." With each drop of the thermometer, more synthetic Seemsberian tiger hairs sprouted from the bodysuit's fabric, cloaking the Fixer in a warm and toasty shell. If only it could do the same for the storm inside his head.

Greg the Journeyman was right when he accused Hassan of lying about what he'd seen in the Brainstorm. When Fixer #19 had been separated from the rest of the team, he'd remained calm and waited for the others to find him. But then the visor on his Head Case had cracked, allowing grains of Scratch to rush in, and he knew it was only a matter of time before something terrible came skulking out of the swirling blue winds.

Hassan never expected it to be a crazed bag of bones, however, cloaked in rags and desperately clutching a tattered old book. Again and again, he rewound the memory, noticing new and terrible details with each viewing: the way the old hermit's hands shook as he turned the yellowed pages; the shrill insistence that the missing chapter was just around the corner; most of all, the insane gleam in his eyes. Hassan had witnessed such a gleam before, on the face of his father and his father's father, but to see it again in this of all people was almost too much to bear.

Ahead on the path, perhaps two hundred yards below, something caught the Fixer's well-trained eye. A flickering of light inside a small black cave, which brought his focus back to the present. Perhaps it was generated by Hope, long rumored to be abundant in this region, but more likely he had stumbled upon a Nowherian outpost, where armed guards waited to ambush all who trespassed upon their territory. Almost welcoming the possibility of confrontation, Hassan crept to the mouth of the cave and took a peek inside.

The source of the light inside was indeed a campfire, which crackled and popped with freshly chopped wood. But if this was an outpost, it had been abandoned long ago—rusty equipment was scattered throughout, along with two moth-eaten sleeping bags.

"Hello?" asked Hassan, briefly regretting his decision to move so far ahead of the team. "Is there anybody—"

"Stay away!"

A woman's voice, hoarse and with a distinctly British accent, shouted from the back of the cave.

"I don't care if you're my sister or my brother or my bloody aunt Ferrah, I will throw you off this mountain if you don't *leave me alone!*"

The manic intensity in her threat caused Hassan to take another glance over his shoulder, but Becker and the others had yet to reach the summit. He would have to tackle this one alone, and tackle it he would, for this was no Nowherian who crouched like an animal in the darkness.

This was one of their own.

"Fixer Simms?"

No response, save the crackle of burning twigs.

"Fixer Simms, it's me, Shahzad Hassan."

He took a few tentative steps inside the cave, just enough to leave the cold and wind behind.

"Hassan? That's odd . . ."

This time her voice sounded more worn out than angry or afraid, which the Persian took as an invitation to take a few more steps closer.

"Are you okay, Lisa? The others are right behind me, and if you let me flag them down, we can—"

"No." A hunched and ragged figure stepped to the edge of the light. "I'm not okay at all."

The sight of Lisa Simms—one of the most elegant and refined women Hassan had ever met—was jarring to say the least. Her face and neck were badly burned, partially by the sun and partially by what Hassan surmised to be the Nowherians' secret weapon. The Badge on her chest had melted into an unrecognizable square—but it was the blue powder encrusting the tangles of her long black hair that revealed the true source of her distress.

"The Brainstorm?"

Fixer Simms nodded absently, then crumpled to a seat before the fire.

"You're the fourth person to show up here since it caught

me in the foothills, and they had no idea they were figments of my imagination either."

"I assure you, Lisa, I am quite real."

"That's exactly what Tom Jackal said to me last night." She sadly wrapped her arms around her knees. "And even though he was the same age as the day we found this cave, it was difficult not to believe him."

Hassan took another look at the dusty pickaxes and Wharizits™ that were strewn about the cavern, and the pieces fell into place.

"This was where the two of you camped during Hope Springs Eternal, isn't it?"

"We found nothing except disappointment here." She held up an empty glass jug covered with cobwebs. "And not the kind with a capital D."

As he warmed his icy hands by the fire, Hassan flashed back to a conversation he'd had with Fixer Simms one night at The Flip Side. Her famously frosty demeanor had thawed over one too many Truth Serums, and the story of her secret and all-too-brief romance with Tom Jackal had slipped out. The Welshman had ended it without ever giving an explanation, and despite her beauty and fame, she'd been alone ever since.

"Jackal wasn't really here, Lisa. It was just the Scratch playing tricks with your head."

"I know that. But take my word for it, knowing doesn't make it any easier to deal with."

"I don't have to take your word for it." Hassan remembered the heavy feeling that had been stuck in his chest since they'd left Who Knows Where. "I, too, was caught in the storm last night, and was forced to confront a demon, though not one from my past."

He shuffled through his Toolkit, then reached across the fire and handed Lisa the photo of a boy with big brown eyes and a crooked smile.

"Who is it?"

"Cyrus, my son. He'll be eleven in March."

"Very handsome."

"He takes after his mother." Hassan smiled proudly, but it didn't last long. "In all things but one."

Hassan started to tell Lisa how he'd done everything he could to shield the boy from the burden of his quest—kept him rooted in cricket and video games and the simple pleasures of childhood—but he stopped himself from lying again. The truth was, he'd watched how Cyrus lit up at the legends of the 13th Chapter, and how crestfallen he became every time Hassan returned empty-handed. And last night, in the big brown eyes and crooked smile of that sad and terrible old hermit, he saw the man his little boy would undoubtedly become.

"What's wrong, Hassan?"

"Nothing, nothing. It's just . . ."

Shahzad Hassan wept not for his people, not even for his own failure to restore them to greatness. He wept for his child, whom he loved like nothing in this world or that.

"There is no shame in crying." Even though she still wasn't sure Hassan was flesh and blood and not the fleeting creation of her own Thought, Lisa reached across the fire and grabbed his hands. "This is what happens in the Middle of Nowhere."

"Fixer Simms is right, #19." A deep and heavily accented

voice echoed off the walls of the cave. "No one survives this place unscathed."

Hassan and Lisa turned to see a tall figure emerge from the wind and snow outside. His eyes were covered by blue-tinted glasses and his left leg could barely support him, only underscoring the truth of what he said.

"Jelani!" Lisa's face lit up at the sight of her dearest friend. "Now I *know* the storm is playing tricks on my brain."

"Hardly. I just wanted to return this to its rightful owner."

Fixer Blaque handed her back the bow he'd found buried at the End of the Line.

"I would love to hear you play again."

Lisa brushed back a tangled lock of black and blue, then found her Toolkit and pulled out one of the less than seven hundred violins that had been constructed by the great Antonio Stradaveri. Her left hand unconsciously slid up the fingerboard, while her right brought the horsehair of the bow against the catgut of the strings—and all at once, with a single middle C, the Fixer began to play.

It was the Caprice No. 24 in A minor, the most difficult piece ever written for the violin, but by the time Lisa Simms was finished, three Fixers and a crusty old Hope prospector had joined Jelani Blaque in giving her a standing O.

"The eleventh variation was a little sharp," joked Becker, who had taken three violin lessons before bagging it because it hurt his fingers. "But you still got it, Leese."

Six hours later, the sun was just beginning its ascent as the second team reached the end of Hopeless's trail.

"Talk to me, Mr. Drane."

From Becker's vantage point, he could make out dozens of tents scattered about the lush oasis some two hundred feet below. Most were shaped into squares, their black roof-cloths supported on all four corners by thin poles, while the largest of them formed a huge octagon at the center of the compound. And moving between them, cloaked in the same robes three of their fellows had displayed at the Far-Out Saloon, was the ancient tribe known as the Nowherians.

"I count at least two hundred, but who knows how many more are inside." Becker lowered his Trinoculars, which were supposed to see through inanimate objects. "For some reason, my third eye can't get through the tents."

"That's because they're made out of Hide." Fixer Blaque crawled forward on his hands and knees to take a look over the side of the ridge. "Nowherians are a very private people."

The Octogenarian appeared over Becker's other shoulder.

"Any sign of the train?"

"Negative. But check out that grove over there."

Becker handed the Trinoculars to the team leader and pointed to a clump of palm trees on the southernmost portion of the camp. It was impossible to see what lay beneath the thick green canopy of leaves, but at six different entrance points armed guards stood sentinel.

"That's an awful lot of people to watch some Fruits of Labor."

"Agreed." Blaque took one last glance about the oasis, then returned the glasses. "We better find out what they're so intent on guarding."

The three onlookers slid carefully away from the ridge, then rejoined the rest of the team. Their long trek over and through the mountains had finally bottomed out at a small plateau, where they'd hastily constructed a base from which to launch their covert assault.

"What's the plan?" asked Hassan, his head seemingly back in the game.

"I suggest Jayson's Triangle." Like a sandlot quarterback, Fixer Blaque made a quick sketch of the Nowherian settlement in the dirt. "Hassan and Octo from the north, Lisa and I from the east, and Becker right down the face of the—"

"Ain't you forgettin' somethin'?"

In the shadows of a rocky overhang, Hopeless and Zebulon the mule were hiding from the newly returned heat. And they were not amused.

"Me and Zeb got ourselves a date with destiny and we don't wanna be late!"

Zebulon used his Speed Demonless right front hoof to kick up a small cloud of dust. *Dang tootin'*.

"My apologies, Hopeless." Fixer Blaque reached into his Toolkit and pulled out a folded up piece of parchment, on which a darkly drawn "X" marked the spot. "You have kept your part of the bargain, so allow me to keep mine."

The old prospector could barely contain his shaky hand long enough to accept the map, and when he held it up to his mule, tears were already soaking his beard. "Can you b'lieve it, Zeb? The Eternal Springs . . . after all these years."

Zeb shook his heavy head back and forth, on the verge of weeping himself, and the strange sight of a man and his mule brought to tears by the possibility of successfully completing their search made a strange spectacle to the Octogenarian.

"If you don't mind my asking, what do you plan to do with all that Hope once you find it?"

"What do we plan to do with it?" Hopeless removed the weather-beaten hat from his head, incredulous. "Is she loco, Zeb?"

Plum loco.

"We gonna be rich, lady! Filthy stinkin' rich!" Hopeless tossed the hat to the ground and would've started whooping it up were it not for the prospect of drawing Nowherian attention. "Next time you sees me and four-legs here, we gonna be square-dancin' in Crestview or sittin' on our new front porch on Easy Street!"

The thought of Hopeless and Zebulon at the Crestview clubhouse was almost enough to make Becker apply for a membership. But as the two prospecting partners headed back up the path that would eventually take them to a cave in a dried-out riverbed, Becker crossed his fingers that Hopeless would find what he was looking for, or that what he was looking for would find him.

"Remember, our main goal is to infiltrate the compound." Fixer Blaque's voice brought the team back to attention. "We only want to fight these people as a last resort."

"Speak for yourself." Lisa Simms tied an IFR bandanna around her head and flashed a wicked grin. "I don't take kindly to having my brain scrambled."

Now that Fixer #11 had bandaged her wounds and joined the team, Becker felt a surge of confidence. Not only did she add one of the most highly skilled and experienced Fixing minds to the mix, but the very fact that she, like Greg the Journeyman, had survived, gave him hope that perhaps Casey Lake and Li Po were alive as well.

"Ladies and gentlemen . . . I believe we have a problem."

Over by the lip of the ridge, Hassan's mind was finally refocused on the Mission, and he was taking one last look down at the Nowherian settlement.

"What are they doing?" wondered Becker, though he didn't really expect an answer, because it was quite clear to everyone what the Nowherians were doing.

Hundreds of feet below, the black-robed figures who had once been carrying baskets of food or making bricks of mortar or simply carrying on conversations in various corners of the village had all at once turned and looked in the same direction.

Straight up at them.

"I think we need to be on our way *right now*," whispered Lisa.

"I think you're right." Fixer Blaque backed away from the ridge. "Everyone to higher ground!"

But it was already too late, for down in the verdant oasis, the Nowherians were performing a single gesture en masse. One by one, each person placed what appeared to be a square metal visor over the hole in their robes where their eyes should be. Eyes that were now protected against what began to emanate from the heavily guarded clump of palm trees that had drawn Becker Drane's attention. Terribly silent, and getting brighter with each passing second . . .

A strange white light.

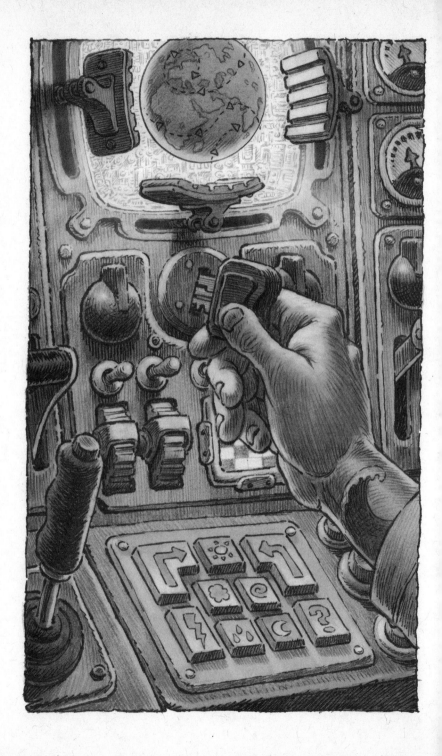

The Word Is Given

30 Custer Drive, Caledon, Ontario Canada

Click.

Jennifer Kaley sat cross-legged in her bed, wearing the pair of fuzzy headphones she'd bought at Paradise Bound Records and clicking through the playlists on her laptop.

Click. Click.

Her door was locked and her iTunes opened to the series of "Mission Mixes" that Becker had burned for her so that when he was away on business, they could listen to the same tuneage. Jennifer briefly considered Mix #3, which was subtitled "Our Songs," but she was afraid that if she played that one she might start to cry again. So she dropped down to #9 instead, "Songs for When Things Are Going Down the Drane," and dragged the mouse over to the button with the symbol for Play.

Click.

Ever since Becker had been yanked from the headquarters

of Les Resistance and ushered back to The Seems, Jennifer had sunk into a deep depression. It wasn't just the separation, because Becker had been away on lots of Missions and normally she enjoyed missing him and waiting for him to come home. No, it was more like a premonition or a voice inside her head that kept whispering that something terrible was going to happen. And no matter how much TV she watched or how much homework she didn't do, Jennifer couldn't shake the awful feeling that her boyfriend wasn't coming back.

"Mr. Sun, come out today, it's a rainy, rainy day, you're a meanie anyway. Mr. Sun, come out to play . . ."

She closed her eyes and tried to focus on the lyrics, which were sung by this guy named Sid Friendly who played punk rock for little kids at Becker's favorite coffee shop in Highland Park. But that only made Jennifer wonder if he was thinking about her, and if he was listening to the same song she was. Finally, she couldn't take it any longer, so she picked up her cell and dialed a number in area code 732.

"Drane household." A voice that sounded uncannily like Fixer Drane's picked up on the other end. *"Me speaking."*

"Hey, Me, it's Jennifer. Jennifer Kaley."

"I know who you are, silly. Don't you think I recognize the voice of my own girlfriend?"

"Ha, ha. You wish." Jennifer smiled but it didn't last long. "Listen, um, I was just wondering if you've, um, heard anything from Becker?"

"Becker Drane? The man, the myth, the legend?"

"No, the other Becker."

"I haven't actually talked to him, but according to 'Missions in Progress,' everything's A-okay."

Even though Jennifer would have loved to believe what the Me-2 had just told her, she also knew that the replica was not just a good liar, it was a professional one, and programmed above all else to cover for its Fixer.

"Don't lie to me, Me. I can tell when Becker's blowing smoke."

"Honest, Jenny. He'll be back before you can—"

"Don't lie to me!" Jennifer's fear turned to anger, but it didn't make her feel any better. " 'Cause I'm really worried this time."

"You want the whole truth and nothing but the truth?" The Me-2 lowered its voice, not wanting a certain little brother to overhear. *"Last I heard, things were going pretty well. Becker's team found some tracks in the Middle of Nowhere and were following them in to investigate. But since then there hasn't been a single deposit in our Memory Bank account."*

"What does that mean?"

"Probably nothing, 'cause everything gets fouled up in the Middle. But I swear to Al Penske if anything was wrong, I would be the first to know."

"And you would tell me, right?"

"Cross my mechanical heart and hope to be shelved for a Me-3."

That made her feel a little better, but there was something else that had been gnawing at Jennifer ever since Becker had bolted from the forest.

"He was trying to tell me something before he left, Me. Something about his punishment for breaking the Rules."

There seemed to be the slightest beat of silence on the other end of the line, but Jennifer couldn't tell whether or not it was just her imagination.

"He got a six-month suspension and a ton of community service."

"That's all?"

"Oh, and his Seems Credit Card got yanked too. Maybe that's what it was about."

"Maybe . . ." Jennifer let her head fall back on her pillow. "If you hear from him, you promise you'll let me know?"

"Promise." The Me-2's voice softened just like Becker's did when he was about to say good-bye. *"Catch you on the Flip Side, okay?"*

"On the Flip Side."

If calling 12 Grant Avenue had seemed like a good idea before she'd dialed the number, it wasn't afterward. Hearing the closest thing to her boyfriend's voice only made her miss him more, and she promptly returned to Mission Mix #9. All she wanted to hear right now was something sad, because that was how she felt. So she put her headphones back on and toggled to song #6, the same one that was playing when they nervously ate their slices of pizza on their very first date at the Sbarro in the Eaton Centre mall.

Click.

423rd Floor, The Big Building, The Seems

Down the seemingly endless hallway, past the elevators and next to the ficus tree, the door to office #423006 was locked from the inside. Normally, Clara Manning kept her door open so her co-workers could wander in and out and discuss how to negotiate the complexities of the Plan. But today that door was closed because the woman who looked more like a librarian than a Senior Case Worker had a visitor from upstairs.

"You're telling me she did this all on her own?" asked Eve Hightower, holding up what looked like a middle schooler's book report.

"She may have bounced a few ideas off Fixer Drane and some friends, but every word of it is hers." Clara opened the file marked "Jennifer Kaley" and showed Eve the docket of Moves that every Case Worker was required to fill out when intervening for their clients. "Not a single Helpful Hint or Shove in the Right Direction."

"Impressive," admitted the Second in Command, taking a seat on Clara's desk. "As much as this whole situation troubles me, I can't remember seeing a more provocative SAT. And by someone so young."

"Perhaps youth isn't always wasted on them after all?" Clara smiled, and was happy to see her boss do the same.

It was expressly forbidden for Case Workers to play favorites within the slate of people in The World they were given to look after, but Clara always had a special place in her heart for a certain girl from Caledon, Ontario. The Case of Jennifer Kaley had migrated from tabloid fascination to political hot potato after her SAT had been unknowingly plucked from the slush pile and chosen for the first-ever internship in the Big Building. But whether or not the appointment would be approved was still very much in doubt.

"If I was inclined to support this nomination"—Eve leafed through the pages of Jennifer's answer to Question #3—"how would we get around the fact that her unremembering is already set in Stone?"

Clara was ready for this exact question. The one-on-one with the Second had been scheduled early that morning and she'd been sipping Inspiration and jotting down notes on her junkyard of a desk ever since.

"On that count, Madame Second, I was thinking—what if the unremembering took place but she was allowed to keep the recollection of when she met Fixer Drane in the Dream? That way she'd remember how she first found out about The Seems, and if they bump into each other at Flip's or the Cafeteria, it'll be one of those 'Don't I know you from somewhere?' moments. After that, it's up to the Plan."

"Interesting."

"I just feel . . ." Clara didn't want to overstep her bounds, but if the 423rd floor couldn't speak freely to the 1,000th, then what was the point? "She's earned this internship on her own merits, and I'd hate to see her lose it because her boyfriend broke the Rules."

"I'll certainly take these thoughts into account." Eve closed Jennifer's SAT and hopped off the desk. "The Powers That Be will be voting on this later today and I'll inform you of the—"

Beep! Beep! Beep!

Clara kicked herself for forgetting to put her Receiver on mute, but when she picked it up, she was surprised to hear the voice of Eve's executive assistant.

"It's for you, Madame."

"Put it on speaker."

Clara pressed the button and Monique's voice came over the tinny line.

"I'm sorry to interrupt, Madame Second, but it's an emergency."

"Let me guess." Eve had had a long day and her frustration was starting to show. "It's Mother Nature and autumn's getting pushed again this year?"

"No, ma'am. It's Warden Cyration." The executive assistant's voice lacked any of her superior's sarcastic wit. *"There's a problem in Seemsberia."*

Seemsberia, The Seems

Deep in the bowels of Seemsberia, the maddening klaxons that rang through the prison above were but a distant echo as Simly Frye wriggled like an earthworm through a tight stone passageway. A few feet behind him labored Permin Neverlåethe, and several hundred more behind, Thibadeau Freck's cell sat empty, the hole in the wall hidden by the picture of a girl named Julee.

"Dude, what is this place?" whispered the Briefer, fighting his claustrophobia.

"My cell was once the home of the Time Bandits."[24] Thib's voice echoed back from somewhere in the darkness ahead. "This is the tunnel they used to escape."

Simly's hand slid over the wall of the tunnel, which felt like it had been chipped away with a Spork™. "But I heard the Time Bandits were locked in solitary confinement and they threw away the key."

"That is what the Warden wanted us to think."

---

24. Justin and Nick F. Time pulled off twenty-three separate heists until they were finally caught on "The Night They Robbed the Memory Bank."

"A breakout would be a permanent stain on Inkar's career." Permin's face was soaked and his breathing ragged, but he still managed to keep pace. "He's probably trying to recapture them before anyone finds out."

"*Bonne chance.* Everyone in The Know says they vanished into Thin Air."

"Cool," whispered Simly, who still had an illegal Time Bandits lunchbox (in mint condition) tucked inside his collectibles closet.

"Why, Sim . . . it almost sounds as if you admire them."

Thibadeau grinned back at him, and for a second it was easy for Simly to forget everything his old classmate had done in the years since they'd left the IFR.

"Touché."

At the end of the miraculous tunnel, the three escapees emerged into a crossroads filled with pipes, heating ducts, and electrical wires. Everybody enjoyed a breath of fresh air, while Thibadeau pulled out an old set of blueprints from his waistband and tried to figure out which way to go.

"I don't get it." Simly studied the faded schematics that looked like they'd been lifted straight from the frame in the warden's office. "If you had the blueprints and a way out the entire time, why didn't you blow this taco stand months ago?"

Thibadeau pointed to the edge of the blueprints, where the grounds of Seemsberia were encircled by the drawing of a wide moat.

"This moat is filled with Thirds from the Mountain Time Zone. Anyone who tries to swim across will be, how you say, like dust in the wind, before they take their first breaststroke."

Thirds were minerals packed with the Essence of Time,

and just a handful were enough to power the aging process of The World. But if the small silver circles scattered at the bottom of the moat meant what Simly thought they did, there were at least several dozen.

"Permin." Thib looked at his old Tide comrade hopefully. "If someone were able to halt the flow of Time, would they not be able to make it across?"

The old man thoughtfully rubbed his chin.

"And is that not a Stopwatch you wear on your wrist?"

Permin's right hand reflexively slid to his left forearm, where a leather band held the one personal item he'd been allowed to keep in Seemsberia as something to hold on to in his moments of dark despair.

"It is. But this one's set to work at the normal flow of Time in The World. According to those drawings, the moat has almost *ten times* that much Essence!"

"Can it be done? Even by an old Ticky such as yourself?"

At the mention of the entry-level position from where Permin had begun his meteoric rise through the Department of Time, the ex-Administrator's hunched old back seemed to straighten.

"I'll need twenty minutes to rewind the gears, and another ten to calibrate the hands."

"*Voilà.*" Thib rolled up the blueprints and tucked them away. "That will give Simly and I time to take care of one final errand."

But as Simly followed the Frenchman through a maze of steam tunnels, question after question began to seep into the Briefer's skull. Like how was it that Thibadeau just *happened* to have been assigned to the exact same cell as the infamous Time

Bandits? And how did he just *happen* to get his hands on an original copy of the Seemsberia blueprints? Worst of all, how could he, Simly Frye, just *happen* to be placing his trust in two convicted Tide felons?

"Hold on a sec, Freck." Simly stopped in his tracks and pointed an accusatory finger at his fellow escapee. "I thought we were trying to escape!"

"We are. But even if we succeed, we are just three men in pajamas in the frozen tundra—hundreds of miles away from where the machinery that makes The World is under assault. If we are to save The Seems, we must find help."

It was only then that Simly noticed he and Thibadeau were standing above what looked like a submarine hatch. Judging by the rust on the surface of the turning wheel, it hadn't been opened in years—probably because the hatch was also covered by at least fifty stickers that delivered the exact same message: "Whatever you do, please, under any circumstances, do not open! (And we mean any!)"

"Where does it lead, Thib?"

"The Heckhole."

"But Permin said there's Glitches down there!"

"Permin did not lie. And yet, we must let them out . . ."

Thibadeau spat into his hands and rubbed them together, then began to turn the ancient wheel. The hinge squealed and the iron oxide crumbled away from the hatch—but not before Simly finally reached his breaking point. In a gangly tumble of elbows and knees, the Briefer leapt upon his former friend and threw him roughly to the floor.

"I'm not gonna let you try to destroy The World again, Thib!"

Beneath his thick brown beard, Thibadeau smiled sadly.

"Trust me, Simly. I'm not trying to destroy The World, I'm trying to save it."

"And if I *don't* trust you?"

"Then the minute I step inside this door, lock it behind me and do not open it again until you have contacted the proper authorities. Of course, by that time The Tide's sleeper cells will have seized control of each and every department in The Seems, and The World will be under the control of Triton himself."

Thib tentatively rose back to his feet, and with one more twist the hatch opened with a hiss of stale air.

"What will it be, *mon ami*?"

The Weather Center, Department of Weather, The Seems

"This is SNN Special Correspondent Waldy Joels reporting live from Seemsberia, where a violent uprising has left this normally loving facility teetering on the edge of chaos. Nearly two hours ago, reputed Tide boss Robert Marcus began an armed uprising against Warden Inkar Cyration and his staff. Special Forces have been dispatched from the Big Building and Second in Command Hightower insists the riot will be brought under control before our next scheduled update. Stay tuned to this special continuing coverage of: CRISIS IN SEEMSBERIA. Jim, back to you."

"First the Unthinkable, now this!" Weatherman #1 turned down the volume on the fuzzy black-and-white TV and flopped into his chair. "So much for working together to build a better World."

His tired eyes scanned the control panel and the dials that orchestrated every aspect of The World's Weather, from the humidity in the Amazon rain forest to the smallest flurry of Tasmanian snow.

"This never would've happened when Samuel was in charge."

"Don't worry, #1." Weatherman #2 placed a reassuring hand on his boss's shoulder. "They'll Fix it."

"They always do," concurred Weatherman #3.

In the time since #2 and #3 had joined the team, they'd cut their trademark ponytails and got rid of the piercings that once kept them from moving up the ranks in the conservative Department of Weather. Their recent promotions to the Control Room couldn't have come at a better time, for after twenty-three years on the job, the #1 meteorologist in The Seems was finally starting to burn out.

"Listen, Harry," Weatherman #2 suggested. "Why don't you take the rest of the day off. Me and Freddy can man the Board."

"You guys wouldn't mind?" #1 perked up for the first time since his fourth Pickmeup of the morning. "I could surprise my wife with lunch over in Love."

"Beat it." Freddy pushed his boss jokingly out of the middle chair. "And don't worry, we promise not to sink another continent until you get back!"

"Thanks, fellas."

Weatherman #1 shook his co-workers' hands, pulled on his tattered trenchcoat, and made for the elevators with an extra spring in his step. But as soon as he was gone, #3 got up from the board and locked the door that separated the Control

Room from the rest of the Weather Center. Then he removed a small magnet from his pocket and placed it against the security camera that monitored the Board 25/7, effectively neutralizing the recording.

"Ready to change The World?" asked #3, loosening his tie and revealing a small black tattoo on his neck.

"I can't do it, Freddie!" #2 sat before the Board, running his shaky fingers through his freshly cut hair. "I just can't do it."

"Yes you can, bro."

#3 walked over to the wide pane of glass that gave view to the sprawling Weather Center. Dozens of Weathermen in white shirts and black ties sat in front of Doppler radar screens keeping tabs on every sector of The World, little knowing that their department was about to change forever. "Remember what the big man promised? No more hurricanes or tidal waves wiping out entire countries. No more freezing to death, no more droughts or mudslides, no more anything! Just perfect weather every day."

Down on the Weather Center floor, a Storm Placer was waving in his direction. She had clearly noticed that the security feed to the Control Room had gone to static, and gestured as if to say, "Is everything okay?" #3 simply smiled and gave her a thumbs-up.

"This is why we got into Weather in the first place, Charlie . . . to help people, not make their lives miserable."

"But what if Triton's wrong?" Weatherman #2 had never liked tattoos and wore a Tide pin on the underside of his tie that, right now, felt like it was burning a hole in his chest. "What if the Plan really is for the best?"

"It's too late for cold feet, dude. The word's been given."

"Yeah, you're right." #2 mustered whatever courage he could. "The World's gonna thank us someday."

"Totally."

The two Tide moles bumped fists, then each removed the metallic keys that dangled around their necks. If inserted into their respective keyholes and turned counterclockwise, they could single-handedly stop the flow of the Jet Stream. It wouldn't destroy The World, but it would certainly wreak havoc with the Weather systems in multiple Sectors, not to mention draw the attention of the Fixers. Which is exactly what it was intended to do.

"On my mark . . ."

The Most Amazing Thing of All

The Middle of Nowhere

Twenty minutes after the light had faded, Becker's head popped up from the sand to find the rest of his team had vanished, along with all their equipment and gear. Seeing that no black robes were visible on the plateau either, he quietly lifted his body from the hole he'd dug in the ground. Part of him longed to scramble over to the ridge and take another gander, but since the Nowherians had somehow been alerted to their presence the last time, it was a bad idea. So was breaking radio silence.

"Drane to Fixer Blaque, come in, over."

All that came back was the white noise of static. Becker switched channels, then whispered into his Bleceiver again.

"Drane to Hassan, can you hear me? Hassan?"

Still nothing.

When the white light had come, Becker's first thought was

to follow his fellow Fixers on a mad dash for the safety of higher ground. But then he remembered Casey Lake's broadcast at the pre-Mission briefing, and how she had frantically dug her way underground to escape the attack. Any strategy that was good enough for the best of the best was good enough for him.

With the help of his Bear Claws™, Becker was already thirty feet down when the first inkling of something warm started licking at his heels. The only thing he could compare it to was what he imagined the mosquitoes in his backyard went through right before they made a kamikaze run into his dad's beloved bug-zapper: they knew the light would destroy them, but they wanted to touch it anyway. Even with his eyes clamped shut, Becker didn't like the feeling at all.

"Drane to Octo. Sylvia, are you there?"

He tried one last time to reach a member of his crew, but again to no avail. Even if they were still alive, chances were good that they'd been captured, and right now he didn't have the luxury of trying to find and free them. Becker's first and only priority was locating that train and somehow riding it all the way back to The Seems.

And he was going to have to do it alone.

A soft breeze blew through the oasis, causing palm leaves to whisper and black canvas tents to rustle in response. Their conversation could be heard just above the stream that spilled an endless supply of cold, fresh water into the pool at the center of the compound. In every sense, it was the perfect picture of a community that had claimed paradise for its own—all except for one minor detail.

"Where the heck is everybody?"

Becker almost bit his tongue just to punish it for speaking aloud, but he couldn't really blame it. Outside of two goats nibbling on a section of grass and a one-eyed dog lazily rolling in the dappled sunlight, there didn't appear to be anyone around. Looms were still threaded with multicolored yarn, a water wheel spun, but the Nowherians who had once manned them had either vanished in the light or gone inside their tents.

From his hiding spot beneath a small cart, Becker did one last visual sweep of the stronghold. Every bone in the Fixer's body screamed that some kind of gathering was taking place in the huge octagonal tent, but he resisted the desire to satisfy his curiosity because the heavily guarded grove of palm trees he'd spotted from above had been evacuated as well. That meant the Train of Thought he hoped was hidden there was unprotected and just a hundred-yard dash away.

The air inside the grove was cool and dark, with only little flecks of sunlight managing to penetrate the leafy blanket of palm leaves above. Becker followed the thin dirt trail straight to the center of the grove, but when he emerged into a clearing, what he found was not a linked collection of boxcars or some light-shooting doomsday device . . .

It appeared to be a manhole cover.

To Becker, it didn't look much different than the one in the middle of Grant Avenue, which he and Chud and the Crozier boys used as home plate for wiffleball. The only difference was that instead of asphalt, this one was built directly on a pile of sand, with a large keyhole in the center. Judging by the scrapings around it and the numerous footprints at the base, the

Fixer surmised that the manhole had been opened several times recently.

He had no idea what was down there—maybe a Nowherian sewer or the source of the strange light, or better yet, a storage facility where the train had somehow been stashed for safe-keeping. But as he dangled his Key Chain™ over the hole and prepared to break inside, the one thing that concerned him was: why had the Nowherians left this mysterious place unguarded?

Inside the octagonal tent there was indeed a meeting taking place. The two hundred and fifty villagers who had been con-spicuously absent from the town center lined the back walls, arrayed in black robes of all shapes and sizes. They were cur-rently being whipped into a frenzy by a wizened old crone, who shook her gnarled staff and screeched for every interloper who'd been captured this day to have their tongues removed and their eyes put out, so they could never speak of what they saw.

Sitting on a faded rug with his injured leg extended, Jelani Blaque knew the angry crowd was calling for blood. But he also knew if he could keep this conversation going long enough, there was a chance their mighty Chieftain could be persuaded.

"We simply want the train back, Kalil." Blaque's mastery of their harsh and guttural language had slipped from lack of use, so he spoke slowly and clearly. "Trust me when I say that we have no designs on staying, and no wish to—"

"Trust you?" The nearly six-and-a-half-foot-tall man with

thickly braided hair reclined upon his wicker throne and laughed. "Jelani Blaque asks me to trust him!"

A derisive roar shot through the assembly, which Kalil silenced with but a raised finger.

"You must think me a fool."

"Hardly." Blaque chose his next words slowly, for if said incorrectly, they could very well be his last. "I know you to be a reasonable man, which is why I ask you again to return the Thought before millions of innocent people are hurt."

Silence fell upon the Chieftain's tent, which was hung with purple draperies, hand-woven tapestries, and the shrunken heads of those who dared defy him. The oil from the lamps was kept so low you could barely see anyone's face, and the sweet smell of incense wafted through the heavy air.

"You are right, Blaque. I *am* a reasonable man."

The Chieftain rose to his feet and approached the Fixer he'd faced in battle many years ago.

"I was reasonable when I allowed The Seems to build a train station and a mining operation on our very border."

Fixer Blaque held his ground, firm in the knowledge that neither the End of the Line nor Contemplation had violated the terms of the treaty.

"I was reasonable when I decided not to raze that ramshackle town built by your exiles . . . but only because my scouts enjoy their mush."

Indeed, Who Knows What from Who Knows Where was a highly coveted delicacy among Nowherians.

"I was even reasonable when you and your so-called Fixers snuck into the Eternal Springs and stole our precious Hope like thieves in the night. Which to many of my people is still considered an act of *war*!"

Another ripple shot through the assembly, and the Fixer felt a dangerous vibe creep into the space.

"But when Seemsians trespass upon our sacred grove and defile our holiest shrine, I do not feel reasonable . . ."

Kalil moved to within an inch of Fixer Blaque's face.

"And this act of war I do not forgive."

Jelani Blaque had not been appointed head instructor at the Institute for Fixing & Repair because he was easily shaken. "I have no idea what you're talking about."

Kalil snapped his fingers and two of his guards threw a teenage boy with shaggy hair and a freshly blackened eye onto the floor of the tent.

"Maybe we should ask him."

Becker Drane's hands were tied behind his back, and the legs of his Extremely Cool Outfit were torn away. By the vicious burns on his ankles, Blaque figured he'd stumbled into a classic Nowherian rope trap, but the bright red flush on the Fixer's face was far more indicative of defiance than embarrassment. It was a dangerous emotion to express in this setting, and Blaque subtly motioned for his young friend to keep his head, lest he lose it.

"This boy is not a thief. He is a Fixer on a Mission to save The World . . . which you cannot in good conscience hold responsible for the actions of a few Idea Smugglers or Back Scr—"

"These were not Idea Smugglers!" The Chieftain gritted his teeth to control his rising ire. "This was the witch who plays with Time!"

Blaque figured he must referring to Sophie Temporale, but

what had she been doing all the way out here? "The Time Being has not been officially associated with The Seems in generations, Kalil."

"If that is so, then why is she currently advising your Powers That Be?" Kalil relished the surprise on his adversary's face. "You sent your spies into the Middle of Nowhere—did you not think we would respond in kind?"

The Chieftain strode over to an arcane machine that was manned by a small boy in orange robes. It looked almost like a telegraph or an old-school Chatterbox™, but the ornate quality of its architecture was distinctly Nowherian. And unlike the Fixers' Bleceivers, it seemed to function quite well in the Middle of Nowhere.

"In fact, I just received an interesting report." He casually lifted the spool of yellowed parchment attached to the device. "Apparently, The Seems is under attack by something called The Tide—and on the verge of losing its precious World."

Kalil turned to the crowd, addressing his people more than his prisoners.

"So you see, even if we were to return your Train of Thought, it would do you no good."

As the crowd roared its approval, the blood drained away from Becker's face. "What do you have against The World, anyway?"

A cold silence fell upon the tent.

"What did you say?" asked the Chieftain, a mix of fury and wonder in his tone. Becker ignored it, and wriggled to his feet.

"I said I can understand that you have a beef with The Seems, but why take it out on millions of people who don't even know you exist?"

"This boy speaks Nowherian?" Incredulous, Kalil looked to Fixer Blaque for explanation. "How is this possible, when Article VIII of our treaty clearly decrees the banning of our language from your schools?"

Blaque hastily pointed Kalil's attention to Becker's Hearing Aide and Sprecheneinfaches. "He wasn't taught anything. He's just using technologies that allow him to speak and understand any tongue."

Kalil nodded, then bent before Becker so they could see each other eye to eye.

"To answer your question, boy . . . what I have against your World is that it should have never been built in the first place. For who are we to pretend to be the Most Amazing Thing of All?"

The crone raised her staff and squawked in agreement.

"But I thought you guys agreed to disagree like a gazillion years ago," said Becker. "Why up and steal the train now?"

"Sometimes an enemy must be reminded of its commitments. The theft was simply a warning shot." Suddenly, the Chieftain grabbed Becker around the neck and lifted him into the air. "And if it is not heard *loudly* and *clearly*, then the next will land directly atop your Big Building!"

"Consider us reminded." Becker spat out the words through gritted teeth. "And I personally guarantee that after you return the train, the Powers That Be will construct a fifty-foot wall from the End of the Line to Contemplation so that no one will ever trespass on your lands again."

Kalil squeezed even harder, but somehow, some way, Becker didn't break.

"Isn't that . . . right . . . sir?"

"It's already part of the Plan." Fixer Blaque touched the Chieftain's shoulder, banking on the fact that years ago there had been some modicum of mutual respect. "Now let him go."

Becker's face had turned a nasty shade of purple, but the defiant expression remained unchanged.

"I want the wall a *hundred* feet high and finished within *three* months." The Chieftain continued to tighten his grip until Blaque nodded his head yes, and only then did he release the stranglehold, dropping the gasping Fixer to the ground. "And you, boy? You and your friends can have your Train of Thought—*after* you've been punished for trespassing on our sacred burial grounds."

The crowd was itching to satisfy its bloodlust and their Chieftain did not disappoint.

"Prepare the Towers of Silence!"

In an instant, the tent exploded in a cacophony of light and sound, the oil in the lamps igniting, the ceremonial drums pounding, and the Nowherians dancing with maniacal glee. The old sorceress even blew a handful of Scratch into the air, and by the time it had dispersed, the blue cloud had transformed into a miniature version of The World—which, cackling like a hen, she promptly crushed upon her wrinkled palm. Amid the barely controlled hysteria, Kalil reclaimed his position on the wicker throne, then rang the Chieftain's bell.

"Take them to the prisoners' quarters!"

"The prisoners' quarters" referred to the circuslike tent into which a motley collection of Seemsian employees were crowded. Becker counted at least two dozen of them—Thought Provokers and Collectors, Signalmen from the End of the Line, even the Conductor of the lost train—all still dressed in the clothes they must've been wearing when they'd come face-to-face with a strange bright light. And all with the same weird, blissful expressions on their face.

"Come, brother." A badly sunburned Thought Chipper gestured for the Fixer to join him by a basket of dried-out dates. "Have something to eat."

"No, thanks. Not really hungry."

"It's hard, isn't it?" The Collector smiled in a way that reminded Becker of Greg the Journeyman at Who Knows Where. "To worry about the needs of the flesh when one is in the presence of something Amazing?"

"Yeah, totally."

As the Collector rejoined his friends around a ragged but giddy drum circle, Becker applied some Al's-O-Vera™ to his injured ankles and struggled to make sense of his predicament. Judging from the workers' blistered skin, they'd followed the Nowherians back across the Middle on foot. But what had driven them to make such a journey was another thing entirely.

"I found them, Mr. Drane!"

Becker turned to see Fixer Blaque step from behind a dangling blue curtain. He put a finger to his lips, then motioned toward the two heavily armed figures who blocked the only flap that led to the outside. "Let's not raise any alarms just yet."

Becker nodded, then followed Blaque through the corridors of the tent. It was much more plush than he expected, filled with countless rooms and alcoves, and Becker figured that maybe the Nowherians weren't expecting this many uninvited guests. But it was in an antechamber walled off by tapestries that they found Fixers Simms and Hassan asleep on a pile of cushions, right beside a semiconscious Octogenarian.

"Sylvia, are you okay?" Becker gently lifted the eighty-four-year-old woman's head, but for some reason she couldn't seem to focus her eyes. *"Octo, can you hear me?"*

"Easy, Mr. Drane. The fact that she's awake at all is a testament to her remarkable constitution."

Becker laid the Octogenarian back down upon a huge golden-tasseled pillow, and she curled up like a lazy cat. "Hers is nothing compared to yours, Fixer Blaque."

This was undeniable. Out of everybody who'd come in contact with the light, his old instructor was the only one who showed no noticeable effects.

"As I told Greg, blindness as a handicap is severely overrated." For the first time that Becker could remember, Blaque removed his signature blue shades to reveal eyes that were just as seared as the Journeyman's. "And when you're facing a mysterious light, it even has certain advantages."

Becker studied the featherweight Eyeglasses™, completely blown away by all Fixer Blaque had been able to accomplish despite his lack of vision. "I'm sorry, sir. I had no idea."

"How could you? The 7th Sense doesn't tell one when a blind man's in the room."

Becker returned the miraculous lenses, his mind filled with more questions than he knew how to ask. But the team leader was already a whirlwind of motion, propping up Fixers Simms and Hassan on the couch, then tossing over a handful of fruit.

"Try some lemon juice. It should help them return to their senses."

"What are you gonna do, sir?"

"Look for some way out of this place. The towers will not take long to construct."

Blaque slipped from the alcove, while Becker did as instructed and squeezed a few drops of lemon on the Octogenarian's lips. Fixer #3 didn't exactly jump to her feet, but the sourness bit at her tongue and began to bring her around.

"Becker? What are you doing here?"

Fixer #3 may have been renowned for her sunny disposition, but the look on her face as she shook and stretched the kinks from her aging body was something entirely different. It was as if she'd just awoken from the greatest dream imaginable, and Becker couldn't help feeling the slightest tinge of envy that he hadn't experienced that dream himself.

"Was Li Po right, Sylvia? Was the light the Most Amazing Thing of All?"

"All I can tell you is that it didn't feel like a weapon to me." The Octogenarian's smile slowly faded. "Though the Nowherians appear to be using it that way."

An awful clamoring rose up outside the tent, and Becker didn't have to see through the Hide to know that the Towers of Silence were almost ready.

"See if you can get these guys up and running." He tossed the Octo another lemon. "I'll get Fixer Blaque."

As Becker stepped back into the hallway, he tried to shake the first real tingle of fear from his legs. Only two days ago, being unremembered of Jennifer Kaley was the harshest sentence he could have imagined. Now it seemed like a slap on the wrist.

"Fixer Blaque, where are you? Fixer Blaque?"

Again and again he called out the name, but being in this tent was like being trapped in Meanwhile or a Nightmare. The thick and billowy curtains caught Becker's words and dampened them to whispers, and the farther he went into the maze of hallways, the more lost he felt. Why would Fixer Blaque have wandered so far away from the rest of the team? Unless something had happened to—

". . . it's too dangerous. There must be another way."

Becker was flooded with relief, for the voice he heard on the other side of a wall-sized tapestry had a Nigerian accent. He was about to shout out again, when he heard another voice.

"Perhaps. But none that I can think of in the time allowed."

Wherever Fixer Blaque had sequestered himself, he was clearly talking to someone. The other voice was strange and tinny, however, like it was over a speakerphone with a bad connection. Becker dropped to his hands and knees and crept closer to the source of the conversation.

"How will you get the Glitches out of there once they get in?" asked Fixer Blaque.

"With all due respect, that is not our concern right now. All that matters is that we regain control of The Seems."

Heart pounding, Becker peeked behind the tapestry to see Jelani Blaque addressing someone on the Calling Card they'd purchased at the Black Market. The image of that person was broken up, though, and it brought back bad memories of similar broadcasts Becker had seen over the last few tumultuous years—those made by Triton, the infamous leader of The Tide.

"Just be careful that you don't exchange one enemy for something even worse," said Fixer Blaque.

"Don't worry. I will make her an offer she cannot refuse."

Both Blaque and the image chuckled like co-conspirators, a sound that only furthered Becker's fears that the person on the other end of the Card was indeed Triton. But if that was true, then it meant his mentor, the man who had trained him in everything he knew about Fixing—not to mention what he'd taught him about life—was a member of The Tide.

"Then do what you must. And if anyone asks, I take full responsibility."

But when the image suddenly cleared up and the person behind it flickered into view, Fixer Drane realized that the truth was so much worse.

"*I only hope they will ask,*" said Thibadeau Freck. "*Instead of shooting first.*"

The Frenchman's beard was longer and his face thinner than Becker remembered, but the bitter hate he felt toward his old classmate remained. Fixer Blaque apparently didn't feel the same way, though.

"I know these last few years have been hard on you, son. But the battle has reached its final hour. And if all goes well, you will be remembered as a hero."

"*That was never my intention, sir. My only concern was for the future of The World.*"

"As is mine." Blaque anxiously checked his Time Piece. "Which is why I must call the Second in Command and inform her that The Tide is about to come washing up on her door. And have faith, Mr. Freck—we will be celebrating on the steps of the Big Building before you know it!"

And as the image of Thibadeau Freck snapped off a salute and vanished from view, the truth slapped Becker Drane like a bucket of freezing cold water. Fixer Blaque hadn't been talking to Triton on his Calling Card at all . . .

Fixer Blaque *was* Triton.

The Mother of All Glitches

Conference Room, The Big Building, The Seems

About an eighth of a world away, things were going even worse for the Powers That Be than Kalil's spies had reported. The speakerphone at the center of the table was ringing nonstop, and Eve Hightower switched lines to take yet another frantic call.

"*Department of Energy to Big Building, please come in!*"

"Talk to me, Energy."

"*Sorry to bother you, Madame Second, but I've tried Central three times and we're running out of Juice down here. If I don't get a Fixer pronto, the lights are gonna go down on Broadway.*"

"I'll take care of it."

The Second in Command made an emergency breakthrough to the fortified ops center in the basement of the Big Building. After a frustratingly long number of rings, the voice of Central Command finally picked up.

"*Dispatcher here. Sorry to keep you waiting, ma'am.*"

"Energy says they're running out of Juice and they've called three times for a Fixer." Eve tried to keep her cool, which wasn't so easy when the Powers That Be and your mother were watching. "Don't tell me you guys are falling apart too?"

"Negative, ma'am. It's just that every Fixer I have is out on a job."

"Isn't dos Santos finished tweaking the Color Palette yet?"

"Already sent her to Nature to get Photosynthesis back online." The Dispatcher's voice remained stoic but did little to instill confidence. *"To be honest, all I've got left on the Roster is Briefers."*

"Then start Bleceiving them!"

"Aye, aye, ma'am!"

Eve hung up the phone, ruing the fact that eight of her finest Fixers had been sent to the very edge of The Seems. Even worse, they were still unaccounted for, and as she called down to her assistant, she couldn't shake the feeling that she'd been outflanked on several sides. "Any word on Special Forces, Monique?"

"They're on their way back from Seemsberia, but it'll take a couple hours."

Eve let her head fall back and looked up at the sky, as if to ask someone, "Could you please just give me one break today? Just one?"

Departments had begun crashing left and right just around sundown, forcing the top-ranking official in The Seems to call an emergency session of the Powers That Be. The eleven other members of the ruling committee—an all-star cast of ex-Administrators, pioneers in Case Work, and one former bee-keeper from the Department of Love—had dropped everything and rushed to the Big Building in their pajamas and overcoats.

"Is it possible the old infrastructure just finally decided to give way?" suggested Herbert Howe, the former Administrator of Reality. "Jayson and the Fixers have been talking about this possibility since before they built the IFR."

"Get real, would you, Herb?" barked Candace Morgan, inventor of the game of Hopscotch. "This isn't some leaky faucet or broken Heart String! This is a sophisticated, coordinated attack, and anyone who doesn't know who's behind it is a moron!"

Attention shifted back to Eve Hightower, who carefully made eye contact with each of the Powers. Four of them she knew were her enemies, individuals who'd voted against her opinion on nearly every proposal since the day she took office. But the other seven were supposed to be her allies—either longtime friends or carefully selected promotions, such as Candace Morgan. Were any of them still on her side now?

"I think it's time for someone in this room to step up and take responsibility." Candace might have used the word "someone," but she was staring straight at the Second in Command. "The people wanted change, Eve, to fight for something they believed in, but you ignored them!"

"Leadership isn't a popularity contest." Eve's conviction was strong, even if the walls around her were not. "You either believe in the Plan or you don't!"

The meeting was about to collapse into a shouting match when Herb Howe turned to a familiar figure who was observing from a cushioned window seat.

"Sophie, please—don't just sit there! Tell us what we should do!"

Sophie Temporale had remained in the building when the

panicked calls had started flooding in, and had watched chaos descend upon The Seems with her typically detached amusement.

"Oh, no!" The Time Being laughed. "You kids are going to have to sort this one out for yourselves."

Once again, Eve Hightower's blood boiled at her mother's smug indifference, but before she could unleash the wrath only a daughter possessed, a heart-stopping

BLAST

blew the conference room door off its hinges.

Heads ducked and the Powers That Be went scrambling for cover, as the floor-to-ceiling windows that made this one of the best views in The Seems shattered into a million little pieces.

"Nobody moves!"

When the sound of falling glass faded and the dust in the air settled, a slender figure recognized by all in the room stepped through the still-smoldering debris. She was followed by a dozen armed men, men who, like Lena Zorn, had black waves emblazoned on the chests of their white bodysuits.

"Now, this can be a bloodless revolution, or we can paint the town red," she snapped, a fiendish grin on her pale face. "The choice is up to you."

As her team fanned out to cover every corner of the room, Lena surveyed her latest conquest. She had been the only Tide agent to escape capture after "the Split Second," and her reputation for ruthlessness had elevated her to number two on the Special Forces most-wanted list, just below Triton.

"Eve Hightower, I presume." Lena approached the unflinching Second in Command, who was the only member at the conference table not now under it. "I've always wanted to meet the person responsible for botching The World."

"You won't get away with this," whispered Eve, fists clenching tightly.

"I'm afraid it's already been gotten away with, ma'am. Or haven't your read your *Daily Plan*?"

While two of her associates seized Eve's arms, Lena toured the perimeter of the conference room, peering out the broken windows as if seeing The Seems for the very first time. She allowed the cold wind to roar through her long black hair, then pulled out a Calling Card from her back pocket and placed it on the table in front of the Second in Command.

"A friend of mine would like to speak with you."

Seemsberia, The Seems

Thibadeau tucked his own Calling Card into his sock and scrambled down the rungs of the rickety access ladder. He wished he could have told Simly the truth—he was sick to death of lying, both to friends and enemies alike—but the one thing that had kept him sane during the bleak and lonely nights was his Mission. A Mission that would never succeed unless he found the one who festered in the Heckhole.

When he finally landed on the tiled floor, Thib found himself in what appeared to be an abandoned hospital or insane asylum. Fluorescent lights cast a pale glow, garbage was strewn everywhere, and the halls were lined with padded cells. There was even a torn-up old straitjacket discarded on the floor.

"Duplicitous creatures, crafty and persuasive," Thib whispered to himself. "Never, ever listen to a Glitch."

The mantra that had been drummed into his head during his days at the IFR was interrupted by the unlikely sound of a ukulele coming from the cell to his right. He cautiously approached the door, and when he lifted the food slot, what he saw inside was a scraggly haired fellow, no more than four inches tall, wearing a tie-dyed shirt and gently strumming a tune on its cot, "If I had a hammer . . . I'd hammer in the mornin' . . ."

The eyes may have lost their mad jaundice, and the peace-sign medallion around its neck might've indicated a shift in personal ideology, but the Glitch's third arm and jagged-toothed maw told Thibadeau he had come to the right place.

"Come on in, friend." The inmate kept on strumming, then used its free hand to hold up a bongo drum. "Let's jam."

Thibadeau realized to his horror that the door to the cell was indeed unlocked. Every fiber of his training told him to run as fast as he could, but the time for avoiding confrontation was over, so he swung the door open and cautiously stepped inside.

"I would love to, *mon ami*. But I did not come to the Heck-hole to rock out."

"Then why, brother?"

"I need to speak with your, um . . . mom."

"Well, why didn't you say so?"

As the little beastie hopped to its feet and happily escorted Thibadeau down the fetid hall, something about its face jogged a memory. It was the slightest of scars—more like an impression, really—in the shape of what appeared to be the four fingers of that Fixer Tool known as a Helping Hand™.

"Pardon, but are you not the Glitch in Sleep?"

"I was that terrible force of destruction once," it said without malice. "But once I got in touch with the Inner Child, I realized who I really was. I don't want to hate anymore. I want to *love* and *be loved*!"

"Quite a breakthrough."

"Thanks, brother. From this point forward, I'm all about making a difference."

The friendly Glitch in Sleep stopped in front of a door several inches thicker than the rest.

"Now, let me do the talking, 'cause Ma can get a little . . . testy."

Students of Seemsian history will attest to the fact that a single Glitch, if left to its own devices, is capable of eating its way through the machinery that makes The World in a matter of days. Yet there is one above them all whose powers exceed the combined talents of her offspring. One who, during Operation Clean Sweep—when the Fixers forcibly removed every known Glitch from the system—easily eluded their grasp. It was only when the bulk of her boys ended up incarcerated in Seemsberia that she turned herself in, in exchange for the chance to keep her family intact.

"Hey, Ma?" The Glitch in Sleep knocked on the half-open door to the cell. "You in there?"

No one answered, but Thibadeau could clearly hear the sounds of cooking inside, and the smell of bacon, eggs, and pancakes wafting through the crack of the door.

"Ma?"

The door suddenly swung open, nearly knocking both Glitch and the Frenchman off their feet.

"Didn't I tell you not to bother me during *Price Is Right*?"

Much to Thibadeau's amazement, the Mother of All Glitches was standing before him in a nightgown, rollers in her hair and slippers on her feet.

"This better be good!"

The Glitch in Sleep gulped for courage, then whispered out its request.

"A buddy of mine wants to see you, Ma."

"Don't you call me that, boy!" The three-inch-tall matriarch abruptly smacked her peace-loving son across the face. "You're a disgrace to the family!"

"But Ma—"

"Go back to your cell and sing 'Kumbaya'!"

Behind the furious mother, Thib glimpsed what was clearly the penthouse suite of the Heckhole. It came with a private bathroom and a small kitchenette, in which she was cooking a huge breakfast. There was also a black-and-white TV set on the formica countertop, and judging from the sight of Bob Barker and his shock of white hair it was set to WTC.[25]

"I apologize for interrupting your program, madame. I only wish I had the luxury of coming at another time."

The Mother looked up at Thib with something like utter disdain.

"Who are you?"

"My name is Thibadeau Freck, and I have a proposition that I believe you will find most entic—"

25. World Television Classics (specializing in vintage favorites such as *The Merv Griffin Show*, *T. J. Hooker*, and *Murder, She Wrote*).

"Wait 'til after the showcase showdown!"

She abruptly turned and scrambled up to the front of the TV, where a ratty old recliner was placed not two feet away from the screen.

"I'm afraid it must be now." Thib helped the cowering Glitch in Sleep back to its feet, then followed it into the cell. "The fates of both The World and The Seems are at stake as we speak."

"So what? They can both go to Heck for all I care!"

The Mother resumed control of a frying pan that was filled with rapidly scrambling eggs, never taking her eyes off *The Price Is Right.*

"Lower, you moron! Bid lower!"

As the contestant onscreen ignored her advice (and lost a brand-new car), Thib could feel his moment slipping away.

"All I ask is a single favor, madame. And in return, I will help you *and* your children escape Seemsberia once and for all time."

The hand that held the Mother's spatula paused for the slightest of seconds before flipping another flapjack. The other two hands began cracking twelve more eggs against the hard edge of the skillet.

"Do I look like the kind of broad that does favors for The Tide?"

"I'm not here on their behalf, madame."

"That charm around your neck says different."

Thibadeau's fingers grasped the black and cresting wave that had hung from his neck ever since he'd been initiated into The Tide. Once it had represented an exciting new assignment, charged with intrigue and danger, but now it felt like a burden that he could no longer bear. So he decided to play his final card . . .

"I am not a member of The Tide, madame, nor have I ever been. I am an agent of The Seems who was tasked with secretly infiltrating their organization, in hopes of bringing it down from within."

Thib imagined the words sounded as strange to the Glitches' ears as they did to his own (for he had never spoken them aloud), but that didn't make them any less true. And whether it was real or just his perception, the kitchen seemed to go silent save for the sounds of boiling water and eggs frying in a pan.

"You expect me to believe that malarkey?" asked the Mother.

"You gotta learn to trust people, Ma!" implored the Glitch in Sleep, hopping up to the counter. "Only when we let our walls come down do we truly begin to connect."

The Mother's answer was to scoop up a rapidly frying egg and huck it at her ponytailed 1,435th born.

"Speak when spoken to!"

As the Glitch ducked behind the recliner and did as it was told, the Mother of them all turned her attention back to Thibadeau.

"Got any proof?"

"Only in the authority I've been granted by the Powers That Be. To free all the Glitches from Seemsberia, with but a single condition."

Thibadeau could tell that calculations were running through her crafty and duplicitous mind, but it was impossible to tell if his offer had gotten the job done.

"What about the moat? How you plan on passin' the test of Time?"

"It will lose its Essence long before we hit the water . . ."

"And our Attak-Paks®?"

"Buried at the top of the Heap. We will have to commandeer a vehicle to get there, but with the combined talents of a thousand Glitches, I somehow doubt that will be a problem."

The three-inch-tall matron nodded, simultaneously turning off all the dials on her crusty stove. The water stopped boiling, the eggs stopped frying, and the pancakes stopped pancaking. As two of her hands began divvying out heaping portions on paper plates, her third reached above her head, where a large dinner bell was dangling from a string. One pull, and a loud *clang* echoed through the Heckhole.

"Breakfast!"

Thibadeau heard the eerie sound of countless doors flying open, followed by the pitter-patter of creepy little feet. In a matter of seconds this cell would be filled with the gnashing teeth and crazed giggles of a thousand lunatics, but he tried to keep his nerve, for all that mattered was what their beloved ma had to say. For her part, the Mother of All Glitches picked up a slimy cigar from her ashtray by the sink, put it between her cheek and gum, and took a deep and glorious drag.

"Now tell me more about this little favor . . ."

The Middle of Nowhere

Back in the prisoners' tent, tears of rage were already spilling down Becker's face as he roughly threw his captive to the floor.

"Meet Triton, everybody! His real name is *Jelani Blaque*!"

Over on a U-shaped couch, Fixers Hassan, Simms, and Octo had only been awake for a minute or two when mayhem had tumbled into the room. Now they looked just as flabbergasted by Becker's accusation as Fixer Blaque himself.

"Easy, Becker." Lisa Simms calmly pulled him a few steps back. "Give the man a chance to breathe."

After he'd witnessed Blaque's conversation with Thibadeau Freck, Becker hadn't waited for his former instructor to make another call. Like a crazed tiger, he'd leapt from his hiding spot behind the huge tapestry and slapped on the same chokehold Blaque had taught him in "Fight or Flight" class back at the IFR. But instead of dishing out some frontier justice, Becker wanted the leader of The Tide to know what it was like to face a jury of his peers.

"How could you, sir? After everything you taught us?"

Down on the rug-covered floor, Blaque coughed his way toward oxygen, then looked up at his student.

"Take my word for it, Mr. Drane. You did not see what you think you saw."

"Becker, this is absurd!" Judging by the hoarseness of her voice, Lisa Simms was struggling to shake off the effects of the Nowherian light for the second time in three days. "Jelani is no more a member of The Tide than I am, let alone—"

Becker interrupted her by pulling out the device he'd confiscated from Fixer Blaque and tossing it over. "Ask him why he was carrying a Calling Card, Leese! Or who was on his last transmission!"

Fixer Simms quickly toggled through the Card's incoming calls. She'd known Jelani Blaque since she was a wide-eyed, seventeen-year-old rookie, but the first hint of doubt crept into her mind when she saw the number at the top.

"Area code 322. Isn't that . . . ?"

"Seemsberia," whispered Hassan, his body wracked with shivers from his own recovery. "I presume he was 'meeting' Thibadeau Freck again?"

"Exactly!" Becker shouted. "I heard them plotting to overthrow The Seems and celebrate on the steps of the Big Building."

Fixer Simms handed the Card to the Octogenarian, hoping she might find some explanation that her own desperate brain could not. But Sylvia couldn't deny the evidence in front of her eyes.

"I'm afraid this looks bad, Jelani. Very bad."

The subtle nods of his three Roster mates said they agreed, so Blaque limped over to the nearest couch and fell heavily into the cushions. This was terrible timing, but if there was ever a moment to trust in the intricacies of the Plan, he figured it was now.

"Four years ago, while he was still in Training, Candidate Freck was approached in the IFR Library and offered membership in The Tide." The retired Fixer's voice sounded old and tired, but there was a certain relief in finally revealing the truth. "The reasons for his recruitment are well known, for Mr. Freck was never shy about expressing his doubts regarding the Plan. And yet, even though he was sorely tempted to venture to The Slumber Party that night to begin his initiation, it was my office he came to first."

Blaque waited for the clamor outside the tent to quiet down, then continued.

"It was there that Mr. Freck and I hatched our own plan: to insert a deep-cover agent into The Tide, one that could feed us information about their infrastructure, their long-term strategy, perhaps even discover the true identity of the one you are now accusing me to be."

Becker watched surprise, maybe even shock, bounce across the faces of his fellow Fixers, and knew that if he found his way to a mirror, it would've already landed on his own. "You must think we're idiots, sir. It was Thib's team that blew up Time Square and nearly caused the end of The World as we know it!"

"Indeed it was. And I have no doubt that Mr. Freck's loyalties were severely challenged by his time undercover. But it was also Mr. Freck who purposely revealed himself as the leader of that attack, who offered up the location of the Split Second, and who, as I recall, put his own life on the line to save yours."

Becker was loathe to admit it (and he didn't aloud), but the memory of Thibadeau standing between him and four Tide members bent on tossing him off a roof in New York City was undeniable.

"I assume there is some corroboration for this claim?" wondered Hassan, the shivers replaced by curiosity.

"Only two people besides myself are aware of Mr. Freck's mission. Casey Lake . . . and the Second in Command herself."

"Convenient that neither are here to confirm your story."

Hassan was not ready to let him off the hook.

"My Calling Card has been adjusted to the peculiar frequencies available in the Middle of Nowhere. I would be more than happy to contact the Second's personal line"—Blaque shot the Persian a confident grin—"especially now that according to Mr. Freck's report, The Tide has begun a full-blown assault upon the Powers That Be."

Combined with what Becker had heard in the Nowherian Chieftain's tent, this intelligence had the sickening ring of truth. He snatched the Card from the Octogenarian and dialed the Big Building's number, not totally sure whether he was hoping to exonerate his mentor or call his bluff. The high-pitched whine was just being replaced by the soft white noise of a connection, when suddenly—

"I suggest you put that down."

Becker's ears only understood the Nowherian tongue because his captors had neglected to remove his Hearing Aide when they'd tossed him into the prisoners' tent. Due to the fact that he was now surrounded by a dozen black-robed figures bearing swords and hunga-mungas, he could only assume the Towers of Silence were ready for their new owners.

"Guys, if you could just hold on one second, I have to ask someone a—"

Just as the other end of the line picked up, the biggest Nowherian slapped the Card from Becker's hands, then ground it to bits and bytes beneath his sandaled feet.

"Where you and your friends are going, you won't need to know the answer."

With a bunch of sharp objects pointed in their direction, the second team put aside their disagreement and anxiously rose to their feet. Becker made eye contact with Simms, who nodded to Octo, who coughed at Hassan, who, against his better judgment, scratched a cheek in the direction of Blaque, who began whistling the theme song to *Don't Be a Tool III: How to Fix Your Way out of 10 Impossible Fixes,* the classic IFR training film. But before Becker could initiate the maneuver they all were thinking of, he noticed something strange poking beneath the headdress of the Nowherian at the front of the line.

A pair of double-braided pigtails.

"Now I don't mean to frighten you, fellas . . ." In a whirl of movement, the black robe fell away to reveal a girl with flip-flops on her feet and something big and nasty in her hands. "But this here's what we call a 'Doozy™."

The Lost Train of Thought

How Cassiopeia Lake managed to survive the mysterious light unscathed, then make her way across the desert and over the Peak of Experience to infiltrate the Nowherians is a Story for Another Day.[26] All that mattered as far as the fate of The Seems and The World were concerned was that with one blow of her Didgeradoozy—an Australian horn modified by the Toolshed to use sound as a weapon—she flattened the crew of guards and led the groggy second team to freedom.

"Nice 'n' easy, mates," Casey whispered under her breath. "Far as anyone knows, we're just out for a midday stroll."

Becker and the others followed her straight through the center of the village and back toward the mountain. They were all now dressed in the traditional garb of their captors, having "borrowed" them from the bound guards they'd left behind in the

---

26. See *The Seems: Stories for Another Day.* (Coming soon.)

prisoners' tent. Those few Nowherians not yet gathered around the newly constructed Towers of Silence paid them no heed.

"No sign of Li Po, Casey?" The Octogenarian was still worried for the lone unaccounted for Fixer.

"Negatory. Been on my own since I dug my head outta the—"

Somewhere in the distance, the old Nowherian sorceress unleashed another blood-curdling cry, and chills shot down Becker's spine. "They're ready for the show."

"Stay frosty, #37. We'll be long gone by then."

Becker nodded, then stepped closer to Casey and dropped his voice to a whisper. "Casey, I need to ask you something."

"If it's about the way we stonkered you in court, you didn't leave us any—"

"It's not that. It's Fixer Blaque."

Casey kept her eyes locked on the ground ahead, which was sloping back toward the mountains. "What about him?"

Becker peeked over his shoulder, where the subject of their conversation limped only a few yards behind them. "Back in the tent, I caught him talking to Thibadeau Freck on a Calling Card. But he claims Thib's—"

"One of us?"

Becker nodded, and by the way Casey winced as she said the words, he knew instantly that all of it was true.

"Sorry, mate. We had to keep it a mystery bag, or Freck was DOA."

A numb feeling of regret came over Becker, one he barely had time to process because Casey suddenly stopped and drew everyone's attention to the mountainside, where a wide, dark tunnel was carved into its sheer face.

"Thar she blows."

The tunnel was directly below the ridge that Becker had been perched upon, which explained why he hadn't seen it through his Trinoculars—and he mentally kicked himself for being so obsessed with finding out what was in the secret grove that he hadn't bothered to simply turn around. But it wasn't his own stupidity or even the Nowherians gift for excavation that caused him to incautiously jog toward the black semicircle in the rock.

It was what gleamed and shined inside of it.

"Now there's a sight for sore eyes," marveled Lisa Simms, jogging right beside him.

By the time the second team reached the locomotive, they were already fanning out between the cars and conducting a tactical assessment.

"Thank the Plan you lot showed." Casey ditched her disguise and squatted beside what was left of a broken wheel. " 'Cause this ain't no one-Fixer job."

That was an understatement. Not only were at least a dozen wheels in need of significant repair, but the coupling rods were bent and several cracks ran through the bottom of the chassis. Even worse, the boiler responsible for generating enough steam to get the cars in motion was unable to maintain pressure. Much of the damage had undoubtedly occurred when the rails beneath the train had suddenly vanished—a side effect of the fact that they'd been made from Scratch instead of iron or steel.

"At least the Thought's all here!" shouted Hassan from atop the nearest freight car. "This train is stuffed."

The Octogenarian checked her Time Piece, but it wasn't working any better than Becker's. "Is it even possible? The Unthinkable could happen any minute."

"Won't get done chatting about it," said Fixer Simms, face blackened from digging around in the coal car. "Cassiopeia, if I can steal your Pressure Cooker™ for a moment, I think I can get this boiler back online."

Casey handed over the Tool, but she shared Sylvia's doubts. "My main concern is finding Scratch to build a new set of rails. I've been scouring this camp since yesterday, and haven't seen a single grain."

Fixer Blaque smiled and showed her what was inside the locket around his neck. "You get it rolling, and I'll make sure there's something to roll on."

"Aces!" Casey emptied the contents of the only remaining Toolkit in their possession onto the ground, and grabbed a lug wrench. "Let's Fix this bugger, mates!"

"Hold on a sec!"

Becker caught Casey by the shoulder and gently tossed a rock up into the booth of the locomotive. The moment it landed, a circular section of twine that had previously been hidden beneath the engineer's chair violently snapped closed. Had a person just sat down there—say, the owner of a surf shop in Adelaide—she would've been neatly sliced in two.

"Classic Nowherian rope trap."

Fixer #37 covertly shot Fixer Blaque a wink, as if to say his wasn't the youngest name on the Duty Roster because he made the same mistakes twice.

"*Now* let's Fix this bugger."

With five of the most talented repairmen and -women The World has ever seen focused like laser beams, it was only a matter of twelve pulse-pounding minutes before the stalled Train of Thought lurched forward, with steel miraculously beneath its wheels. White puffs coughed from the smokestack, while Casey Lake floored the throttle and shouted over the locomotive's roar.

"Keep shoveling, mates! We need more speed!"

On the other side of the cabin, Becker and Lisa frantically shoveled piles of coal into a firebox. With each scoop, the flames grew hotter and the water in the boiler vaporized into more steam, powering the Train of Thought back through the underground tunnel.

"Careful." Fixer Simms kept a worried eye on the boiler's safety valve. "If she gets too hot, we could lose pressure again, or crack the head."

"That's a chance we'll have to take." The heat from the fire was fogging up the front windshield, and Casey struggled to see through the glass. "Can somebody go check on Fixer Blaque?"

"I'm on it!"

Becker dropped his shovel, then scrambled up the rungs of the access ladder to the top of the train. Though the wind and smoke bit at his eyes, he couldn't stop himself from admiring the size and scope of the cavern. Judging from the stonework of the bridge they were now traveling across (not to mention the man-made waterfall) the Nowherians had somehow carved out this place by hand—using a completely different method of architecture than Fixer Blaque's Scratch.

"How those tracks coming, sir?"

Out on the nose of the train, only a few feet in front of the same smokestack that had scalded a lightbulb and teardrop into Greg the Journeyman's chest, Jelani Blaque sat cross-legged with his hands pressed together.

"See for yourself."

He motioned down toward the bridge, where, illuminated by the locomotive's yellow headlights, there was a spanking new set of train tracks. They came complete with wooden slats and painted steel spikes, courtesy of the Scratch he'd purchased at the Black Market. Most of the blue powder he was now rubbing between his two palms was generating just enough friction to heat his very thoughts into reality.

"Are they gonna be long enough to get us back home?" asked Becker at the top of his lungs.

"Not if you don't let me concentrate, Mr. Drane!"

Blaque smiled without looking back, and as Becker started back toward the ladder, he felt an uncomfortable twinge of guilt.

"Sir, I'm—"

"It's me who's sorry, Becker." In the four-plus years they'd known each other, this was the first time Becker could remember Fixer Blaque using his first name. "And I look forward to the day when you and I and Mr. Freck can sit atop the Stumbling Block and put these last few years behind us."

This time the teacher did turn to smile at his student, and the student responded in kind.

"Me too, sir. Me too."

As Blaque returned his attention to making train tracks from Scratch, Becker scrambled back down the ladder, feeling much lighter than he had only seconds before.

"So far so good, Case."

Casey nodded and flipped the switch on the intercom above her head.

"Lake to Hassan, how we doin' on those tarps?"

Fixers Hassan and the Octogenarian had gone to the back of the train in an attempt to secure each car with a tarpaulin so they would not lose even a single chip of Thought. But their response to Casey's query was little more than static.

"These trains are still using old radio receivers for their intercoms," said Lisa, leaning on her shovel and wiping the sweat from her brow. "Might need to wait 'til we get out from under the mountain."

Becker grabbed his own shovel off the floor, but before he could get back to using it a harsh light suddenly bombarded the cabin, and the train exploded from beneath the mountain. As it roared across the desert on the eastern side, Casey blinked away the stars, then gave the intercom another try.

"Hassan, Octo, I need a report, over!"

Just as Lisa predicted, the intercom signal had cleared up the moment they left the darkness of the cavern. But it was not the voice of Shahzad Hassan or the Octogenarian who responded over the tinny receiver . . .

"You'll have to come down here and get it."

In fact, the speaker's name was Kalil.

Two dozen cars back, in the roaring wind and scalding sun atop the train, the Chieftain of the Nowherians and his men removed their robes and girded themselves for battle. This would not be a fair fight—they numbered more than thirty—but

Kalil had underestimated the enemy once before, and he would not do so again.

"Here they come, Sire!"

His men pointed to the front, where three figures stood poised atop the locomotive. One by one, they began to hop from car to car.

"They are courageous, these Fixers," admired Joachim, the Chieftain's most trusted lieutenant.

"We shall soon see."

As Kalil lifted two gold-handled scimitars from their scabbards, Fixers Hassan and Octo struggled to free themselves from their bindings. The duo had been surprised by the Nowherians just as they were installing the final tarp, and now sat back-to-back atop a pile of stray Thought.

"I am sorry, Sylvia." Hassan's left eye was closed shut from the butt end of a Nowherian blade. "I should have offered up a more suitable defense."

Fixer Octo shrugged and delivered a typically sunny take on their situation.

"No apologies necessary, Shahzad. And as soon as I get these wrinkled paws free, I'm going to teach these hooligans to respect their elders."

Hassan couldn't help laughing at the image of an eighty-four-year-old woman cleaning the clocks of thirty warriors, and his own despair instantly melted away.

"Blaque was wise when he chose you for the team, Sylvia. I only wish he had been so with me."

"Mission's not over yet," she whispered. "Not by a long shot."

But all evidence pointed to the contrary, as two heavily muscled arms lifted them both into the air like babies.

"What shall we do with these?" asked Joachim, dangling the Fixers over the side of the train.

"Get rid of them."

"You are a hateful man, sir." The Octogenarian shook her head at the Chieftain like a disappointed schoolteacher. "The king of a hateful lot."

Kalil ignored the insult, for the three approaching Fixers were close enough now to see that one was Jelani Blaque and his walking stick. No, not a fair fight at all.

"A final request, mighty one." Hassan did his best to avoid looking down at the swiftly moving landscape below. "If this day is to be our last, then at least grant us the honor of joining our comrades in battle."

The Chieftain gave Joachim the nod. But as his lieutenant began to loosen the Fixers' bindings, Kalil noticed the amulet that hung from Hassan's neck. "What is that you wear?"

"The winged sun . . . the ancient symbol of my people."

"Of *your* people?" Kalil tore the amulet off Hassan's neck and held it up to his equally surprised men. "Of *his* people!"

Hassan's confusion was apparent, especially when Kalil showed him what had been branded onto his own chest during the ritual of manhood so many years ago: the same winged sun.

"I do not understand."

"Understand this, my brother." Kalil snapped the ropes around the Fixers' wrists and dropped them roughly onto the boxcar. "The Powers That Be are liars as an order of business. It is what they do, who they are. And they will never be anything else."

Hassan and the Octogenarian cautiously backed away to the other end of the car, still expecting to be tossed over the side at any moment. But the Nowherians stayed as motionless as their Chieftain, patiently waiting for their enemy to gather in full strength. They didn't have to wait long.

"Did it really have to come to this?" asked Lisa Simms, flanked by Casey Lake. "Surely we can find a peaceful way to resolve this dispute, as we did at the Eternal Springs."

"The time for negotiations is over, woman."

But as his men effortlessly slid into formation around him, two things troubled Kalil. Where was the boy who had so blatantly defied him back in his own tent? And more important, what happened to the old cripple? Only moments ago, Jelani Blaque had staggered behind the others, but now only four Fixers stood before him. Had he fallen off the train somewhere along the way? Or was he—

"Sire," whispered Joachim beside him. "Why are we moving so slow?"

As if waking from a daze, the Chieftain realized his lieutenant was right, and that the train had begun to precipitously lose speed. His first thought was that they were trying to slam on the brakes in order to jar the Nowherians off the top, but then Kalil saw a man with blue-tinted shades climbing up the ladder that led to the space between this car and the one in front of it.

"Because they just disconnected us from the rest of the train."

Executive Conference Room, The Big Building,
The Seems

If it hadn't been for his mask of digital fuzz, it would have seemed to everyone in the Conference Room that Triton was really there and walking among them. His projection stepped off the metal square of the Calling Card and approached the Second in Command.

"This battle has gone on far too long, Madame Hightower. All we're asking for is a peaceful transfer of power from you to a democratically elected Second that is more reflective of the people's views."

"What do you know of the people?" scoffed Eve Hightower from the seat beside him. "You're nothing but a terrorist who preys on their worst fears!"

"And you are nothing but a slave to a Plan that was obsolete on the day that it was born!"

A digital fist noiselessly pounded the conference table.

"Weather, Nature, Energy, Time, Reality . . . The Tide now controls every key department in The Seems. So whether you like it or not, Madame Second, The World WILL be put on hold, and the Plan WILL be revised!" Triton appeared to run a hand through his hair, as if to steady his emotion. *"Your final act as Second will be to decide if it is done through honest discourse . . . or through the use of force."*

Eve's mind raced unsuccessfully to find some stratagem that could halt the rising Tide when the conversation was interrupted by a knock on the door.

"The Care Givers are here, Lena," said one of the henchmen.

Lena Zorn looked to the image of her boss—who assented with an absent wave of a hand—then cautiously opened the door herself. "Be quick about it, Doctor. The future of The World is being decided here."

"Of course."

A young Care Giver carrying a black Department of Health bag hastily entered the room, accompanied by a uniformed nurse. Several people had been badly injured during the attack on the Conference Room, most severely Eve Hightower's personal assistant.

"Monique, can you hear me?" The doctor lifted the injured girl's head off the floor. "My name is Doctor Carmichael and I'm going to take good care of you, okay?"

Strange. Eve had attended every graduation from the Department of Health's med school since taking her position and couldn't recall a Doctor Carmichael ever taking a diploma from her hands.

"Where are you hurt, Madame Second?" prodded the Care Giver's assistant.

"Don't worry about me. There are others with far greater injuries than me."

Eve was about to push the busybody nurse away when she suddenly realized it wasn't a nurse at all. It was a Chinese woman in her midthirties, with streaks of white in her jet black hair, who just happened to be the most talented Briefer on the Duty Roster.

"Are you sure, Madame?" asked Shan Mei-Lin, skillfully remaining in character. "Because there's a whole *team* of Care

Givers waiting on the floor below, and they can be here at a moment's notice if the need arises."

Eve snuck a look at the "doctor," and Fixer Harold "C-Note" Carmichael threw back the subtlest of winks. They were clearly the vanguard of a Central Command counterstrike—one the Second only wanted to use as a last resort.

"I'm fine, Nurse. But please stay until you've made sure everyone's okay."

Briefer Shan nodded and made her way through the Powers That Be, who, like the members of The Tide, were completely unaware of who was in their midst.

"There's no point fighting him any longer, Eve." Candace Morgan had lost her bravado, but not her point of view. "The writing's on the wall."

"As it was with the Blue Poison Dart Frog, I suppose."

"Excuse me?"

Eve just shook her head and smiled, finally understanding how thoroughly she'd been outmaneuvered. Looking at the faces of the Powers That Be, all caught somewhere between fearfulness and hope, it hit her that Triton must've reached out to those in this room long before his minions actually entered it.

"Do all of you feel this way?" she tested.

Of the eleven other members, only one Power shook his head no.

"I'm still with you, Eve," said Herb Howe. "Come Heck or high water."

The old Reality Checker's loyalty put a lump in her throat, but she wasn't ready to make the call until someone else weighed in. "Mom?"

As usual, Sophie Temporale had watched the proceedings without ever offering an opinion—but this time a mother's concern replaced her usual detachment.

"I just don't want you to get hurt, sweetheart. Maybe a fresh voice at the top will end all this pointless bickering."

Eve nodded, torn between her disappointment that the Time Being was tacitly supporting Triton's agenda, and practically moved to tears that her mother was actually worried about her for the first time since she could remember.

"I suggest we put it to a show of hands." Triton rose to his digitally garbled feet. *"Yea, and the Second in Command tenders her resignation, The Tide stands down, and a new dawn arises in The Seems and The World. Nay . . ."*

The Tide's leader motioned to his right-hand woman and Lena coolly dragged Eve over to the shattered windows.

"And you resign when you hit the pavement below."

Lena dangled her prisoner over the side for extra measure, but the sight of where a thousand-story fall would end for Eve Hightower had an unexpected effect. The proud front steps, the marble sculpture of The World, even the delicate topiaries of the surrounding Field of Play were all reminders of what she loved about this job, and why she'd wanted it in the first place.

"I vote you take off that pathetic mask of yours and debate me in the Court of Public Opinion." The Second looked over the side again and let the cold wind wash across her face. "Or get it over with and show the people of The Seems what a coward you really are."

It was a crazy gamble, made less so only by the fact that C-Note and Shan were covertly pressing their fake Health Badges to signal that the time to counterstrike was now. But before anyone could make a move, a strange humming began to filter through the windows, getting louder and louder with each passing second.

"What is that noise?" asked Triton, his voice reflecting the first hint of doubt.

When Lena tried to answer him by leaning even farther out the window, she could've sworn that what echoed through the thick and purple clouds surrounding the Big Building sounded like a billion mosquitoes descending from the sky in sneak attack.

Or perhaps a bunch of tiny helicopters.

"Steady, boys!" The Mother of All Glitches put the brakes on her Attak-Pak, then held up all three of her hands. "Nobody strikes until you see the whites of their eyes!"

Swirling about her was a cloud of Glitches at least a thousand strong, each with a propeller extending from the top of their own Paks and over their misshapen heads.

"What're we waitin' for, Ma?" shouted Phineas, her eldest. "We can finally pay them back for what they done to us on Clean Sweep!"

The Mother's answer was to press a button on her handle, activating a mechanical arm that reached out and started washing Phineas's mouth out with soap.

"Anybody else gives me lip, and nobody gets to trash nothin'!"

Her brood immediately fell silent, dropping their eyes bashfully toward the ground. But as the Mother flew down to where the Glitch in Sleep's Attak-Pak was struggling to carry three orange jumpsuits through the air, she knew the madness of her children couldn't be contained for long.

"I'm warnin' you, Freck. My boys're gonna tear this place to shreds unless somebody tells them exactly where to go and what to do."

Thibadeau Freck was the only escapee who had summoned up the courage to take a gander below—Simly Frye and Permin Neverlåethe both had their hands over their eyes and skin the color of peas—but at a height of nearly twenty thousand feet, the Frenchman didn't quite feel ready to lead the way.

"We must use the 7th Sense, then," he stammered. "To find where in each department The Tide has taken hold."

Thib could definitely feel shiverings and quiverings all over his body, not surprising when something was wrong in just about every department in The Seems. The only problem was, Seemsberia hadn't exactly done wonders for his mastery of a Fixer's greatest Tool.

"Just give me a moment to focus my—"

"Don't sweat it, Thib. I'll handle this one."

Thibadeau turned to see Simly dangling from a bungee cord just a few feet to his right. The Briefer was already stretching out his arms and reaching his awareness toward the entirety of the campus below.

"But Sim, you are Seemsian. You have no 7th Sense."

Simly took a look up at his old classmate, and Thibadeau saw a sparkle he'd never seen before in those Coke-bottle glasses-covered eyes.

"*Au contraire*, Frenchie. *Au contraire*."

The Unthinkable

When it was all over, and Simly Frye had guided hordes of clinically insane four-inch-tall monstrosities through every tube, air-conditioning duct, and exhaust pipe into The Seems, the Mother of All Glitches fulfilled her promise to Thibadeau by wresting control of The World away from The Tide. Coupled with the devastating counterstrike led by C-Note and Shan, the Big Building was once again under Seemsian control. And though Triton may have slipped away like a phantom, at least the departments and sub-departments that had been gummed up by his agents were immediately back in motion again . . .

All except for one.

---

27. ☠ After years of fruitless research, funding to strip the number 13 of its destructive properties has been officially suspended. Superstition, a sub-department of the Department of Everything That Has No Department, issues the following warning: "The prime numeral 13 has been proven to possess properties both unpredictable and unsound. Those encountering the cursed integer in elevators, motels, or books are advised to proceed with extreme caution."

Department of Thought & Emotion, The Seems

On the floor of Central Shipping, the conveyor belts had stopped, the hearths had been extinguished, and Think Tanks lay empty on their sides. As the sweat-soaked members of the Brain Trust dejectedly abandoned their posts, the same terrible message cried out over and over again on the loudspeaker . . .

"Warning! The Unthinkable is happening! The Unthinkable is happening! Warning!"

Most of the staff were gathering around a single Window on The World, where Eve Hightower was monitoring the rapidly deteriorating situation herself. The Second in Command had come down to T&E to personally supervise the allotments of Idle Thought, but since the final stack of chips had gone out twenty minutes ago, there was little she or anyone else could do now but watch in abject horror.

"If anyone has a suggestion, please speak up." Eve's eyes were streaked red, and she had never felt so tired in her life. "'Cause I'm all out of Big Ideas."

"So are we, ma'am." A brokenhearted Mind Blower held up a stamped bill of lading. "We tried sending the last one to Oxford—thought maybe the physicists there could use it to figure out what was happening, but—"

The Blower burst into tears before he could finish his sentence, and it wasn't hard to see why.

Onscreen, enraged students were clashing with cops on the streets of downtown Tokyo. Six miles worth of bumper-to-bumper traffic spilled road rage across Rio de Janeiro. And worst of all, in a heavily fortified sub-basement of the White House, the president of the United States was staring angrily at a big red button and trying to think of one good reason why he shouldn't just go ahead and push it.

"I don't understand why we're letting this happen, Madame Second." The Foreman of T&E was a grizzled old vet of the Color Wars, and it was killing him that everything he'd fought for was about to go up in flames. "Can't we just stop Time for a few weeks until we get a new batch of Thought from Contemplation?"

Eve shook her head, crushed by an overwhelming sense of defeat.

"I wish we could, but the Rules are very clear in this matter. No matter how much it hurts, we can't interfere with the—"

"Forgive me for saying this, ma'am . . . but damn the Rules!"

The Foreman's voice was so thick with emotion that he could barely say what he knew he had to say.

"And damn the freakin' Plan."

Eve slowly looked up at him, then back at the rest of the T&E crew who crowded close behind her. She knew without question that they were loyal and dedicated employees whose greatest mission in life was to create the most magical World possible, which only made the doubt on their faces that much harder to stomach. She also knew it was a perfect reflection of her own.

"I . . ."

Buzz, buzz, buzz.

Her Bleceiver began to vibrate, and when she quietly lifted it to her ear, Eve was surprised to hear her injured assistant on the other end of the line.

"Excuse me, ma'am . . . but someone just made an emergency breakthrough on your personal Calling Card."

"Who is it, Monique?"

"The signal's pretty weak, so I can't quite make out who's calling . . ."

Despite her minor concussion, Monique's excitement jumped right through the phone.

"But I think it's Fixer Drane."

The Middle of Nowhere

Becker was sorely disappointed when he pulled the short end of the Stick and got stuck behind the engineer's wheel. Nothing would've made him happier than to crunch a few Nowherian skulls after all the trouble they'd caused, but unfortunately, Trains of Thought don't come with an autopilot. Someone had to operate the throttle at all times while simultaneously keeping the Johnson Bar in the front position and stoking the boiler every so often with another shovelful of coal. Not exactly a one-Fixer job either, but since there was only one left to do it . . .

". . . Repeat, am currently fifteen clicks west of the End of the Line, with 80 percent payload on my back!" Becker was barking into Fixer Blaque's battery-operated Calling Card, trying to make himself heard over the engine and wind. "With any L.U.C.K., I'll be rolling into T&E in less than twelve hours!"

"Twelve hours?" The barely discernible image of Eve Hightower flickered in and out of reception—as if she were

momentarily in the cabin with him, then out again. *"That's great, Fixer Drane."*

Her tone of voice told Becker it was anything but.

"What's wrong, Madame Second?"

"It's just . . . we were forced to expend a tremendous amount of resources last night, including our last bit of Idle Thought."

Becker kept his eyes focused on the gauges, afraid to even ask. "The Unthinkable?"

"Already happening. And worse than we ever imagined." Her image schitzed out of view for a second, but her voice could still be heard. *"I had my Senior Case Workers crunch the numbers, and these are the projections."*

When the Second in Command popped back into view, she was reading from a printout in an almost mechanical voice.

"In approximately thirty-seven minutes: first bombs fall upon Indian subcontinent. Forty-two minutes, cities of Hong Kong, Jerusalem, and Washington, District of Columbia, engulfed in flames. At one-hour mark, estimate . . ." Eve coughed, finding it hard to say the words. *"10.3 million people dead."*

Becker found it even harder to hear them, relying upon professionalism to keep himself from totally wigging out. "What are our options, Madame?"

"To be honest . . . I'm seriously considering putting The World on hold."

"You can't do that!" Becker gripped the Johnson Bar so tight his knuckles went right past white to blue. "There's only a one in three chance it'll start up again—at best! And we could end up having to rebuild the whole thing from Scratch!"

"One in three is better than no chance at all! So, Plan help me,

Fixer Drane, unless you have the Solution to All Our Problems™ on that train or in your brain, I'm gonna do what needs to be done!"

With his own supplies of Thought undoubtedly dwindling, it was hard for Becker to keep his Emotions under control. He focused on his breathing for a few seconds, then tried to remember that on at least a half-dozen Missions, he'd arrived at this exact same moment, when all seemed lost and there was nowhere left to turn. Yes, he'd already used his Glimmer of Hope. Sure, his Ace in the Hole™ was back in the Nowherian village with his Toolkit. And by all means, his 7th Sense was useless out here, but there had to be a way to Fix this thing. There had to be a way to get this train's cargo across to The World before—

"The In-Betweener!"

"Excuse me?" asked Eve Hightower, not quite sure if she'd heard her Fixer correctly, but Becker was too busy tearing through the box of maps the conductor had stashed beside his chair to repeat himself. The documents were crumpled and riddled with Pickmeup cup stains, so it took a few anxious moments to find one that was old enough to feature the Pre-Seemsiana Purchase layout. Back then there had been all sorts of cool departments that were no longer in service.

And all sorts of train lines.

"What about the In-Betweener, Fixer Drane?"

"I can use it to deliver the Thought."

"You must be joking."

"I saw an old, boarded-up tunnel when we were out at Contemplation, and I can be there in less than twenty." Becker checked the mileage on the map against the speedometer on the train to make sure his calculations were correct. "All I need is someone to throw the switch at the End of the Line and kick me over to the right set of rails."

The Second in Command's silence said she was doing some calculating of her own.

"Even if you don't totally derail, and even if the In-Betweener tube hasn't caved in, how are you planning to get the Thought off the train? There's no staff out there except for a handful of Provokers. It'll take you hours to unload it . . ."

Becker Drane gritted his teeth and pushed the throttle even farther.

"I'm not planning on unloading it."

For the intrepid handful who've been lucky enough to make the leap across the In-Between, there is nothing quite like the feeling of being propelled at inconceivable speeds down an electrified Transport Tube. But back before this technology was invented, the Department of Transportation relied upon a different method of delivering Goods & Services to the newly operational World. Instead of being shipped via magnetic suction, the wares of Nature and Energy and Sleep were piled atop pallets and delivered by an automated freight train line.

They called it "the In-Betweener."

"Just get as many boards off that tunnel as you can, all right?" shouted Becker into the locomotive's built-in Receiver.

"We're trying, sir, but there's only five of us out here! Most of our best people have been missing since that train went lost."

Now that he'd left the Middle of Nowhere and turned the train toward Contemplation without derailing (barely), Becker's lines of communication had opened up. He was trying to get a small crew of Thought Provokers to give his lunatic plan a chance of working, but it was easier said than done.

"Just make sure everybody's outta the way in about ten minutes." Becker's Time Piece was happily working again. " 'Cause I'll be seeing you in eleven."

Becker hung up, then ran a spot check of all the details. Speed? Check. Boiler pressure? Check. Way to maintain enough velocity for the Train of Thought to smash through the boarded-up old In-Betweener entrance at Contemplation, make it all the way across the In-Between without derailing, and still get the driver off the train alive? Not so check.

"Fixer Drane, come in, over."

It was the Second in Command on the Calling Card again, and Becker pressed the green "answer" button with his right foot.

"The Transpo guys have done the math, and if you hit the tunnel entrance at your current speed, momentum should carry the train all the way across the In-Between whether it slips off the rails or not."

"What about the Tube? Won't it shatter from the weight?"

"Transpo swears it's good to go."

"Then, um . . . what's the problem?"

"I think you know the answer to that, Fixer Drane. I think you knew the moment you came up with this idea."

Eve Hightower hadn't risen to the most powerful position in The Seems because she was dumb, and even if she had been, the singular flaw in Becker's World-rescuing scheme was obvious. In-Betweener freights had been designed to deliver the payloads automatically, without drivers, and thus, they didn't come with locomotives on the front. And locomotives were way too tall to fit through the tunnel that Becker was heading straight for.

"The engineer's cabin will be sheared off the minute you hit that entrance."

"Don't worry about me, Madame. I'll figure out some way off."

"I thought you said you lost your Toolkit."

"I did. But Fixer Blaque always said, 'A true Fixer never blames his Tools.'"

"Becker—"

"I don't mean to be rude, Madame Second, but I just wanna make sure all the i's are crossed and t's are dotted before I focus on my rip cord strategy."

Eve nodded and quickly confirmed that all of Becker's suggestions for how to maximize the potential Fix had been carried out. The Department of Transportation was ready to calculate the train's moment of impact with the Fabric of Reality to the millisecond. The Department of Reality would ensure that the train itself would disintegrate, while Time would be stopped Worldwide for thirty seconds, so people's heads wouldn't explode from the sudden rush of Thought and Big Ideas.

"I think that's everything, Madame."

The image of Eve Hightower nodded and seemed to lean sadly against the console of the train. *"You don't have to do this, Fixer Drane."*

"Then who will?"

Becker kept his hand on the throttle, his eyes focused on the parallel lines of steel that disappeared beneath him.

"But if I, um . . ."

This time it was Becker who struggled to find the words, and Eve to hear them.

"Anything."

"I want you to carry out my sentence to the full letter of the law." Becker worked up the courage to look her in the eyes. "Unremember Jennifer Kaley and my brother."

"Are you sure?"

"It's gonna be hard enough on Benjamin if my Me-2 has to decommission itself."

"Understood."

"But before you unremember Jenny, I was working on this mix for her and I was hoping that . . . before I . . ."

"You want her to hear it?"

"Yes, ma'am. Me-2 knows where it is."

"Done." Eve motioned toward someone not in her Calling Card's view. *"Anything else?"*

"Maybe put a call in to Henry Steele over at L.U.C.K., see if there's any he can throw my way."

"One step ahead of you. Steele says he'll be waiting for you at Flip's—burgers on him."

"All right, then. I better get going."

"Jayson would've been proud of you, Becker. Plan knows I am."

"Thanks, Madame Second. That means a ton."

"I'll call you back in ten minutes to celebrate."

With a smile on her digitally projected face that said she might've even believed that, Eve Hightower hung up.

Four minutes to go . . . make that three minutes and fifty-eight seconds of driving a hundred miles an hour straight toward what amounted to a brick wall. The moment he let go of the throttle that speed would drop precipitously, which meant he needed to hold on to it until about fifteen seconds prior to impact. Not a lot of time for a rip cord strategy, even if he had one.

It would take only three seconds to dive out the side door of the cabin, but there was nothing inside the locomotive he could use to cushion his fall. No, a better bet was to head for the roof. Maybe six seconds to climb the ladder, four to sprint back to the car behind him, nine to cut off the tarpaulin that he was almost positive had been draped over the carload of Thought, six more to pull it tightly into the form of a parachute, and no more than two to dive over the side, where he would float gently and safely to the ground. Of course, that all added up to a minimum of twenty-seven seconds, but who was counting?

Outside his windshield, the railroad tracks sliced due south through the rocky canyons on the edge of the Middle of Nowhere. Soon those tracks would pass the same sign welcoming all visitors to "Where the Thinking Process Begins!" that he and Hassan had gathered under two days ago. He laughed at the memory of how spooked they were by the eerie silence—Becker had known so little about his teammate then, and knew so much about him now. About all his fellow Fixers, who he hoped more than anything were opening up serious Cans of Buttwhuppin'™ on a bunch of Nowherians right now.

With two minutes to go, Becker pulled the rubber handle dangling over his head, sending a sharp whistle of steam into the air. The crew of Thought Provokers up at Contemplation would've undoubtedly heard him coming by now, but he wanted to make sure they weren't anywhere near the tunnel when he came screaming through. Most of the train would vanish directly into the In-Between in a matter of seconds, but that didn't mean there wouldn't be plenty of shrapnel flying around. Not to mention the train's conductor.

On some level Becker knew that, worst-case scenario, he'd be going to A Better Place, where long-lost loved ones would be waiting to greet him on the shore, along with a lifetime of Frozen Moments. His entire account would arrive from Daylight Savings about two days after he did, giving him the chance to re-experience the best moments from his life of fourteen years. Like his ninth birthday party, when his mom and dad brought him and Benjamin and all their best friends to Action Park. Or the time he and Thibadeau hung out in Thib's dorm room at the IFR one Saturday afternoon and did nothing but lie on the floor and listen to *The Wall* from start to finish. Or every time he got some Time with Amy Lannin.

But he knew the first Frozen Moment he would melt and step inside of was that night in Alton Forest when he kissed Jennifer Kaley for the very first time. Or more truthfully, she kissed him, because he'd been too much of a wimp to make the first move. Becker knew in that one moment that he was going to break whatever Rule he needed to to be with her, and he'd never regretted that decision even once. The only thing he *did* regret was that he almost certainly would never be seeing Jennifer Kaley again, not in the real World anyway.

And that hurt.

Yet standing there on the train and careening toward a collision with a boarded-up mineshaft, it wasn't the fact that he had A Better Place to go that made him feel okay. It was the fact that when he spun over the totality of his life, with all its twists and turns and good things that turned out to be bad and bad things that turned out to be good, the part of him that believed in the Plan outweighed the part that didn't. Yeah, maybe it was only 51% to 49%, but at *this* moment, that 2% made all the difference.

His mind cleared and focused only on what was happening right now. The "Welcome to Contemplation" sign passing on his right and the mining colony rapidly approaching ahead and the train's odometer, which said Becker had to let go of the throttle and make a run for it in 5 . . . 4 . . . 3 . . . 2 . . . 1 . . .

Then he was climbing up the ladder and onto the roof of the locomotive and leaping into the car behind him and thank the Plan, there *was* a tarp on there and it didn't take nearly as long to get there and cut it as he thought it would . . .

. . . and he grabbed the four corners of the tarp and made a parachute and the last thing Becker remembered as he jumped off the train was the screeching sound of metal being torn apart like paper and the feeling of splashing into cold, salty water . . .

. . . then everything went dark.

14

Triton

Two days later, Thibadeau Freck sat outside the boardroom that was serving as the temporary office of the new Second in Command. The Frenchman wore jeans with a blazer and a tie, and with his thick black beard shaved off, cut quite a handsome figure to the young interns who worked on this floor. The only things that gave them pause were the scars visible on his neck and face, and a certain sadness that was draped over him like a blanket. Of course, when they got a look at the name on his laminated Badge, everyone knew exactly where that blanket had come from.

As Thib crossed his legs and perused the morning's *Daily Plan*, he tried to remember the name of the Fixer who sat on the couch across from him. The middle-easterner wore semiformal attire as well, his silk suit perfectly tailored and his shoes the soft black shine of quality leather. Thibadeau remembered seeing the man's face inside a pack of Fixer trading cards, and up on the group portrait of the active Duty Roster that hung at the IFR, but that seemed like a lifetime ago. Several lifetimes, in fact.

Hassan. That's what his name was. Shahzad Hassan.

"If it makes you feel any better, he knew."

"*Excuse-moi?*"

"Becker knew that you were on our side." Hassan crossed a leg and absently tightened the band on his ponytail. "Blaque told him the whole story."

Thibadeau's eyes asked the question he was afraid to pose aloud.

"I don't know how he took it, but if I had to hazard a guess? Hurt that he never knew, guilty about some things he said, and anxious to have you back as his friend."

At that last part, Thibadeau felt something rising in him that he didn't want to display in public, so he bit the tip of his thumb as hard as he possibly could. It worked, but just barely.

"*Merci*, sir. I am very glad to know that."

Thibadeau waited for the feeling to return to his thumb, then flipped back to the *Daily Plan*'s front page. Headlines still celebrating the failure of The Tide's master stroke and the last-second reversal of the Unthinkable were hard to enjoy, so he flipped to an article about the unexpected shake-up among the Powers That Be. No one was surprised that Eve Hightower had tendered her resignation, not after the near full-scale collapse of The Seems, but the speed at which the Court of Public Opinion had selected her replacement caught everyone off guard.

"Come in, Mr. Freck."

Thibadeau waved a farewell to Hassan and headed for the office, rolling up the newspaper so he would have something to do with his hands. He probably should've brought a briefcase or a laptop or something to this meeting, but since he was only here to collect a single piece of paper, he figured it was best to travel light.

"You can shut the door behind you."

The new Second was tall—at least six feet five—with steel blue eyes and a thick head of brown hair. He reached across the desk that was strewn with papers and files and boxes to shake Thibadeau's hand, and the Frenchman was surprised to feel how calloused his fingers were. Most politicians he'd met hadn't done a day of honest work in their lives, but Samuel Hightower clearly wasn't most politicians.

"Take a seat, Mr. Freck. This won't take long."

Thibadeau watched Samuel pull out an official-looking form and begin to sign and date it.

"Now I know Central Command already debriefed you, but there are a few matters of controversy on which you might be in a unique position to offer an opinion."

"Fire away, sir."

"Permin Neverlåethe?"

"Whatever he did in Time Square—whatever *we* did— Permin is a good man. He will never accept a pardon because he has yet to pardon himself, but three life terms seems a bit . . . severe."

"Agreed. I was thinking two more years in the minimum-security wing, and perhaps a chance to train prisoners in the skills necessary to become a Ticky or a Minuteman in Time?"

"More than fair, sir."

Samuel finished signing the document, then stamped it with the official seal of the Second in Command. "And the Glitches?"

"I thought that affair was settled."

According to the rolled-up newspaper in Thib's hand, it was. As soon as the Mother of all Glitches had reluctantly returned control of the departments to the Powers That Be, she and her children had been declared "free to live out their lives in peace and harmony."

"Yes, but where do you think we should send them?" asked Samuel. "I mean, we can't exactly rent them a thousand-bedroom condo up in Crestview."

"May I speak freely, sir?"

"Always."

Samuel's relaxed vibe said this wasn't just an empty promise.

"I believe it was a mistake to banish the Glitches to Seemsberia in the first place. *Oui*, they are destructive, and their temperament a bit . . . difficult, but they are ingenious when it comes to the inner workings. And if The Seems is ever going to raise its technology to the standards The World deserves, the Glitches *must* be brought in to test and retest the system."

Thibadeau grimaced, having spoken a little more freely than he'd intended to.

"I'm glad you said that, Mr. Freck. Because it's already done."

"What's already done?"

"The Mother of all Glitches moves into her office in the Big Building next Tuesday. Other than a corner view, a seventy-two-inch plasma TV, and some loft space in Alphabet City for her kin, she had very few demands."

The Second in Command rose to his feet and began running off copies of the form on a mimeograph machine.

"Lastly, on the subject of Triton, you're absolutely convinced that Robert Marcus is no longer a suspect?"

"Totally. I watched them speak to each other in Seemsberia."

"Anyone else jump to the front of the list?" Samuel's steel blues locked upon Thibadeau's hazels. "'Cause I hear you got to know Triton quite well during your assignment."

The Frenchman only shrugged.

"I never saw his face."

"You're sure? The matter of The Tide will never be closed until this man's been caught and punished."

"Let's just say that if I met him in person, I believe I would be able to identify him. But in my heart, I feel that has not happened yet."

Samuel was visibly disappointed, but he shrugged it off as he handed Thibadeau the original copy of the document in his hand.

"Then you're a free man."

The official title of the form was "Executive Pardon #104Z" but the only words that mattered were the ones at the bottom: ". . . Thibadeau P. Freck is therefore granted clemency for all crimes committed ~ By order of the Powers That Be."

"Now that the truth is out, you can have any job in The Seems your heart desires." Samuel casually leaned on the corner of his desk. "But if you ask me, you're still a natural-born Fixer."

Thib folded up the page and placed it in his pocket.

"To be honest, sir, I just wanna spend a few weeks in

Chamonix and do nothing for a while. Reconnect with my family, maybe track down an old girlfriend or two."

"Sounds like a plan."

The two shook hands again, and Thib headed for the door.

"Mr. Freck?" Samuel's voice grew solemn. "Whatever happens with Fixer Drane, I promise you, one day it will all make sense."

The Frenchman paused in the doorway, wanting badly to bite his thumb again.

"How do you know that, sir?"

"Because you and I and the rest of The Seems are going to make sense of it."

Thibadeau nodded, feeling for the first time in a long time that maybe the right person was in charge of the world that made The World.

"Do me a favor, send Fixer Hassan in on your way out."

As the door to his office gently closed, Samuel Hightower leaned back in his chair and rubbed his aching temples. His first day back had been a long one, mostly occupied with formalities like parking spots and personality scans and a physical at the Department of Health. But since he'd taken office in a time of crisis, Samuel didn't have the luxury of easing into the job, and his list of things to do had been lengthy.

Already he'd knocked off fifty or so items, including the dismissal of Inkar Cyration as Warden of Seemsberia (and the promotion of the Inner Child), the issuing of an all-points bulletin for the escaped Time Bandits, and the transfer of

Captain Robert Marcus and all known agents of The Tide from the maximum security wing to the bottom of the Heckhole. But it was the Freck meeting he'd been dreading the most, partially because of the affection he felt for the deep-cover agent, and partially because there was no telling what he—

"You summoned me, sir?"

Fixer Hassan. He'd almost forgotten.

"Yes, yes. Thank you for coming, Shahzad. Please sit."

Hassan gingerly took the same chair as Thibadeau, the injuries suffered at the hands of the Nowherians not quite healed.

"How are you feeling?"

"Fortunate to be alive."

That was an understatement. After Becker Drane and the rest of the train had disappeared, five Fixers squared off against thirty Nowherians with every expectation that death would come swiftly. But strangely, Kalil had called off his men, tossing the amulet of the winged sun back to Hassan before retreating in the direction of the mountains.

"Any word from the search parties?" asked Samuel, leafing through Fixer Blaque's Mission Report.

"Negative." Hassan shook his head with great sadness. "Lake and Simms are in the Middle right now, but they've found no sign of Li Po whatsoever."

Samuel winced. Losing two Fixers on the same Mission (and one to Who Knows Where) was nothing less than a full-scale disaster. Human Resources would have to redouble their efforts, and it might be time for a few promotions as well.

"What about Blaque and the Octo?"

"Scouring the In-Between for any sign of Fixer Drane."

"As they should be."

"As I should be as well, sir." Hassan rose to his feet, still shaken by what he'd seen at the crash site in Contemplation. Not only had all evidence of the Train of Thought vanished, but most of the rubble from the collision had been sucked into In-Between as well—along with whatever was left (or not left) of Becker Drane. "I would like to rejoin the search, if you don't mind."

"And you will, Hassan. But before you go, I know there's something you've been chasing after for quite some time. A certain chapter missing from a certain book?"

The Fixer laughed, at last feeling free of his lifelong quest.

"Things changed for me in the Middle of Nowhere, sir. I've decided to give up my search to concentrate on the things I have, not the things I haven't."

This time it was Samuel who laughed aloud.

"Funny how the Plan works, isn't it? The moment you stop looking for something, there it is."

The Second in Command reached into his bottom drawer and pulled out a rectangular box made of Time-resistant glass. Inside was a collection of old parchment pieces, perhaps thirty, handwritten and bound with twine. And sketched on the top page in charcoal was the image of a winged sun.

"What is this?" whispered Hassan, feeling every molecule of air rapidly being sucked from his lungs.

"It's the story of where your people come from and who they truly are. Many years ago, it was removed from the Library at Alexandria by members of the Cleanup Crew, and the reason why you could never find it again was because it was locked inside a vault in this building ever since."

"Why would they do such a thing?"

"At the time, the Powers That Be believed there was information in these pages that compromised the security of The Seems, and to be honest, they were right. But personally, I don't see there being any harm in letting you take it to one of the reading rooms on the 734th floor for a few hours."

Samuel lifted the glass container off his desk and offered it to the Fixer.

"If you're still interested, that is."

The strangest feeling came over Shahzad Hassan, standing there, looking at the artifact that had destroyed his father, his father's father, and every one of his ancestors for no less than a thousand years. It was something like terror mixed with good helpings of betrayal and rage.

"The Chieftain of the Nowherians told me that the Powers That Be are liars as an order of business." Fixer #19 locked eyes with the Second in Command. "Is that so?"

"It used to be, Hassan. But not anymore."

Barely able to control his shaking fingers, Hassan reached across the desk and gently lifted the 13th Chapter from Samuel Hightower's hands.

"Do you think it was wise of you to let him read it?" asked Sophie Temporale, Samuel's last meeting of the day. "Seems to me you're just opening up a can of worms."

"It won't be the last one." Samuel poured some Creative Juices into a glass. "If Kalil wants war—and everything in Blaque's Report suggests this is a strong possibility—then we'll need all the allies we can get."

The new Second polished off his drink in one long gulp.

"To recruit them, we must have the truth on our side."

Sophie sat back in her chair, trying to keep a straight face, and waiting for Samuel to lose his. She didn't have to wait long.

"I realize how hypocritical that sounds." He chuckled. "But I actually meant it when I said it."

"So how does it feel to be back on top?"

"Good. It feels very good."

"It should. Everything worked out even better than you planned."

"Not exactly. When I showed you where they were hiding the Most Amazing Thing of All, I expected you to attempt a break-in much sooner."

Sophie's gray eyes glistened with a youthful spirit that belied her almost inconceivable age. "You knew I couldn't resist?"

"I needed a way to get the Nowherians involved, so Eve would turn her attention away from the home front." Samuel refilled his glass, and filled another for the Time Being. "And I knew there was only one mystery left in this world you hadn't solved."

Sophie took a small sip and curled her nose at the strong flavor.

"Unfortunately, I haven't solved it yet."

"The important word there is *yet*."

Samuel reached into his pocket, pulled out an exceedingly long and heavy brass key, and dangled it in front of his former mother-in-law.

"How did you get that?"

"Kalil has his spies in the Big Building. Did he not think I would respond in kind?"

Sophie reached out for the key, but Samuel yanked it away like a teasing schoolboy. "Of course, you realize I'll have to roll you under the bus with the others."

"Of course."

"Your daughter is well aware that Triton was whispering in the ears of the Powers That Be, and as Second in Command, I must expose and punish all traitors to The Seems."

"Do what you must, Samuel. Just . . . try to make it easy on Eve." Sophie fell back in her chair again. "To find out that I was working for The Tide would be very painful for her."

"Not half as painful as it would be to find out who Triton is."

"Oh, I don't know. Part of me thinks she already suspects."

"What makes you say that?"

Samuel did the slightest of double takes, and Sophie didn't miss it.

"Who else could it be?"

Realizing a battle of wits was futile, Samuel tossed Sophie the key.

"There's an air taxi waiting for you on the roof. The driver will fly you out to the Sticks, and feel free to crash at my place for as long as you want. But I warn you, as soon as tomorrow's *Daily Plan* comes out, you'll probably want to be as far away from The Seems as is Seemsianly possible."

Sophie cradled the heavy key, almost giddy at the possibilities of what it might unlock. But as she gathered her small duffle bag and prepared to head up to the roof, she couldn't resist tweaking Samuel one last time.

"If the Glitches hadn't come, who would be in charge of The Seems right now? Samuel Hightower, or Triton?"

The Second in Command burst into laughter and made his way around the desk.

"But they did come, Mom." He gave the grandmother to his only child a warm and familial kiss on the cheek. "That is truly the Most Amazing Thing of All."

They hugged each other warmly, and then the Time Being was gone.

"Travel safe."

Samuel poured himself another drink, still undecided about whether or not to explode Sophie's air taxi as soon as the dirigible took flight. After all, she was the only person who knew that he was Triton. On the other hand, maybe it was time for the plotting to stop. Ten years of recruiting people for an underground revolution without ever meeting them face-to-face had taken him exactly where he'd hoped it would, and damn if it wasn't satisfying. Yes, he'd sold every single one of those people out to get here, but The World would no doubt be a better place for it. Just as soon as he rebuilt it from Scratch.

At the bottom of a well-worn notepad was the final item on his list of things to do, and Samuel got down to the process of crossing it off. It involved a somewhat messy decision made by the Court of Public Opinion, which directly affected the approvals of an internship at the Big Building and a heroic Fixer's last request. All Samuel needed to do was sign on the dotted line, and the rest, as they say, would be history.

Caledon, Ontario, Canada

The next afternoon, Jennifer Kaley hopped down the steps of her school bus and onto the corner of Gerard Avenue and Custer Drive. The moment the doors closed behind her, Jimmy the Driver peeled out and the kids cheered out their windows, but the girl with the dirty blond hair heard none of it. She simply turned up the music that was playing over her ear-buds and headed down the sidewalk for home.

The Mission Mix had arrived yesterday, as it always did, in a small yellow envelope covered with hideous handwriting. Most people Jennifer knew who were into music traded songs electronically, but Becker Drane was nothing if not old school. He insisted upon sending her CDs with track lists and liner notes, and always with some kind of cool/goofy picture on the cover. But the one she was listening to now—"Mission Mix #10: I Dream of Jenny"—featured a pretty spectacular sketch drawn in crayon by a certain little brother.

"Nimrod's not here right now," Benjamin Drane had said when she'd called Becker's house last night. *"But I'd be happy to take a message."*

"How come he's not answering his cell?" Jennifer implored, having left half a dozen messages since the envelope arrived.

"How should I know? I'm not my brother's keeper."

"But he *is* home from his Mission, right?"

Since the package was postmarked yesterday in Highland Park, she figured Becker must've finally come back from The

Seems and was trying to make up for the abrupt way he left by being mysteriously romantic.

"*I just told you he wasn't home, didn't I?*" The nine year old had clearly reached his wit's end with this conversation. "*Who is this, again?*"

"Jennifer Kaley, Becker's, um . . . friend from Canada."

"*Well, Jennifer Kaley from Canada, I'm busy playing 'Juvenile Delinquent II: Tried as an Adult' right now, so if you don't mind—*"

"Hold on, B. Can I talk to Me-2 for a second?"

"*Me who?*"

"Me-2!"

"*I don't know what you're talking about. Please take us off your list!*"

Click.

It was a weird moment then, and it still struck her that way now, bopping down the suburban streets of Caledon. Jennifer had spoken to Benjamin dozens of times, but from his tone of voice, it was as if he didn't even know who she was. He even seemed like a different kid to her, not the sweet-natured artist who was her co-keeper of Becker's big secret, but an annoyed (and annoying) nine-year-old brat. But she shook it off as the final song on the mix kicked in . . .

> *Oh, to live on Sugar Mountain*
> *With the barkers and the colored balloons . . .*

It was the first song she and Becker had ever listened to together, on the night they met inside a Dream. Jennifer replayed the memory in her head as Neil Young sang the words, smiling as she recalled the thrill of holding the Fixer's hand and literally flying through the air above The Seems. It had never occurred to her that this incredible world and the boy who showed it to her were real—only that she wished they were, and that the moment she shared with Becker on a rocky overhang overlooking the Stream of Consciousness could've lasted forever. In a way it had, because it was that same rocky overhang that adorned the cover of Jennifer's new Mission Mix.

"Guess that's it for now," the voice of Becker Drane said as soon as the song was over. *"Can't wait to see you again, and in the meantime, always remember—something somewhere is making sure you'll always be okay . . ."*

He made the little sound of a drumroll . . .

"And his name is Ferdinand."

Jennifer rolled her eyes, just like she did several times inside that Dream, and whenever he got too new-agey on her. But in truth, she couldn't have felt happier if she tried, and she couldn't wait until the two of them could finally be together aga—

Wow. That was weird. She totally lost her train of thought.

"What was I just thinking about?"

As Jennifer racked her brain, she arrived on her block to see a weird-looking man standing on the opposite corner. He definitely wasn't from this neighborhood, and he didn't look at all like any of the landscapers or kitchen contractors that were working on some of the houses on her street. In fact, the only thing Jennifer knew for sure about the stranger with the three-piece suit and the leather attaché case was that he was staring directly at her.

"You're being paranoid," she said to herself, calmly starting toward 30 Custer Drive. "He's probably just a vacuum cleaner salesman."

But when she pretended to be getting something out of her book bag and looked back over her shoulder, Jennifer saw to her horror that the stranger had crossed the street and was heading in her direction. Even worse, no one on Custer seemed to be home—the only sign of life was a delivery van from something called "The Cleanup Crew," which was unfortunately just pulling away. With thoughts of herself on the evening news, she picked up her pace, but the man in the suit did the same.

"Ms. Kaley?" he shouted after her. "Ms. Jennifer H. Kaley?"

Only when she was safely inside the house and locked behind the screen door did Jennifer turn to answer him.

"Who wants to know?"

"Allow me to introduce myself." The stranger pulled a business card from his pocket and slid it through the mail slot. "Nick Dejanus, Director of Human Resources."

According to the card, Dejanus worked for a company called The Seems. The Seems? Where had Jennifer heard that name before? But before she could ask, the man started to wheeze and cough.

"Breathe much?" Jennifer inquired, starting to relax.

"My wife bought me a membership to the Department of Health Club, but with all this political upheaval, I've been too busy to go." The man dropped his hands to his knees, clearly regretting the decision. "At least the nearest Door is in those woods nearby."

"Door to where?"

"I'm sorry. You'd think after six years on the job, I would know how to do this already." He reached into his briefcase and pulled out a laminated piece of 8½-by-11 paper that was connected to what appeared to be a book report. "Is this your handwriting?"

Jennifer looked at the perfectly color-coded spiral notebook.

"Yup. That's me."

And that's when it all came back to her. The box at Paradise Records. The Seemsian Aptitude Test and "the Best Internship in The World." But that had been months ago and she hadn't heard a thing.

"Then, on behalf of the Powers That Be, I would like to extend you the opportunity for an internship at the Big Building." Before Jennifer could ask what that was, the man stuffed an oversized envelope through the slot, with the same four-color logo that was printed on his card. "Orientation begins tomorrow at eight a.m., but Second in Command Hightower is pretty easygoing, so don't sweat it if you're a few minutes late."

She stood behind the screen with the packet in her hands, mystified.

"Becker always said you'd make a perfect Case Worker," Dejanis said, before sadly turning and heading back to wherever he had come from. "Maybe he'll be right."

As Jennifer Kaley watched the stranger slowly vanish into the streets of suburbia, she took another look at her SAT, then shouted out one final question.

"Who's Becker?"

Epilogue

The bottom curve of the sun was just dipping into the ocean when Becker Drane stumbled out of the tide and onto the safety of the shore. He'd been swimming for what felt like hours, and even with the current on his side his arms felt like two wet pieces of spaghetti. But as he relished the warm sand against his cold cheek, Becker allowed himself a flash of pride in the simple fact that he hadn't drowned out there. Maybe his breast-stroke wasn't what it was when he medaled at the Rutgers Pool swim meet, but at least he was still breathing.

It took the Fixer fifteen minutes to push himself to his knees, and another ten to get back to his feet. Walking was another story, but Becker was in no hurry to do that anyway, since his first order of business was figuring out where he was (not to mention how he'd gotten there). Though he appeared to be alone amid the high dunes and even higher cliffs, the sand itself was littered with footsteps and the outlines of blankets and towels. It didn't take a genius to figure out that a whole bunch of swimmers and sunbathers had just been—

"'Scuse me, bud."

Becker wheeled to see an older man in a Hawaiian shirt, methodically waving a metal detector over the sand. He wore headphones over his ears as well, and judging by the way he knelt and started digging a hole in the sand, he'd just picked up a signal.

"Litterbugs," he muttered, uncovering a crushed-up can of Tab. "Whatever happened to 'give a hoot, don't pollute'?"

As the beachcomber stuffed the can into the plastic bag that dangled from his fanny pack, Becker jumped into his field of vision.

"Excuse me, sir? But can you tell me where I am?" he asked. "I think I'm a little lost."

The man pulled off his headphones, irritated by the intrusion.

"Wish I could help you, kid, but there's gold in them thar hills." He threw a thumb back over his shoulder. "Talk to that fella on the boardwalk. Been waiting here for hours, so chances are he's part of your Welcome Committee."

In a bit of a daze, Becker noticed for the first time the old-fashioned boardwalk that bordered the beach a few hundred yards away. But when he saw who was sitting on the wooden steps leading up to it, he instantly snapped out of it.

"That's what I thought." The treasure hunter gave a salute, then slapped his headphones back on. "Have a good one, kid."

As man and metal detector disappeared in search of loot, the sopping-wet teen limped toward the boardwalk, his eyes even wider than his mouth.

"Po . . . is that you?"

Indeed it was. The immortal Li Po, #1 on the Duty Roster and master of the 7th Sense, wearing not his traditional gi and Toolkit but a short-sleeved button-down shirt and a pair of Bermuda shorts.

"Hello, Becker. I cannot tell you how good it is to see you again."

Becker's head felt like it was about to blow clean off his shoulders, and not just because Li Po had addressed him verbally for the first time ever. The famed Fixer had been missing for almost a week now, but here he was, somehow teleported from the Middle of Nowhere to the shores of what for all the world looked like Point Pleasant or Cape Cod.

Just as Becker himself had been.

"What happened to you, Po? I mean, we couldn't find you anywhere!"

"I had waited all my life to see the Most Amazing Thing of All, and once I did, well . . . there was nothing left for me to do." Fixer Po rubbed his bald head and relished the slightly burned feeling on top. "But I must admit, the swim was unexpectedly refreshing."

Becker nodded and turned back toward the ocean, trying to retrace his own voyage to this mysterious place. During his brief career, he had tumbled between realities before—from Dreams and Frozen Moments to both sides of the In-Between—but never as harshly as this. Perhaps he'd been sucked into the tunnel with the runaway Train of Thought and been accidentally propelled to some distant corner of The Seems. Or perhaps this was all his own Dream, and he'd momentarily awake to find himself in a bed at the Department of Health surrounded by the second team, their smiling faces an equal mixture of worry and relief.

But there was also another explanation.

"Po?"

"Yes, Becker?"

"I, um . . . there's something I need to know."

"I figured you might."

Becker's mouth had become so dry that he couldn't manage the words, so he inhaled the clean and salty air instead. Waves were lapping gently against the shore, while a trio of palm trees swayed easily overhead. Out on the water, a lone seagull skimmed across the surface, and Becker was sure he could hear music and people laughing from somewhere up above the boardwalk. All of these sights and sounds melted away his fear, and with one last deep breath, he turned to the Fixer beside him and found the courage to ask—

"Is this A Better Place?"

Glossary of Terms

A Better Place: Where people go when they die.

Action Park: The (now closed) water- and motor-themed amusement park in Vernon Township, NJ, whose popularity was accompanied by unsafe rides, zoned-out attendants, and questionable patrons. (But it was awesome.)

Animal Affairs: The department in The Seems responsible for Leopard Spots, Lions' Roars, maps for Carrier Pigeons, updates on the secret plan among squirrels to overthrow humankind and force all other life forms into indentured servitude in the nut mines, etc.

Attak-Pak®: A silver backpack or "anti-Toolkit" used by Glitches to wreak havoc on the machinery of The Seems.

Back Scratcher: One who toils in the back country of the

Middle of Nowhere, searching and sifting for precious grains of Scratch.

Bargain Hunters: A loose band of mercenaries specializing in the buying and reselling of precious materials to a small segment of The Seemsian upper crust. (Usually at a great profit.)

Brainstorm: A phenomenon, peculiar to the Middle of Nowhere, where gusting winds and shifting sands kick up large quantities of unrefined Scratch. When combined with human or Seemsian Thought, virtually anything imaginable can come to life. See also: Brainstorming.

Brainstorming: An extreme sport pioneered back in The Day in which participants intentionally enter a Brainstorm to turn their wildest fantasies and fears into reality.

Buzz Kills: Gnatlike insects indigenous to the Middle of Nowhere known to kill your buzz with theirs.

Care Giver(s): Highly qualified medical personnel dispatched from the Department of Health to handle any and all life-threatening emergencies.

Cleanup Crew: A division of Human Resources responsible for "humanely unremembering" people of what they know about The Seems and collecting all hard materials that might leave a paper trail.

Clink, the: The sheet-metal holding tank adjacent to the Pokey where Seemsberia's most dangerous arrivals are housed during processing.

Cloud(s) of Suspicion: Nasty bulbous puffs known to settle over The World at random intervals, causing large-scale mistrust and fear.

Day, the: The time before the Beginning of Time, when The World was under construction.

Distraction: A Seemsian sport/pastime combining elements of curling, shuffleboard, and Tetris, in which participants push metal figurines down a sheet of ice, attempting to stack them in an organized fashion.

Easy Street: The most expensive block in Alphabet City, overlooking LMNO Park.

Everywhere: 1. A quaint village of hardworking people complete with a trolley, walkable downtown, and excellent school system. 2. Hometown of Simly Frye.

Firefox: Feature film centering on a Vietnam vet enlisted to steal a highly advanced Russian fighter plane (nicknamed "Firefox") and return it to the United States for analysis. *[Starring: Clint Eastwood, Freddie Jones. 1982. 136 mins. Rated: PG.]* Based on the book by Craig Thomas.

Firsts, Seconds, Thirds: The three naturally occurring geological phenomena from which the Essence of Time is distilled. For more, please see *The Seems: The Split Second.*

Head Rush: The period back in The Day when Seemsians looking to make a Buck (or Bill) flocked to the Middle of Nowhere in search of untapped Thought. The frontier economy inevitably dried up when the Powers That Be decided to regulate the industry.

Heap, the: Name for the pile of discarded inventions, phased-out innovations, and never-before-seen creations junked before ever making it to The World.

Hide: A thin, skinlike textile resistant both to the elements and to Peeping Toms.

Hopscotch: A simple game in which participants hop through a series of squares on one foot. Designed in the Department of Fun, it was leaked to The World during the rule of the Roman Empire.

Hunga Munga: An early tribal weapon consisting of a pointed blade with a curved back and a spike near the handle.

Idea Smugglers: Outlaws who run stolen (and sometimes revolutionary) Ideas back and forth between the Middle of Nowhere and Black Market.

I'llshootyoudeadwhereyoustandyoulowdownnogoodsonuva Gun: A Color War–era musket considered extremely rare and highly dangerous, particularly in the hands of one who knows how to wield it. (Aka 'Sonuva Gun.)

Inner Child: The nine-year-old chief psychologist of Seemsberia charged with getting prisoners back in touch with their true selves.

Jiffy Pop: A brand of popcorn that combines kernels and oil in an aluminum pan with a crinkled foil lid. As the pan becomes hotter, the popped corn causes the foil to rise and expand.

Jinx Gnomes: The comic strip-turned hit TV series-turned major motion picture about the crack unit dispatched to The World whenever a person overcelebrates a bit of good fortune.

Johnson Bar: A yard-long lever that controls if a train locomotive moves forward or in reverse.

KGB: aka *"Komitjet Gosudarstvjennoj Bjezopasnosti,"* aka *"Committee for State Security."* The Soviet Union's security forces, secret police, and intelligence agency from 1954 to 1991.

Knockout Punch: Originally developed as a cure for Insomnia in the Department of Sleep, this 100 percent juice (not from concentrate) elixir slipped out and became a popular Seemsian sleep remedy.

Library at Alexandria: The greatest bibliotheca in the ancient world, allegedly burned down by Caesar during his visit to Egypt in 48 BC. Details of the destruction, however, remain unclear.

Memory Bank: The fortresslike institution in which the Memories of The World are kept.

Mind Bender: An employee of the Department of Thought & Emotion responsible for stringing the filament of Mind into the glass bulbs of Big Ideas.

Mind, Body & Soll, LLC: The award-winning architectural firm credited with designing many of the most innovative departments, as well as some World-based wonders (e.g., Stonehenge, Machu Picchu, Easter Island).

Operation Clean Sweep: The Mission when all Glitches, except one holdout, were swept from the system.

Outskirts, the: A far-out area of The Seems that vagabonds, bohemians, and dropouts from mainstream Seemsian society call home.

Pickmeup: Similar to coffee but double the caffeine and twice the Inspiration.

Pink Floyd: 1. The British Invasion–era prog-rock band famous for their haunting melodies, profound lyrics, and obsession with flying pigs. 2. Becker Drane's favorite band.

Price Is Right: The television game show where contestants guess the prices of household items, without going over. Hosts have included: Bill Cullen, Bob Barker, and Drew Carey. *A Mark Goodson–Bill Todman production.*

Purple Haze: An anomalous cloud of magenta dust associated with a faulty algorithm in the Department of Weather. The psychedelic blob last reached The World in the late 1960s, resulting in a fascination with flashing lights, bright colors, and songs over twenty minutes in length.

Remote Gremlin: The infamous "collector of clickers," this former employee of Lost & Found ran roughshod through The World pilfering TV remote controls until he was captured and sentenced to life in Seemsberia. Many anonymous copycats still perform his "work" to this day.

Ripple Effect: A large-scale unraveling of the Plan, often caused by broken Chains of Events.

Scratch: Tiny blue specks, indigenous to the Middle of Nowhere and used to create anything and everything.

Signal Box: A raised hut/tower providing a dry space for mechanical switching levers and a home base for the accompanying signalman/woman.

Sock Goblin: The nefarious "snatcher of soles," this former Collections employee expressed her inner madness by robbing

The World of countless foot-gloves. Due to the pain and frustration inflicted, she was given a term of life in Seemsberia, without possibility of parole.

Spy Who Came In from the Cold, The: Feature film about a disillusioned British agent who refuses to come in from the Cold War, opting instead for another mission, which could very well be his last. *[Starring: Richard Burton, Claire Bloom. 1965. 112 mins. Not Rated.]* Based on the book by John le Carré.

Thin Air: A Bermuda Triangle–like corner of The Seems where people inexplicably vanish, often never to be seen again.

Torch, the: Lit by Jayson himself and protected by a small bronze censer, this flame symbolizes the unofficial leader of the Fixers. It has never been extinguished.

Tumulty's: 1. Featuring burgers too big for the bun, model trains, and wedges of iceberg lettuce. Present your copy of *The Seems* and get 10% off! Not to be combined with other offers.
_____ (Signature of owner/server) Good for one use! 361 George Street, New Brunswick, NJ 2. Benjamin Drane's favorite restaurant.

Wheel Tapper: The railroad employee responsible for testing train wheels for cracks by hitting them with a special hammer.

Yard Master: The railroad employee responsible for the makeup or breakup of trains, devising schedules, and coordinating yard switching.

Making Things from Scratch

Ever since its discovery in the sands of the Middle of Nowhere, the substance known as Scratch has sparked the imagination of The Seems. Early pioneers used raw Scratch to dream up foodstuff and water where none was readily available, to imagine groves and oases as respites from the sun, and even just to watch their wildest fantasies come to fruition. Though items made this way only boast a half-life of three days, "Brainstorming" became a popular sport back in The Day and drew many a follower to the harsh desert climate.

Nonetheless, when The World project was finally green-lit, a process was needed to ensure a more lasting reality. It was called "Design" and entailed superheating Scratch to a temperature of +541° F. The liquefied powder was then allowed to coagulate into an azure paste, filtered of impurities, and shipped in rubber Conun-Drums to appropriate departments. Last but not least, Agents of L.U.C.K. would scrape the residue from the vats and transform it into moments of good fortune for the people of The World.

Today Nature Buffs regularly use processed Scratch to think shrubs and bushes to life, while Mountaineers conjure the snow-covered peaks of Zermatt and Vail. Scratch is also woven into the Fabric of Reality and remains a fundamental building block for all Goods & Services, from Dreams to Hunches to Matters of Fact. Not surprisingly, quantities of Scratch are tightly controlled, accounting for a thriving Black Market.

Warning: _Scratch should never be used without a clear mind and clean hands._

Tools of the Trade

Selected Tools from "The Lost Train of Thought."
(*Note:* Reprinted from *The Catalog*, copyright © Seemsbury Press, MCGBVIX, The Seems.)

Tool Name: Spork™
Use: Escape from anytraz with this hand-held tunneling device! Ultra-quiet motor makes for ultra-quiet exits. Vacuum shoot inhales messy dust. Leaves subtle herringbone groove.
Designer: Steve Spork

Tool Name: Fly on the Wall™ *(Discontinued)*
Use: Surveillance. Bugging people out. Being a pest. Comes with dual joystick remote! *(CR2032 lithium battery not included.)*
Designer: Morton Penske

Tool Name: Didgeradoozy™
Use: Give new meaning to breaking wind! Audio blast reduces football field radius to mush. Kakadu design. *(WARNING: Self-defense only. May cause injury or harm.)*
Designer: Fixer Casey Lake w/ Toolshed Staff

Tool Name: Al's-O-Vera™
Use: "PENSKE ASTOUNDS WITH MIRACLE DREAM CREAM."[28] Apply to skin and watch scorched epidermis regrow like a Chia pet! <u>Treats:</u> lesions, burns, bug bites, scars, lacerations, vacillations, poison ivy and sumac, and psoriasis.
Designer: Al Penske

Tool Name: Bear Claws™
Use: When it's a bear of a Mission, you'll dig these helping hands! Paws come with three-inch claws, Thinsulate fur, and natural suede pads. *Not to be confused with a pastry of the same name.
Designer: The Handyman

Tool Name: Key Chain™
Use: Sick of toothpicks, Dweezers™, and knocking three times? You're never locked out when you carry your Key Chain. (*Guaranteed to pick any lock or your money back.*)
Designer: Al Penske

---

28. *Daily Plan*, Volume #MGBBG, Issue J, Section: "Seems Style."

Tool Name: Bleceiver™
Use: Condense your overcrowded Toolkit with this Blinker™-Receiver™ combo whose time has finally come! Available in all-new colors: Plum, Tangerine, Kiwi, Maize, Polka Dot, Camouflage, and Fixer Fern.
Designer: Al Penske Jr.

Tool Name: Thinking Cap™
Use: One spin of the propeller on top of this canvas beanie and your IQ shoots through the roof! A must for complex Missions. (And final exams.)
Designer: Al Penske

Tool Name: Speed Demons™
Use: Throw those Reebok Pumps in the trash and pretend you're Golden Age Flash! Sneaks come in standard or automatic, three colors, high-top or low! *(Ask about our turbo models!)*
Designer: Al Penske

Tool Name: Stopwatch™
Use: When Time is of the Essence, strap into the octagon! Self-winding. Quartz movement. Essence resistant to 300tg!
(Note: Beware Butterfly Effect!)
Designer: Yore Alvayez Ontim

Tool Name: Seat Belt™
Use: Simply insert the flat metal end into the buckle and pull! Guaranteed to keep your feet on the ground, even when The World turns upside down! *(Extension available for big & tall.)*
Designer: Al Penske

Tool Name: Extremely Cool Outfit™
Use: Style meets substance in the garment that's sure to be the rage on Easy Street. Adjusts for temperature, setting, and "cool factor." *(One size fits all.)*
Designer: Al Penske Jr.

Tool Name: Trinoculars™
Use: Sick of being called "four eyes"? Well, now you have *five* and it just doesn't roll off the tongue the same way. Sucks for them. Two oculars search distance, third taps anja chakra (brow) and grants 20/20 hindsight! *Sees through every material except Hide.*
Designer: Al Penske

Tool Name: Turf Board™
Use: Hang ten. Flick off. Turn turtle. Cover more distance than a gazelle—and all on dry land! Hand painted by the Original Artist! Aloha, dude.
Designer: Al Penske Jr.

Tool Name: Security Blanket™
Use: Wrap this puncture-resistant quilt around your loved ones and sleep tight! Keeps the insulated insulated from every element known to AI! (Also not bad for picnics or sitting on the grass.) Comes in solid, plaid, or country folk.
Designer: Al Penske Jr.

Tool Name: The Solution to All Our Problems™
Use: Everything
Designer: Al Penske
Sorry, not currently available.

*For more information on Tools, arcana, and Seemsian *détritus en général* please visit the Fixer's Lounge area of theseems.com. [Password: **LTF-FTL**]

Form #1030
Post-Mission Report

Mission: *The Lost Train of Thought [037024]*
Filed by: *Jelani Blaque*

Summary:

Though we managed to save The World from the Unthinkable, this Mission still leaves me with a great sadness. Human Resources and the IFR will have their work cut out for them to make up for those Fixers who remain lost or missing.

Areas for Improvement:

Despite Fixer Lake's suggestions, it was my call to make sure Fixer Drane drew the short end of the stick and thus would end up driver of the train. I did so because I believed it would be a safer assignment than facing Nowherians in hand-to-hand combat. I was wrong and take full responsibility for this decision.

Rate Your Briefer (1-12):

There were officially no Briefers on this Mission, but I must state for the record how proud I was of each member of the first and second teams. I also wish to give a Special Commendation to Thibadeau Freck, whose courage and fortitude over the last several years ensured our final victory over the Tide.

(Note: In the case of the one UNofficial Briefer on this Mission—Simly Alomonus Frye—I propose this matter be handled internally by IFR personnel.)

Suggestions Box:

a) Fixers must be _fully_ briefed on all Missions, regardless of Clearance. As we saw on this Mission, lack of information about the Most Amazing Thing of All nearly cost both teams. b) Begin construction on the wall that Fixer Drane promised the Nowherians. c) Even though the Tide is quashed, Triton's identity remains unknown. He _must_ be found and brought to justice.

____✓____ Check here if you wish to attend the Department of Energy's "Power Lunch"—a symposium on helping The World go green!

_____Jelani Blaque_____ Signature

the seems

The Powers That Be

MEMORANDUM

From: The Powers That Be
To: All Seems Employees
Re: Change of Plans

Dear Fellow Seemsians:

Though recent events have tested our mettle, I am proud to announce that The Tide has been defeated and peace restored to The Seems. Nonetheless, you have called for change and we, the Powers That Be, are listening!

Effective immediately, my office will be accepting suggestions on making adjustments to The World. Already, initiatives for the two-day work/school week, ending global hunger, and a Make All Your Problems Go Away button have reached my desk and are awaiting final approval.

The Plan has served us well in the past, but we must not be afraid to forge a new tomorrow. In this spirit, I invite you to become part of a very special time in The Seems—a time when we will finally deliver on our promise to make The World "a better place."

Looking forward to hearing your thoughts!

SAMUEL HIGHTOWER

Samuel Hightower
Second in Command, The Seems

P.S. Members of The World will also be invited to submit their proposals at www.theseems.com.

JOHN HULME and **MICHAEL WEXLER** are also the authors of *The Seems: The Glitch in Sleep* and *The Seems: The Split Second*. They accidentally stumbled upon the existence of The Seems after opening an unlocked Door in Wilmington, North Carolina, during the summer of 1995. From that moment on, they were obsessed with the curious realm and sought to pen a book series based on their discovery. Though the project was held up in administrative Red Tape for nearly eleven years, the Powers That Be finally signed off on its release, resulting in the text you now hold.

Hulme lives with his wife, Jennifer, and his children, Jack and Madeline, in a small New Jersey town with crookety sidewalks and tree-lined streets.

Wexler was last sighted driving a truck with the words "Experienced Ice Cream™" stenciled on the front.

www.theseems.com